PRECIOUS
CARGO

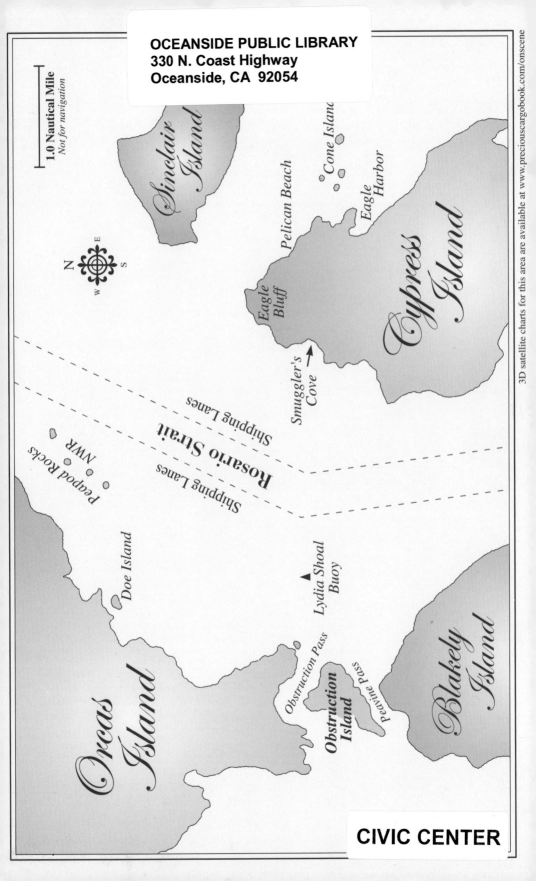

1.0 Nautical Mile
Not for navigation

Sinclair Island

Cone Island

Pelican Beach

Eagle Harbor

N
E
S
W

Eagle Bluff

Cypress Island

Smuggler's Cove

Shipping Lanes

Rosario Strait

Shipping Lanes

Peapod Rocks
NWR

Doe Island

Lydia Shoal Buoy

Obstruction Pass

Obstruction Island

Peavine Pass

Orcas Island

Blakely Island

CIVIC CENTER

3D satellite charts for this area are available at www.preciouscargobook.com/onscene

PRECIOUS CARGO

A Novel of Suspense

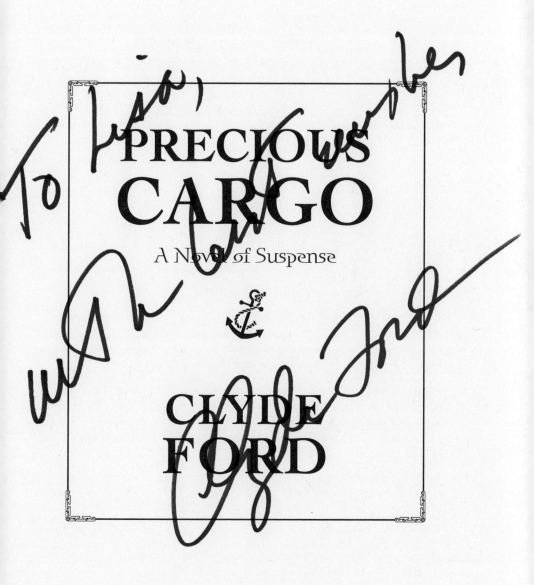

CLYDE FORD

Vanguard Press

A Member of the Perseus Books Group

Copyright © 2008 by Clyde W. Ford

Published by Vanguard Press
A Member of the Perseus Books Group

Books published by Vanguard Press are available at special discounts for bulk purchases
in the United States by corporations, institutions, and other organizations. For more information, please contact the Special Markets Department at the Perseus Books Group,
2300 Chestnut Street, Suite 200, Philadelphia, PA 19103, or call (800) 810-4145 ext. 5000,
or e-mail special.markets@perseusbooks.com.

DESIGNED BY JEFF WILLIAMS
Set in 12.5-point Fournier by the Perseus Books Group

Library of Congress Cataloging-in-Publication Data

Ford, Clyde W.
    Precious cargo : a novel of suspense / Clyde W. Ford.
       p. cm.
    ISBN 978-1-59315-485-1 (alk. paper)
    1. Noble, Charlie (Fictitious character)—Fiction. 2. Private investigators—Fiction.
3. Prostitution—Washington (State)—Fiction. 4. San Juan Islands (Wash.)—Fiction.
5. Bellingham (Wash.)—Fiction. I. Title.

PS3606.O724P74 2008
813'.6—dc22

                                                                                      2008019463

10 9 8 7 6 5 4 3 2 1

To Chara:
Nothing is more precious than our love.

prologue

arabande swayed gently at anchor off Cypress Island. Marvin Baynes clutched his coffee cup, savoring daybreak from the pilothouse bench. A pale blue sky backlit the crisp white dome of Mount Baker. Muted cries of seagulls broke the early-morning quiet. The coffee's rich aroma seduced Marvin, relaxed him, the warmth of the cup a buffer against the morning's chill. He smiled and sank into the leather seat.

Outside, the buzz of an outboard engine grew steadily louder. When the engine throttled back to a soft, steady hum, Marvin stood. He slid open the pilothouse door. A skiff floated nearby.

"CJ, that you?" He called to the woman in the skiff.

"Stopped by to say hi," she said.

"You're up early." He raised his cup. "Care to come aboard for some coffee?"

"Love to but not today. Boating season's begun and I've got lots of work to do. Tree falls on some of the paths need clearing."

"And there's no one to help you?"

CJ smiled. She raised her arm, made a fist, and tapped her biceps. "I'm one tough broad." She laughed. "I can outwork any man they've ever sent me. Besides, with cutbacks the department only has the budget for one ranger on Cypress. Though I might get an intern this year."

Marvin took another sip. "You've been out here what? Five, six years?"

"Almost ten."

"And by yourself no less. I admire that."

"It's . . . well . . . sometimes difficult being alone on the island, but I love it here."

"This summer's our last cruise north," Marvin said.

"Last?"

He gripped his cup. "It'll be the fortieth year Angie and I have cruised the Inside Passage." He sighed. "Much as we love it, we're getting old and being aboard for three months is getting harder."

"Old? Marvin, you look great."

"Stop or you'll make an old man blush."

CJ laughed. "Come back by when you return from Alaska and we'll celebrate."

Marvin waved. "We will."

CJ stepped back to her helm. The engine revved. She spun the skiff around. Marvin watched her head toward the far shore as *Sarabande* rocked gently in her wake.

Marvin stepped back inside the pilothouse. Forty years. Five boats. One wife. He sipped coffee, then raised his cup forward in a toast toward the berth where Angela slept. Then he sipped some more, raising his cup this time in honor of the boats that had marked the passage of their lives together: *Prelude,* the twenty-six-foot wooden sailboat that he'd taken Angela on for their first date; *Allemande,* a thirty-foot ketch they'd bought the first summer of their marriage; *Minuet,* the fast, thirty-three-foot fin-keel sailboat they'd raced for years; *Cantata,* the steel sailboat they'd built with the intention of making a circumnavigation.

Marvin winced, clutching the coffee cup even tighter, recalling the times spent on *Cantata* with their daughter. After losing Amy, he and Angela had found it difficult to sail *Cantata,* so they'd purchased *Sara-*

bande, their current boat, an older motor sailer that chugged along at seven knots, with an inside helm where they could escape harsh Northwest weather—a perfect boat for two retired concert musicians, two aging sailors.

"Time to weigh anchor?" Angela's voice rose from below.

"Almost," Marvin said.

The boat creaked and rocked as Angela ascended the spiral pilothouse steps. The khaki pants and dark gray woolen sweater she wore matched Marvin's. Angela carried her floppy, wide-brimmed hat in one hand. Marvin reached for her and gently pulled her down to sit with him. They held hands in silence. Through thinning skin, his pulse throbbed against hers.

Marvin tapped his feet to the rhythm of waves lapping softly against the hull. From the tree-lined shore, a raven's clucking recalled the striking of a wooden block. The raucous cries of seagulls mimicked blaring trumpets.

Marvin let go of Angela and stepped behind *Sarabande*'s wheel. Then, like a conductor waving a baton to cue an orchestra, he turned the key. A high-pitched buzzer sang out. *Sarabande*'s diesel sprang to life with a pulsing bass tone and rhythmic tenor overtones. Angela tamped her hat down onto her head. She opened the pilothouse door and stepped out onto the deck, walking slowly toward the bow. Once there, she turned back. Marvin flashed her a thumbs-up. Angela stepped on the large, black rubber footswitch. The winch whined. The main engine groaned under the load. Metal clinked and scraped against metal as the winch pulled the anchor chain in.

Sarabande glided forward as the chain rose. Then, with a clunk, the chain stopped. The winch whined louder. Marvin stuck his head out of the pilothouse window. Angela cupped her hands and called to him.

"I guess we set the anchor really well."

"It's mostly a mud bottom," Marvin said. "I'll drive over the anchor and see if I can break it free." He eased the gearshift and the throttle forward. *Sarabande* moved ahead. "Try it now," Marvin called out.

Angela stepped on the footswitch, and the chain jerked up a few feet before stopping again. With the chain pulled tight, the boat began to swing in a circle. "Maybe we've snagged an old logging cable," she said.

"Damn," Marvin said. "Some way to start our cruise. Look, I'll try rocking the boat back and forth."

He threw the gearshift forward, powered the boat ahead until the anchor chain grew taut, then reversed gears and moved backward. Between each forward and reverse movement, Marvin waved to Angela and she tried the winch, but it only moved the chain slightly. Angela shook her head.

"Stop," Marvin said. "We'll burn out the winch motor." He sighed, and then let the boat idle in neutral. He pushed open the pilothouse door and stepped out, grabbing a red and white float. "We'll have to unhook the chain from the boat and attach a float to it so we can retrieve it later. We'll throw the chain overboard. Then we'll go back to port and hire a diver to come out and see what we've snagged."

"That's too bad," Angela said. "It means we won't get going to Alaska for several days."

"We'll lose three hundred feet of chain and an anchor if we don't come back for it," Marvin said. "Then we'll have to buy a new anchor and new chain."

"Okay," Angela said. "Give me the float. I'll tie it on while you unhook the chain."

Marvin walked back toward the pilothouse. He'd just reached the door when he heard the winch motor whir and Angela cry out. When he turned back, he saw her reeling in anchor chain.

"The motor's working," Angela said. "A little." She held her thumb to her index finger. "It pulls in about a foot of chain and then stops. It might take time, but let's see if I can pull the anchor up this way before you unhook it."

Marvin nodded. "Maybe we broke free. I'll go back inside and stand by the controls."

The engine rumbled beneath Marvin as he watched Angela step on the switch, then wait. Step, then wait. The chain moved slowly, link after link winding up and over the bow roller, before dropping into the anchor well. Angela moved slowly too, bent over the railing, directing spray from a nozzle to wash down the muddy chain. A twinge of pain stabbed Marvin each time Angela stiffened and rubbed her hip. Perhaps the problem lay not with the anchor but with the winch motor, like the two of them, old and losing strength.

Suddenly, Angela screamed. She staggered backward from the bow, then crumpled to the deck. Marvin rushed from the pilothouse. "Not now," he whispered, shaking his head. "No, please. Not now. One more trip north together. Please, just one more trip."

Marvin knelt beside Angela, picked up her hand. She breathed in short, sharp puffs, which released small steam plumes into the cold morning air. A tortured look enveloped her face. Her eyes registered fear. She opened her mouth but no words came at first. Her arm flopped out, finger pointed toward the bow.

"There," she said, her voice hoarse, raspy. "Marvin, it's Amy. . . . She's there."

Marvin needed to get Angela medical attention. He also needed to finish pulling in the anchor so they didn't drift into the rocks. He walked to the bow, looking over and down at the muddy anchor emerging from the dark green waters. A clump of seaweed snaked around the shank.

Marvin gasped.

Beneath the seaweed, the sharp point of an anchor fluke stuck into the pallid flesh of a young woman's lifeless body.

one

Sunlight set the rear deck of the *Noble Lady* ablaze. A sailboat just pulling away from its berth glided by, sending a gentle wake under the *Noble Lady*'s hull. When the rocking stopped, I set a green and white folio of music on the stand in front of me. I opened to the Prelude of the *English Suite* by John Duarte, written for Andrés Segovia in honor of his second wedding.

My hand trembled slightly as I reached down beside me for my guitar. I loved the *English Suite*. But would I remember how to play it, or would I have to completely relearn the piece? Would I ever play it as well as I once did? I took in a deep breath and held it. My head flopped back onto the cushion. Sun bathed my face. I exhaled to the words of Frederico Oller, my guitar teacher, which floated through my mind. "The past is not the prelude; the present is. Perfection is not the goal; love is. Love of the guitar. Love of music. Love of life."

I took another deep breath before grasping my guitar by the neck and easing it from its case. I cradled it in my arms. Then I reached down for the card lying on top of the crushed red velour lining the bottom of the case. I opened the card and re-read it as I had so many times in the past months. *Please don't drink this alone. Kate.* I smiled and warmth flushed through my body. Kate had left the card for me last fall, along with a bottle of Red Mountain Reserve wine—a gift for the successful conclusion of my first case.

I didn't drink the wine alone that night. I didn't call Kate either. At least, not at first.

"Mr. Noble."

"Charlie."

Two voices rang out like bells, one high, one low, startling me from my musings and my music. Marvin and Angela Baynes stood on the dock looking in. They moored their boat just a few slips down from me, spending their winters in Arizona and their summers cruising the Inside Passage.

"Permission to come aboard?" Marvin asked.

"Permission granted," I said.

I laid Kate's card in the bottom of the case and set the guitar down on top of it. Marvin swung the boarding gate open. The boat dipped as he and Angela stepped aboard. They reminded me of bookends, dressed in matching khaki shorts, green floral shirts, and wide-brimmed straw hats.

"We haven't disturbed your practice, have we?" Angela asked.

"No. I've simply been finding ways to avoid beginning a new piece. Have a seat."

They sat across from me on the padded, curved bench that followed the contour of the *Noble Lady*'s stern. Glum stares replaced their bright smiles, which ordinarily lit up the dock.

"I heard about what happened at Eagle Harbor," I said. "It must have been hard. You're still taking your summer cruise up the Inside Passage, aren't you?"

Tears welled in the corners of Angela's eyes. Marvin pursed his lips and clenched his jaw, deepening the furrows along his brow.

"Yes, we're still going," Marvin said. "But before we leave there's something we'd like to ask of you."

"Certainly," I said.

Angela sighed. Her voice wavered as she spoke. "Mr. Noble, would you find out who that young woman was and why she ended up on our anchor?"

"Shouldn't the police and the Coast Guard do that?"

"Yes, they should," Marvin said. "But they won't."

"Won't?"

"Well, at least it's not a priority for them," he said. "Angela and I met with the police and with the Coast Guard this morning. We're not next of kin. So all they'd commit to is keeping us informed. Even after we explained why, they didn't understand how much it means to us to find out whom that girl belonged to; who loved her."

I looked back and forth between them. Their faces appeared older, more wrinkled with sadness and pain. "I'm afraid why this means so much to you both is not obvious to me either."

Angela sniffed back tears. "Amy," she said.

"The girl's name?" I asked.

Marvin winced. "No, our daughter's name."

I shook my head. "I'm not sure that I'm following you."

Marvin sighed. He took off his straw hat and slicked back his full head of silver hair. "When Amy was thirteen we took her camping by a small lake in eastern Washington."

Angela's eyes were red. "Our Amy was a young girl with her whole life ahead of her."

Marvin blinked back tears. "She left camp one morning to go for a walk, and we never saw her again. We searched the woods and hills surrounding the campground for almost a week. Many of the other campers helped. The police dragged the lake. But we never found Amy."

"Do you have any idea what it's like to try to continue with your life after the death of your only child?" Angela said. She closed her eyes and shook her head.

"I don't," I said.

"She just vanished," Marvin said with a snap of his fingers. "We never knew if she'd been abducted and murdered, run away or—"

"Our Amy didn't run away," Angela said. A tinge of anger colored her voice.

Marvin turned to her. "Dear, I'm not saying she did. I'm just saying that after all these years we still don't know."

"And somewhere a poor mother or father is wondering about that young girl we pulled from the bottom of Eagle Harbor," Angela said. "Right now, they don't know either."

"No one should ever have to go through what we went through," Marvin said. "That's why we'd like you to find out who she was and where she came from, so her family can at least begin healing from her death."

"It's hard to let go, to move on without the truth, without the body of a loved one," Angela said. "Years afterward, even though we were sure our Amy was dead, some part of us held out hope that a miracle had taken place and she'd return to us. We jumped every time the telephone or doorbell rang.

"We've talked about it, and we both feel that finding out about this young girl we pulled up on our anchor would, in a strange way, help us finally let go of our Amy."

"It sounds crazy," Marvin said. "But for years we've gone to church and prayed for Amy's safe return."

I shook my head. "It doesn't sound crazy at all. Even six years after her death, I often imagine my wife calling to me from the dock, then stepping aboard the *Noble Lady*."

Angela gasped. Her hand went to her chest. "I'm so sorry," she said. "How insensitive of me. I'd forgotten. Why just a moment ago I asked if you had any idea what it's like to continue with your life after the death of a loved one. . . . Of course you do."

"It's hard," I said. "Sometimes you don't know when or how to let go of the past in order to grab ahold of the future."

"Will you help us?" Marvin asked.

"I can certainly follow up with the police and the Coast Guard," I said.

Marvin grabbed my arm. For an older man he had a vicelike grip.

"I want you to investigate this on your own, regardless of what the authorities say."

I started to tell them about my plans to go out on the *Noble Lady* for two weeks with Kate, and how we'd both looked forward to this cruise. But one glance at the pain in their faces undercut my resolve.

"I'll see what I can find out," I said.

"No expenses barred," Marvin said. "Follow the investigation wherever it leads. And when we return from Alaska, tell us what you've found out about that poor child."

I nodded.

Outside, a large diesel engine groaned. I turned to look through one of the clear plastic windows embedded in the heavy dark blue canvas enclosing my cockpit. A clutch of people gathered to watch a glitzy white motoryacht, at least eighty feet long, maneuver into the visitor's dock. When I turned back to the Bayneses, they both had smiles. A sparkle had returned to their eyes.

"Thank you," Angela said. She sighed. "I may never be able to erase from my mind the frightful image of that young woman at the end of our anchor, but knowing that you'll find out who she was helps."

"You've lifted a burden from our hearts," Marvin said. "This may be the last year we cruise the Inside Passage. I wouldn't want forty years of fond memories to end on such a dismal note."

"Dear, people must tire of hearing us say that every summer's cruise might be our last," Angela said.

"Doesn't matter," Marvin said. "At our age, each day's a gift. The present *is* the present."

It sounded like something Señor Oller might say.

Marvin patted Angela on the knee. The two exchanged a soft, sweet glance. Then Marvin placed his hat back on his head and tapped it down. He stood. "Come, dear, let's leave Charlie to his Sunday." He reached for my hand. "Thank you, again," he said. Then he reached out for Angela and pulled her up from her seat. They slipped through the plastic enclosure and strolled, arm-in-arm, back down the dock toward their boat.

When Señor Oller said, "Perfection isn't the goal. Love is," he could easily have been speaking about a couple like Marvin and Angela.

I reopened the *English Suite* and picked up my guitar. But the plain white card at the bottom of the case called out to me. I reopened it, too, and placed it on the stand in front of the music.

I'd thought about calling Kate the night she left the wine and the card, but I called my friend Loi Ng instead. I thanked him for his help in solving my first case and I told him we should celebrate together. Then I told him the truth. I hadn't been with a woman in the years since Sharon's death. And the thought of starting over, being with someone else, both excited and scared me.

Loi spoke in rapid-fire Vietnamese to his wife, Minh Thi. Then he put her on the line. Both of them had known Sharon.

"Mr. Charlie," Minh Thi said in her soft, mellifluous voice. I remember laughing to myself, realizing that she hadn't a clue what "Mr. Charlie" would signify to an African American. "No harm try for love. Only harm do nothing, then feel sorry for self. Sharon very nice woman. Very loving. Would want you find love."

Somehow Minh Thi knew.

Before her death, Sharon made me promise that in time I'd find a loving woman. But Sharon insisted that this woman also should love boats as much as she did. Kate Sullivan did love boats as much as Sharon, and Minh Thi would hear nothing of our difference in age.

"Twelve year? Nothing," Minh Thi said. "Muscle of younger person stronger than muscle of older person. But love of older person maybe stronger than love of younger person. Older person has seen more life. Knows more value of love. Mr. Charlie, you call 'wine woman.'"

And I did.

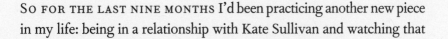

SO FOR THE LAST NINE MONTHS I'd been practicing another new piece in my life: being in a relationship with Kate Sullivan and watching that relationship grow. I'd break the news to her about the change in our cruising plans later. Right now, I wanted to begin the *English Suite*. And after that, even though it was Sunday, I wanted to start asking questions about the young woman that Marvin and Angela Baynes had pulled up from the bottom of Eagle Harbor.

two

After a frustrating half hour of trying to play the *English Suite* from memory, and berating myself because I couldn't, I put my guitar away and stepped off the *Noble Lady*. A tremulous, nasal rendition of "Amazing Grace" filtered through the rising, early afternoon heat. Ahead of me, Leonard Whitehall paraded back and forth between slips, red-faced, a bagpipe squeezed under his arm, his fingers working the tune. Off to one side, sitting on the bow of *Pied Piper,* his wife, Leslie, stroked their two Scotties, one black and the other white.

Leslie smiled as I passed by. "It's an annual ritual," she said. She motioned toward her husband with her head. "Each year, Len welcomes summer and the beginning of our cruising season by playing the pipes."

I stopped to listen, remembering that it was a remorseful, shipwrecked captain of a slave ship who wrote "Amazing Grace" to atone for the sins of his wretched business. I reached aboard *Pied Piper* to stroke the white Scottie, but it narrowed its eyes at me, growled low, tossed its head to one side, and trotted away down the side deck. I pointed to Len.

"He needs a kilt," I said.

"He's got a closet full," Leslie said. "Thank god, he's not wearing one today." She laughed, and then whispered, "His legs looked better thirty years ago."

When I reached Len, he marked time in place, eyes straight ahead, continuing to play while allowing me to pass. In the background, a chorus of sounds accompanied his bagpipe: the drumbeat of hammers, the drone of power tools, and the hiss of pressure washers. Boaters scurried to ready their vessels for cruising.

I took the asphalt walkway around the marina, toward Gate Six. Halfway there, I paused for the view. The snowy white cap of Mount Baker poked above the hills behind the city, jutting into a deep blue, cloudless sky. Off in the distance, beyond Bellingham Bay, the craggy peaks of the Olympic Mountains held a line of clouds at bay. Wind-socks and flags fluttered from the riggings of sailboats, rumoring of light winds. All signs pointed to a Pacific high-pressure front trying to build.

A line of blue dock carts filled with groceries awaited me at the top of the Gate Six ramp. With a low tide, the ramp angled down precipitously. Boaters grabbed a handrail with one hand, their cart with the other, leaning backward against the pull of gravity, while slowly working their way down. A young girl in a bathing suit and flip-flops struggled with her cart. I could see the cart about to get away from her. I raced to the head of the line and lunged for the cart handle just as it slipped from her grasp. She ran to the bottom of the ramp. When I got down to her with the cart, she slowly worked her gaze up the length of my body.

I handed the cart to her. "Can you make it from here?" I asked.

She said nothing. She just stared at me and slowly nodded. She seemed amazed at the tall black man who'd appeared out of nowhere to her rescue.

Three rows over from the main ramp, *Big Ben* sat in a slip with her cabin door open. The wooden, thirty-six-foot Grand Banks belonged to Bellingham police detective Ben Conrad. The sound of metal clinking on metal arose from inside the boat. Then silence. Then, "Shit!"

Apparently, I'd caught Ben aboard.

"Ben," I called out.

"Yeah."

"It's Charlie."

"Noble, that you?"

"Uh huh."

"Good. Just in time to go fishing."

I called back. "Lose a wrench in the bilge?"

A pair of oil-stained hands emerged from the cabin door, followed by Ben's face with a streak of oil across the cheek. "Fucking right. How'd you know?"

"Ahh. The telltale sounds of metal bouncing off metal, then silence followed by loud profanity."

Ben wiped his hands off with a rag then stepped onto the deck. "Lost a half-inch socket along with the wrench. Hell, half the bolts on the damn boat are half-inch. Come on aboard."

Ben waved me on. I swung up onto the rear deck.

"Stainless steel wrench and socket?"

"Uh huh. Expensive suckers."

"Too bad, a magnet won't work."

"What do you use?"

"Never lost anything in the bilge," I said.

Ben looked me straight in the eye. "Bull. If you own a boat, you've lost tools in the bilge."

I laughed. "Duct tape."

"Duct tape?"

"Uh huh. Wad it up, sticky side out. Put it on the end of a pole or piece of stiff hose. Drop the pole into the bilge and fish around until something bites."

Ben pointed at me and winked. "Good idea, Noble. Step in and have a seat. I'll be right up."

I slipped inside and grabbed the helm seat. My legs dangled above huge open pits, where Ben had ripped up the cabin sole, pulling out large parqueted squares to expose the engine, the shaft, and the boat's mechanical guts. He tore duct tape from a roll and mashed it between his two beefy palms. Then he pressed it onto the end of a length of fuel hose. Ben stepped down into the engine well. He bent his knees and started to descend deeper into the bowels of his boat, but he bounced up.

"It's one thing I hate about working on boats," he said.

"Not enough space."

"Especially for tall guys like us."

He dipped down again, burying his head so deep into the bilge that only his wriggling backside showed. I waited and listened to him grunt.

"Biting yet?"

"Hell, no," Ben mumbled. Then, "Come here you little sucker. . . . Damn. . . . Damn."

"Big one get away?"

"Go to hell, Noble."

"Been to bilge hell many times before, and used duct tape to get out."

"Come to Daddy. . . . Come to Daddy. . . . That's right," Ben said.

Then he became silent, though his backside squirmed as if he wanted to squeeze all of his large body into the bilge. Suddenly, he popped up from the engine. His face looked like he'd emerged from a day's hard work in a coal mine. But he held the stem of an oil-soaked socket wrench high in the air like a prized salmon he'd just landed. A smile and a line of white teeth broke through the grime on his face.

"I owe you one," Ben said. "Beer's in the fridge. Grab two. It's time for a break."

I stepped around the gaping openings in the cabin sole and made my way to the galley while Ben washed up in the head. He lowered the parquet squares back in place. I handed him a bottle and we walked outside. Ben unfolded two plastic chairs. We sat on the rear deck, holding our beers.

A twenty-seven-foot coast guard patrol boat zoomed into the harbor, slowing down as it neared us, but still sending a train of waves our way. We bobbed in its wake. Sunlight glared off the patrol boat's shiny aluminum pilothouse, which sat atop its black, inflatable bottom. Two men in dark blue uniforms and bright orange life vests stood on the rear deck of the patrol boat tying off fenders, which trailed in the water. Ben hoisted his beer bottle toward the coast guard boat.

"You miss that?" he asked.

"I worked in intelligence. It's been a long time since I went on patrol."

"Yeah, but do you miss being in the Guard?"

"Sometimes. I miss the travel, and the people I worked with."

Ben took a swig of beer. "Don't know if I coulda done what you did. Refusing an order to doctor an intelligence report. I've thought about it. Janet and I even talked about it. You know, if the chief said I needed to alter a report would I do it?" He took another swallow of beer. "If it meant losing my job . . . I just don't know."

"And if it meant losing your soul?"

"You felt that strong about it, didn't you?"

"Uh huh."

"Maybe you were a better man than I'd have been in the same situation. . . . I just don't know."

I raised my beer bottle to my lips and took a sip. "I hope you're never put in a situation where you have to find out."

"Ain't that the damn truth."

I drank some more beer, then pulled the bottle away from my lips and studied the label.

"Since when are you into Northwest microbrews?" I asked.

"I seem like a Bud guy, don't I?"

"Uh huh."

He grimaced. "Since Janet."

"I see. Added a little class to your life, huh?"

Ben smiled. "You come over to talk about the gals?"

"Not really, but we can. I came over to talk about the young woman raised from the bottom of Eagle Harbor."

Ben took a healthy swig. "Oh, that. Figured you might be looking into it."

"You did?"

"Yeah. I spoke with the folks that found her. They make a cute couple don't they?"

"Sure do."

"Anyway, they wanted us to find out all we could about the woman. Hell, I told 'em we didn't have the manpower or the money. Told 'em to hire an investigator. They said they knew just the person. I figured it was you, since their boat's also moored at Gate Nine."

"But isn't investigating this woman's death your job?"

"Ten, fifteen years ago, the police department woulda been all over this. We did the usual. Medical examiner performed an autopsy. Took a DNA sample. We sent prints and a photo to the national missing persons database. Reported the incident to state and federal authorities. If relatives turn up, or her prints or photo get a hit from another jurisdiction, then maybe we'll give it more juice. Right now, she's on ice at the morgue. The case'll get put at the bottom of our 'to-do list.' We're overworked and understaffed. You know the drill. Truth is, and frankly I hate to say this, this gal's death isn't a high enough priority. Hell, it didn't even happen in our jurisdiction."

"What do you mean not in your jurisdiction?"

"That couple snagged her body in Eagle Harbor. Eagle Harbor's on Cypress Island. Cypress Island's in Skagit County, not Whatcom County, where we are." Ben pulled the bottle away from his lips and laughed. "Hell, the Skagit County Sheriff's Department is overworked too. They were more than happy to hand over the case to us. Since the couple that found her live aboard in Bellingham, it kinda made sense. The chief owed the Skagit sheriff a favor, so we took the lead on the case."

"On paper only." I took a swallow of the microbrew. It had a sweet, chocolate flavor.

"Look, around here we've got more meth labs than pharmacies, drug runners tunneling underneath the border from Canada, and motorcycle gangs ruling like warlords. Add to that a shitload of regulations that Homeland Security wants us to follow—all unfunded, mind you—and we don't have a lot of time for your routine investigation of a dead body." Ben lowered his head and shook it. "It's a damn shame. We're no longer on patrol at the airport. So the airport has had to outsource security to a private firm. And we're damn near outsourcing daily police work to guys like you. . . . It's not why I became a cop."

"Can you tell me anything more about this young woman?"

"I don't know much. Based on the crab feeding, the medical examiner thinks she was in the water for a week or more. Gruesome stuff, ain't it?"

"Did she drown?"

"The ME says no, because there was very little water in her lungs."

"Bruising?"

"On her ankles, wrists, and neck. Maybe vaginally but there was too much decomposition and crab feeding to be certain."

I closed my eyes and let a stream of beer slide down my throat. "Rape? Bondage sex? It gets out of hand, and the guy throws her overboard."

"Could be one of those big-ass party boats, like that one, out for a good time." Ben pointed with his beer bottle across the marina to the eighty-foot yacht, *Longhorn,* sitting at the visitors' dock.

"Or a killer who lures prostitutes onto his boat, has sex, then kills them."

"Great, Noble, the San Juan Islands Killer. Just what we need. Look, I'm thinking she wasn't local. If she was, family or friends would have noticed her missing and filed a report."

"Unless she was a runaway."

"We ran a computer-reconstructed photo of her face against the missing persons database. Fingerprints too. Nothing."

"Doesn't mean she wasn't a missing person."

"I know that. But it doesn't mean she was, either."

"Did you comb the beach?"

"Yep. And we got zip."

"How about dragging Eagle Harbor? Sending down divers?"

Ben nearly spit up a mouthful of beer. "You're kidding, right?"

"No."

"Looking for what?"

"Evidence."

"Chief would shit his pants if I asked for divers and a drag team. Now tell me she had drugs on her, or a bomb, and the FBI, ATF, DHS, Coast Guard, and a hundred other friggin' agencies would be all over Eagle Harbor. Hell, they'd probably try to drain Puget Sound. If a local investigation doesn't smell of terrorism or drugs no one's going to throw big money at it."

"What's this woman look like?"

"Pretty gal. Young. Dark-skinned. Native. Hispanic. Oriental. Maybe Mediterranean. Hell, you should pay her a visit and see for yourself."

"I'll settle for a copy of her photograph."

Ben sighed. "Turns my stomach too. You'd think after all these years I'd be used to staring death in the face." Ben hit the arm of his chair with his bottle. "You want another?"

"Sounds good." I turned up my bottle and finished the last of my beer.

Ben stood up and disappeared inside the boat, emerging moments later with two sweating bottles. He twisted off a cap and handed one to me. "Can we change the subject?" he asked.

"Anything more I should know?" I asked.

"Nothing I can think of, but if I do I'll give you a holler. You'll keep me in the loop?"

"I will. You wanna talk about the women?"

"You read my mind."

"How's Janet?" I asked.

"Wild. Crazy." He hoisted his beer. "Maybe too much for a Bud guy like me to handle."

"Somehow I doubt that."

"You ever see her at the helm of a boat?" Ben smiled. "Yeah, I guess you have, haven't you?"

"That's why I thought you two would hit it off," I said.

"Well, you figured right. Janet's as crazy about boats as I am. Barbara hated boats."

"That'd be tough."

Ben laughed. "That's why she got the house and I got the boat in the divorce. Janet, on the other hand, can handle this boat better than me. Truth is, she's one hell of a nice gal. She's divorced. I'm divorced. We're taking things at a real low rpm. Biggest problem for me is that she's got this wild side. You know, peace, environment, poverty, abortion. She gets all worked up, then goes off to join a group protest. Every Friday she's out in front of the Federal Building, holding up a sign for us to get out of Iraq. Hell, I'm with the guys on the other side of the protest line."

"Sounds like being with her might stretch you a little."

"You taking her side?"

I held up the microbrew. "As far as you stepping up from Bud to microbrew I am. I like this beer."

Ben smiled. "Hate to admit it, but I like it too. Hell, the guys at the station razz me a little because of Janet. The latest thing she's into is a group that wants to stop development along Chuckanut Drive. Some rich Texan bought a tract of land and wants to put in 800 homes . . . 800 homes. A mix of high-rise apartments and single-family dwellings."

"To which you say what? 'Go for it buddy. The more the merrier?'"

"Like hell I do. Truth is, I'm glad people like Janet are fighting to preserve this town."

"You ever tell her that?"

"And spoil the basis for a good argument?"

"Lemme guess. The sex is great when you two make up."

Ben winked and pointed the microbrew at me. "Now tell me how it's going between you and Kate."

I took another sip of beer, then expounded on the virtues of re-learning a piece of music while beginning a new relationship. Ben screwed up his face. Maybe I'd waxed too philosophic for a Bud guy.

He pointed his beer bottle across the harbor toward Gate Nine. "As long as you do the relationship with Kate better than that guy plays his bagpipe."

"You can hear him all the way over here?"

"Like an off-key foghorn."

three

I smiled the entire walk back to Gate Nine. Behind his gruff exterior, Ben seemed pretty happy that I'd set him up with Janet Paulsen. Hey, maybe matchmaking could be a backup career option in case marine private investigation didn't work out.

Walking down the dock toward the *Noble Lady*, I noticed that the boarding gate was partially open and the large zipper on the plastic enclosure pulled up. A sweet lavender smell met me as I stepped aboard, which meant I'd find Kate inside. I opened the door. Kate sat behind the galley table. She raised her head from a book and smiled. My body responded with a rush of blood to my loins.

"You're out of uniform and you look relaxed," I said.

"I should be. I just came from my first hot yoga class."

"And would that be hot as in heat . . . or hot as in sexy?"

"We did yoga in a 105-degree room."

"That would be hot as in sweaty."

She laughed. "Don't worry, I took a shower after class."

A bulging, black, soft-sided suitcase sat at the top of the steps leading down to the stateroom. Kate turned to look at it. "I thought I'd start bringing over my gear today. We still haven't made a list of groceries and we're leaving the day after tomorrow. We need to get busy."

My body stiffened. I took a deep breath. "I've got some bad news."

Kate sat up straight. Her dark blue eyes flashed wide open. "What?"

I didn't have my speech prepared. I hadn't expected to see her so soon. I searched for words, but not fast enough.

"You don't want to go," Kate said.

"No. I do. But I took a job that might delay our departure for a few days."

"You don't want to go."

"I do."

"Then why'd you take a job?"

"I couldn't refuse."

She dropped both hands on the galley table. "You don't want to go."

"I do."

"What job?"

"A couple brought up the body of a young woman from the bottom of Eagle Harbor on their anchor."

"Yes. I know about it. But that's a law-enforcement investigation, maybe involving us at Station Bellingham." Kate pointed at me. "Why are you involved?"

"The couple asked me to investigate."

"And you said yes?"

"Uh huh."

"Are you afraid?"

"No. . . . I mean . . . of what? Am I afraid of what?"

"Afraid of going on vacation with me."

"No."

"Then why'd you take a job when you knew we were supposed to leave?"

I explained what happened, and why Marvin and Angela Baynes needed to find out about this young woman.

Kate jabbed her finger at me. "Did you tell them we were going on vacation?"

"No."

She jabbed at me again. "Did you tell them you had to check with your partner first to see how taking *their* case might impact *our* plans?"

"No."

"You're scared, Charlie. You're scared of being alone with me for two weeks on the *Noble Lady,* aren't you?"

"I'm not scared," I said. But I could feel my conviction lagging.

Kate held up her hands. "Take a deep breath, look me straight in the eyes, and then tell me you're not scared."

I closed my eyes. I took a deep breath and held it. When I opened my eyes, Kate's penetrating stare demanded the truth.

"Okay, I have some fear. But I didn't take the job to avoid going away with you."

"Thanks for being honest. But you didn't think about me either when you took the job."

"I felt trapped. Marvin and Angela stood here"—I pointed down—"obviously in pain. There seemed to be something I could do to help them, even though I knew it meant interfering with our plans."

"We're in a relationship. That means what each of us does affects the other. I need to feel that you'll take me into account when you make decisions that affect us. I don't feel that right now. I feel like you just thought about yourself." Tears pooled at the corners of Kate's eyes. "I don't want to take Sharon's place. I couldn't even if I did want to. I know that I'll never fill the place inside you that she did." She tapped her chest then pointed to me. "I want to carve out my own place inside you, and fill it with me. Are you ready for that? Or did our relationship happen too soon?"

"I think I'm ready."

Kate stood up before I could say anything more. "When you know for sure, give me a call," she said.

Kate snatched her bag from the floor. Her long dark hair whipped around her shoulders. She swept her hair back and brushed past me on her way toward the door. She yanked the cabin door open and ducked her tall frame under the doorway, then slammed the door closed behind her. The *Noble Lady* shuddered as she stepped off.

My sigh must have sounded like a foghorn. I slumped into the seat that Kate had left. Her lavender scent lingered. I parted the window blinds in time to see her car zoom away from the marina. I tried calling her on her cell phone, but she didn't answer. I lowered my head and massaged my brow. Damn. Sometimes being in a relationship felt like navigating through fog—without radar.

I putzed around the boat for the rest of the afternoon, tightening hose clamps that didn't need tightening, replacing a heater switch that didn't need replacing. Between tasks, I called Kate. She still refused to answer. I went over my plans for tomorrow. I intended to hire a diver to scour the bottom of Eagle Harbor. I also rehearsed my apology. "I'm sorry. Yes, I was wrong. I should have spoken to you before I took the case. It's hard starting a new relationship, when I'd planned on the previous one lasting a lifetime. And, no, I don't expect you to fill Sharon's place. I love you for who you are." Wine and flowers might sweeten my mea culpa.

After dinner I tried several supermarkets, but none had our special wine, Red Mountain Reserve. So I settled on a nice bouquet of flowers. The dashboard clock read 9:30 when I pulled into the marina parking lot. Down at the *Noble Lady*, a soft light illuminated horizontal lines from the slats of the blinds on the large galley window. Lavender scented the rear deck. Inside, atop the galley table, a candle flickered next to a bottle of Red Mountain Reserve. But I didn't see Kate.

"I'm in here." Her voice came from the stateroom.

I held the flowers out in front and stepped down into the stateroom, where another candle burned. Kate sat in bed with her back propped against the wall, reading. Only now she wore the black lace negligee I'd given her for Christmas. She slapped the book closed and reached for my hand, drawing me down on the bed beside her. I handed her the flowers. She sniffed them, then set the bouquet on the nightstand.

"I was wrong—"

"Don't," Kate said. "I pushed you and I didn't need to. I'm sorry. I'm scared too. Scared that you won't give me the chance to be in this relationship. Scared that you'll find a reason to push me away. Because

I'm twelve years younger than you; because you're African American and I'm not; because you're afraid that you're not ready for a new relationship."

"So what do we do if we're both scared?" I asked.

"What we do is hold each other."

Kate slid down in bed and pulled me down with her. Then she guided my head toward her and we kissed deeply, passionately. When we came up for air, she said, "You know that's one of the reasons I love you?"

"What reason?"

"Because you care about people like the Bayneses and you're willing to go out of your way to help them."

"And all this time I thought you loved me because I was tall, dark, and handsome."

"That too."

She pulled my head toward her again, and we kissed. This time when we came up for air, she said, "And you love me because?"

"Are you fishin'?"

"Without shame."

"Because you're tall, light, and gorgeous. . . . And because you're sensitive, caring, loving. . . . I could go on."

"And at some other time you will."

Kate pulled me in for another kiss, then she abruptly pushed my head back. "I'm not too beamy? My stern's not too wide?"

"A beamy boat's more comfortable when the seas get rockin' 'n' rollin'. And as for your stern," I slipped my hand under the covers. "My hands-on inspection concludes that it's rounded in perfect proportion to your beam."

"Just like the *Noble Lady*'s."

"Most women would not appreciate being compared to a boat," I said.

"Most women don't love boats as much as I do."

"Which is another reason I love you," I said.

Kate wrapped her hands around my neck and guided me down for another long kiss. When we came up for air this time, she said, "You know I was going to ask if we could postpone leaving anyway."

"What?" I raised my head and looked at her.

Kate's eyes sparkled in the candlelight. The flames set shadows dancing softly over her face. "Two new crews are in from Cape May for training. The station CO asked if there was any way I could delay my vacation to assist. I'd be out on the *Sea Eagle* for a week to ten days."

"As a lieutenant looking to become a lieutenant commander, this would be good for your career."

"Yes, Commander, it would be."

Kate stroked the back of my neck, sending tingles down my spine. "Are you sorry you never reached captain?" she asked.

"God knows I had the years and the experience for that promotion."

"And your former CO offered to reinstate you after you uncovered the reasons why Admiral Ritchie wanted your report falsified."

I sighed. "I couldn't go back. You come to a point in your life where you have to let go of the past in order to grab hold of the future, even if you don't know what that future will bring."

Kate raised her head for a quick kiss. "That's another reason I love you," she said. "You're willing to risk the safety of what you know for the challenge of an adventure. The good news is the CO said if I stayed for this training cruise, he'd give me a three-week leave afterward but write it up as two. That'd mean we could have three weeks of adventure together."

"That's great," I said. I thought about asking why this important bit of information concerning her CO hadn't surfaced earlier. But one look at Kate, shimmering in candlelight, lavender, and lace, convinced me that not all my questions needed answers. Kate pulled me down to her and we kissed again.

"Do you think it's time we got the seas rockin' 'n' rollin'?" she asked. "And test out your theory about the comfort of my beam?"

"I do."

"So do I."

We kissed once more. Only this time, I slipped off my clothes and we didn't surface for air.

THE FOLLOWING MORNING, I awoke to an empty pillow. Kate had left at 0500 to report for duty. For breakfast, I made a smoothie with orange juice and a protein powder that Kate had found at the local food co-op. Despite her cajoling, I hadn't tried it yet. The label read, "No dairy. No wheat. No soy. No eggs. No animal or fish products." Which left me scratching my head about where the protein came from. So I spun the can around and read further. Rice, and more than fifty other herbs, enzymes, and extracts. What the heck. If Ben could switch from Bud to microbrew, I could switch from coffee and toast to something healthful like this shake for breakfast. I took a sip. Vanilla with a pleasant, sweet taste. Not bad when you consider the label also read, "No added sugar."

After breakfast, I set out to hire a diving partner. Every diver learns never to go down alone. It only takes one search-and-recovery operation pulling up the body of some guy who thought he could beat the odds to drive the point home. In over twenty years in the Guard I'd pulled up more than two dozen. I'd heard of a fellow named Dan, who owned Raven Diving and Salvage located here in the harbor.

I took the marina walkway again and caught a glimpse of *Big Ben* as I passed by Gate Six. The path followed the shoreline out to Zuanich Point Park. There, a tall granite statue of a weathered fisherman in rain gear and a cap faced north, in the direction of so many tragic fishing accidents. He stood ready to heave the rescue line coiled in his hands to the souls of his brethren who had never made it back to port.

On the other side of the monument, a woman stood, holding a child's hand. She ran a finger down the list of fishermen lost at sea, stopping at the names etched under the year 1999.

Beyond the statue, the masts of the tallest fishing boats came into view, peeking over the breakwater at Gate Five. Interspersed between the fishing fleet, the white hulls of large yachts gleamed in the sunlight.

Many harbors separate their fishing fleet from their pleasure craft. But here at Squalicum Harbor they were mixed.

At the bottom of the Gate Five ramp, two men wrestled a large net peppered with tiny white floats onto the back end of the *Pacific Master,* a fishing boat over one hundred feet long. One man stood on deck, barking orders to a second man, who stumbled several times before finally feeding the last of the net aboard. I walked over to the *Pacific Master.*

"Excuse me," I said to the man on the dock.

When he turned around, I caught a strong whiff of alcohol mixed with tobacco and rotten fish. The man had bloodshot eyes. He looked me up and down and said nothing.

"I'm looking for Raven Diving and Salvage," I said. "Do you know where I can find it?"

He smiled, exposing a row of yellowed teeth. "Need a bottom job?"

"No. But I do need to find Raven Diving and Salvage."

"Well, that's what he does, don't he? BJs for you fucking fancy yachties." He turned to the man aboard the *Pacific Master* and yelled, "Guy's lookin' for a fuckin' BJ."

"Gary," the man aboard the ship said. "Fuck with 'im. Let's get back to work so we can get outta here sometime soon."

A line of concrete berths to my right held mainly larger fishing vessels. I looked left, past the *Pacific Master.* Gary pulled a smaller net from a cart on the dock. He backed up to toss it to the man aboard. He may have been hung over, because he stumbled as he walked, backing up at an angle into me. I caught him with my hands and gently pushed him forward. He dropped the net and swung around.

"What the fuck you doing, yachtie?" He pushed me back, hard.

I tried to explain what just happened, but comprehension didn't seem like Gary's strong suit. "Maybe you should just go back to work," I said.

"Maybe you should stay outta a working man's way." He pushed me again.

He must have been too drunk to realize that I hadn't even moved from his puny shove. I wasn't looking for a fight, so I turned to walk away. But a moment later, an arm clapped my shoulder. I spun around to Gary's fist heading toward me. I didn't even bother to block it. I threw my weight onto my left foot and leaned to that side. Gary's fist and his body flew past me, headed for the water. I grabbed him by his shoulder. By this time, his friend had hopped down from the fishing boat. I pulled Gary back from the edge of the dock, spun him around, and threw him over to his partner.

"Sorry. He had a little too much to drink last night, eh?" the other man said.

"He's going to get himself hurt throwing a punch like that again."

The other man cuffed Gary by the collar and bundled him away. Gary mumbled, "Fucking yachtie."

I think this is why many harbors separate their fishing fleet from their pleasure craft.

A gauntlet of bows lay ahead of me. Guys like Gary aside, I love walking docks filled with older fishing boats. I passed the *Sea Maiden*, an old wooden trawler about sixty feet long. She had to have been built before World War II. Paint peeled off her hull. Rot ate away at her planks. Rust stains oozed from her bronze portholes.

I stopped and stepped back to admire the old gal, looking beyond her sad decline to the heritage of my *Noble Lady*. She had a pilothouse set well back, away from the area where green water would come crashing over the foredeck. A rounded stern to split following seas. Stabilizer poles to dampen her roll. Some yacht owners might turn up their noses at the *Sea Maiden*. But I'd moor my boat next to her in a heartbeat. Then the *Noble Lady* would be close to the roots of her own family tree.

A gray-haired man, dressed in slacks and an open-collar white shirt, stepped off a sleek fifty-seven-foot Bayliner across from the *Sea Maiden*. He called out to me. "She's for sale."

"The *Sea Maiden*?"

"Hell, I haven't seen anyone on her for years. . . . No, *Happy Hour*," he said, pointing to the Bayliner.

He chuckled. "Best looking boat on this dock."

"It depends on your eye," I said.

He squinted. I looked closer at *Happy Hour*. A "For Sale" sign hung from her deck rail.

"Which one would you take?" the man asked. "That old wooden barge, or this modern fast bullet?"

I smiled. "We're out in the open Pacific. Forty-knot winds. Fifteen-foot seas. Which one would you take? That shallow draft Tupperware bowl, or this solid, deep draft trawler that's been out there and back hundreds of times before?"

"You must be a fisherman," the man said.

"No, but you must be a boat broker."

He smiled. "Uh huh."

"I'm looking for Raven Diving and Salvage," I said.

"Need a bottom job, huh?" He pointed down the dock. "All the way at the end on the left. You should love his boat. It's a smaller version of that." He pointed back to the *Sea Maiden* and frowned.

four

A circular logo in the window of the old wooden boat featured a raven perched atop the arched back of an orca, both drawn with the oval shapes common to northwestern Native American art. I didn't see a sign, but apparently I'd arrived at the corporate headquarters of Raven Diving and Salvage. The boat also had the name *Raven*. She appeared to be about thirty feet long. A weathered bronze plaque on the side of her cabin read, "Wm. Garden, 1942," which to most might mean little, but for a boat aficionado equated to finding "A. Stradivari" on the inside of a violin.

A bilge pump kicked off, startling me as I walked toward the door at the rear of *Raven*. It pumped . . . and pumped . . . and pumped. Caulk needed replacing. Several brass fasteners holding the side planks had popped out. A faded blue tarp, stretched over a scaffold of PVC tubing, covered most of the rear deck. A lot of people erect tarps for temporary protection from the rain. But the underside of this tarp showed several shades darker blue than the top, which gave me the impression that it functioned more as a permanent roof over a leaky vessel.

I knocked on a rear porthole . . . and waited. No answer. I knocked again. Then someone inside knocked back. I waited. Still no answer. So

I knocked once more. Again someone knocked back. I got the feeling it meant "go away."

I called toward the porthole. "I'm looking for Raven Diving and Salvage."

No answer. So I knocked and said, "Is this Raven Diving and Salvage?"

Someone knocked back, while saying, "Not today."

I don't like being told no, especially by someone knocking from behind a porthole. But at least I'd figured out the company's communication style. I said, "I need you to go diving," and I preceded each word with a knock.

The man inside the boat rapped on the porthole three times, "No . . . bottom . . . jobs."

I rapped back, "Don't . . . need . . . one."

Three knocks followed. "No props . . . No shafts . . . No zincs."

I replied with four, "Don't . . . need . . . those . . . either."

The fellow pounded out, "No . . . salvage . . . work."

I hit the porthole, "Not . . . that . . . either."

Four more thuds asked, "What . . . do . . . you . . . want?"

I didn't beat the porthole this time. "I need you to dive for evidence," I said.

The porthole creaked as it swung back, and a Native American man with jet-black hair tied into a ponytail stuck his head out. "Evidence of what?"

"A crime."

"Where?"

I knelt, which placed me eye-level with the porthole. "Eagle Harbor."

"What kinda crime?"

"Possibly a murder."

"Is this some kind of joke? You know, I don't work for the police or the Coast Guard any longer."

"I didn't know that."

The man squinted at me, then rubbed his eyes. "You're not with 'em anyway, are you?"

"I'm not."

"Goddamn government agencies. After 9/11, I had to be certified to dive for them. Background checks. Fingerprints. Pay them money." He pointed a finger to himself. "My land. My water. White people should be certified to be here. Background checks. Fingerprints. Pay us money." He squinted at me again. "But then you're not white, either."

"I'm not."

"You had breakfast?" he asked.

"Yes."

"You need some coffee?"

I laughed to myself, thinking about the protein smoothie. "I do," I said. I'd fallen off the wagon so soon.

"Not much room inside here," the man said. "Hop aboard. Push the gear aside and have a seat on the rear deck. Be out with a cup in a minute."

It appeared that *Raven* functioned not only as the corporate head-quarters, but the CEO's private residence as well. I set two scuba tanks on the rear deck and slid into a seat beside a rusting air compressor. I kicked away a tattered wetsuit from underneath my feet. A moment later, the cabin door handle moved down and the man bumped the door open with his hip. He held a coffee cup in each hand, extending one to me. I reached for the cup.

"Are you Dan?" I asked.

He jerked the cup away and narrowed his eyes.

"I was told the owner of Raven Diving and Salvage was a guy named Dan," I said.

"You were told wrong," the man said. "The owner's name is Raven." He handed me the cup.

"That you?"

He took a sip and nodded.

"Name's Charlie," I said. "Charlie Noble." I didn't bother reaching out to shake. Raven didn't seem like a guy for whom shaking hands held much meaning. He stood at most five feet six, but he was compact and slightly barrel-chested. He wore only boxer shorts and a sleeveless

T-shirt. A fading tattoo on his arm showed a raven set inside the arc of a crescent moon formed by the distorted shape of an eagle. All drawn in northwestern Native American style like his logo.

Raven sat atop an air tank. "Murder at Eagle Harbor," he laughed. "Sounds like a Raymond Chandler novel."

"You like detective mysteries?"

He nodded.

"Me too," I said.

Raven stared into his cup of coffee, and then suddenly lifted his head. "When do we go?" he asked.

"To Eagle Harbor?"

He squinted as though I'd lost my mind. Raven also didn't seem like a guy for whom details held much meaning.

I pointed to his corporate offices. "Going in this boat?" I asked.

"That a problem?"

"Not if she's seaworthy."

"Does she look that way?"

"No."

"I've got a dive boat that'll get us there," Raven said.

"You didn't say anything about your rates," I said.

"You didn't ask."

"What are they?"

"Depends."

"On what?"

"What I have to do once I get there."

"In other words, you don't know."

"Neither do you."

"That's why . . . Look, I want to dive with you."

Raven jerked his head around toward me. "You got diving chops?"

"Coast Guard. Advanced Diving School."

"Thought you said you weren't with 'em."

"I'm not."

"What happened? After 9/11 they wanted to certify you, too?" He chuckled.

"Something like that," I said.

"You got gear?"

"Medium-weight dive suit. Flippers. Snorkel. Weight belt. No mask or tanks."

He snorted. "Vacation gear." He stared into his coffee again, then raised his head and stared at me. Raven had penetrating, dark eyes. "I'll see what I've got."

I pulled back the blue tarp and peeked outside. "Weather looks good. We can—"

Raven cut me off. "Low pressure's moving in, might bring some fog."

"Did the weather forecast say that?"

"Hmmph." Raven stared into his coffee.

I got the feeling that weather reports didn't hold much meaning for him either.

He stood up and reached for the cabin door. "Be back in an hour with your gear." Raven disappeared inside. Only then did I realize that I hadn't touched a drop of coffee. I set the cup down and made my way off the boat.

AN HOUR LATER, I arrived back at Raven Diving and Salvage wheeling a dock cart full of my diving gear. I knocked on the rear porthole but Raven didn't answer. I thought about knocking while calling out his name, like I'd done before, but I decided to forgo the strange ritual. I'd give Raven fifteen minutes before looking for someone else to dive with me at Eagle Harbor. Thirty minutes later, a boat screamed around the breakwater with its bow pointed high. The engine revs dropped precipitously, and the bow lowered to the water.

Raven brought the thirty-foot aluminum craft alongside his wooden boat. It looked like a miniature World War II landing craft. It also reminded me of a modified version of the boats that many Native American fishermen here use, with the exception of the weathered aluminum covering welded to its rear deck, which protected the compressor, tanks, floats, and the other diving equipment.

I tossed Raven my gear and jumped aboard. We zoomed from the harbor bow up. Out in Bellingham Bay, a steady breeze had started from the south. In the distance, near Fidalgo Island, a low-lying cloud bank moved slowly our way. Funny, I'd looked across the bay before returning to Raven's boat. I hadn't seen the cloud bank then. I'd also checked the weather report before leaving the *Noble Lady* with my diving gear. Donna and Craig, NOAA's computerized weather-radio voices, had said nothing about fog.

Raven sat silently at the helm, staring straight ahead. Halfway across the bay he turned and said, "Take the wheel."

Which I did.

Raven walked onto the rear deck. He rummaged through his gear and pulled out a heavy canvas bag, from which he withdrew a large, circular skin drum and a wooden drumstick with a rounded leather head.

We made fifteen knots across the bay, about double the *Noble Lady*'s top speed. While we skipped along the light chop, Raven sat on the rear deck, eyes closed, beating out a rhythm in time with our boat clapping into the waves. Then we rounded Carter Point, the south tip of Lummi Island, and the drumming stopped. I looked over my shoulder. Raven slipped his drum and drumstick back in the canvas bag. He walked into the cabin.

"You want the wheel?" I asked.

Raven walked over to a window and looked out. "SEALs," he said. "Underwater demolition. Desert Storm. I blew out my eardrums more times than I can remember. Sometimes I feel vibration through my body better than I hear sound. Playing the drums helps calm my nerves. Besides, I drummed to ask the spirit world for permission to enter these waters," he added, pointing to the rippled patch of water ahead, just to one side of the dark green buoy marking Viti Rocks.

"You mean the tide rip in the Devil's Playground?"

"One culture's devils. Another culture's gods. Tide rips. Rapids. They signify a threshold, a doorway, an entry point from one realm to another. You step over at your own peril, which is why you ask permission from the spirit world first."

I hadn't thought about tide rips or rapids that way before. "Diving and salvage. Not a good business to be in with blown eardrums," I said.

"It's a business I know."

By the time we reached the Cone Islands, a ghostlike band of mist was floating our away up Bellingham Channel. Raven turned to view it.

"Pressure changes," he said. "I feel them through my body."

I swerved south around the Cone Islands and headed into Eagle Harbor. At the harbor's mouth, we passed a park ranger's aluminum skiff tied to two old wooden pilings. A few red-and-white crab-trap floats bobbed in the water.

Eagle Harbor on Cypress Island is a harbor only in the sense that it provides shelter from northern and western winds. No glitzy marina lines its shore. No docks jut into its waters. Only a handful of mooring buoys await visiting boaters.

Cypress Island is the last large, undeveloped San Juan island. The state owns most of Cypress, and it's managed by the Department of Natural Resources. Eagle Harbor's dark green shores and high rocky cliffs hint at the pristine beauty that must have graced Cypress and the other San Juan islands before humans arrived on their shores.

When I anchor in Eagle Harbor, I usually tuck in close to the five-hundred-foot cliff on the north side, which offers great protection from the wind and still affords a stunning view of Mount Baker.

I love Eagle Harbor, as many boaters do. But word of the dead woman must have spread quickly because no other boats anchored here today.

Raven tapped my shoulder. "What are we diving for?"

"Don't know."

He scanned the shoreline. "Tide's falling. We'll anchor this side of the shallow ledge in the center of the harbor. We'll dive first. Afterward, when the tide's low, we can comb the mud flats on the other side of the ledge on foot."

I swung the aluminum boat into the center of the harbor and we dropped our anchor in forty feet of water. We sat on the back deck, stripping out of our clothes and donning our wetsuits.

"Someone died here?" Raven asked.

"A couple pulled a young woman up from the bottom on their anchor."

He looked around and took a deep breath. "Place needs to be cleansed. Her spirit needs to be released from here and sent on. Bad business diving in an area where someone's died without cleansing it first."

With the top of his wetsuit falling down behind him, exposing his chest, Raven walked over to the canvas bag and pulled out his drum. Then he stepped inside the cabin and emerged with what looked like a bundle of dried grass. He grabbed a lighter and set the end of the grass on fire. He blew out the flames and handed me the smoldering parcel.

"Sage," he said. "Wave it out over the water. Do you know her name?"

"No."

"Doesn't matter. In your heart, tell her soul to follow the smoke home as it leaves the earth."

Raven walked around the rear deck, holding the skin drum over the side of the boat and drumming toward the water. I held the burning sage over the side as well, waving it back and forth in time to Raven's slow, mournful beat. I can't say that I understood what we were doing or why, but I watched as smoke rose from the bundle of sage and mixed with the fog that gathered around us.

Ten minutes later, Raven beat the drum loudly three times, spoke a few words softly under his breath, then stopped. He took the sage from my hand and tapped it on the side rail of the boat. The embers hissed as they fell into the water. Raven carefully wrapped the remains of the burned sage in aluminum foil and stowed it back inside the cabin. Then he put his drum away.

He sat on a bench and pulled the top of his wetsuit over his head. He zipped his suit up, turned to me, and said, "Her soul's grateful that you came. Grateful that you asked me to come. She said we are in the right place, and whatever we find here will bring peace and comfort to those who need it."

I still didn't get what had taken place, but I did feel serenity settling over me in the same way that the fog now settled over the boat and the water. I could no longer see the shore at the head of the harbor.

Raven twirled his finger for me to turn around. He lifted an air tank. I stuck my arms through the straps. I reached behind me for the mouthpiece, stuck it between my teeth, and bit lightly. I breathed a few times to make sure the tank and my air regulator worked. Then I dropped the mouthpiece and turned around to help Raven.

His stare unnerved me.

"Now I understand," he said. "Noble goes where the spirit calls, even if he can't hear his name." Raven nodded, which led me to believe that in his world I'd just passed muster.

We walked through the gate at the back of the boat and onto the swim step, where we sat and put on our flippers. Raven tossed a weighted line into the water. When the weight hit the bottom the line tugged on a float attached to a black-and-red-checkered flag that would tell boaters we swam below the surface. We'd also use that line to make our descent. Then Raven placed a large bag of floats, lines, and lead weights on the swim step before he slid into the water. He held onto the step while he checked his wrist compass. Then he looked up at me.

"We'll swim a grid search pattern. A hundred feet out, move the lines over ten feet, then a hundred feet back. Wait here 'til I set out the grid."

"You need any—"

Apparently not.

I hadn't even finished asking if he needed help before Raven had grabbed a line, a float, and a weight. He lowered his mask and disappeared below the surface with a swoosh. A white float trailed in the soft ripples of his wake. For the next twenty minutes that float rode a stream of bubbles out from our boat then back again, grazing smaller orange crab-trap floats in its path. Finally, the float dipped briefly under water before bobbing to the surface a hundred feet off of our stern.

Raven's flippers occasionally broke the surface as he swam just under the water back to the boat. Then, like an underwater ballet dancer, he arched back gracefully and came to an upright position, treading water. He pulled up his mask and pulled out his mouthpiece. Between spits of water he said, "It's murky down there. . . .We'll travel together along the jackline, holding onto one of the search lines. . . . When we come to the end we'll move the lines ten feet over toward the shore. . . . Watch out for crab-trap lines. Got a knife?"

I patted the knife bound to my ankle and nodded. Then I slipped in beside Raven. I swished water around in my face mask before putting it on. Finally, I took several easy breaths through my mouthpiece and ducked beneath the surface. I pinched my nose and blew gently several times before my ears cleared. Raven hovered nearby. I gave him a thumbs-up, then followed him down.

As I descended through the cold water, an even colder shiver wracked my body. Six years ago I'd scattered Sharon's ashes over Tribune Bay. This marked my first time diving since then. It didn't matter that Tribune Bay lay one hundred miles north. Diving here at Eagle Harbor, I felt like I'd just entered the world where Sharon now resided. I blinked back tears.

"I love you," I said.

The words vibrated against my throat. Raven spun around as though he'd heard them too. He stopped, stared into my eyes, put a hand on my shoulder, and pointed up. I shook my head and pointed down. He nodded and began swimming. I took slow, easy breaths and followed. Quietness filled my senses. The sensation of floating freed my body.

A few small fish swam by as we descended. Once we reached the bottom, I saw that Raven had laid out a rectangle of rope ten feet wide and a hundred feet long. I squinted to see the far end but the turbid water prevented me. Three ropes traveled the length of the grid. He'd run a weighted jackline down the middle with two search lines on either side. Lead balls held down the lines. He'd also attached the white float to the far end of the jackline.

Raven grabbed hold of the jackline with one hand, the outer line on his right with the other. I did the same only to his left, grabbing the jackline just behind his hand. Rescue and recovery divers call this a "jackstay search," and it would have been my choice, too, when faced with the low visibility we had here in Eagle Harbor.

In the muck beneath me I saw several Dungeness crabs skittering along. Raven stopped, checked his compass again, and pointed. We headed away from the boat along the jackline. Fifty feet later Raven's hand flew out to hold me back. Like a magician plucking an object from the air, he pinched a crab-trap line between his fingers. I hadn't seen it. Raven held it out of the way as we swam by.

Suddenly, Raven tapped me on my shoulder, hard. He made exaggerated pointing motions down and to his right just outside the grid. I followed Raven as he swam. The bottom dropped off slightly. At first it looked like we headed toward a rock.

Then I saw it too.

five

I fought hard to keep my mind and breathing in check. We swam in close and came upon the body of a young woman resting on the seabed. Her eyes and mouth seemed shocked wide open. In the murky water, her skin shimmered a ghastly dark green color. Rocks tied to her ankles and wrists weighed her down. Her dark hair trailed up toward the surface. A small crab crawled out from between her lips.

Raven whipped an underwater marker from a bag tied to his waist. He fastened a line around the dead woman's wrist, then pulled a cord, which inflated a small balloon that shot to the surface. He motioned for me to follow him up.

We ascended slowly. I ripped off my mask when I broke the surface. Raven lifted his above his eyes. Fog shrouded Eagle Harbor. I couldn't see the dive boat or the shoreline. The marker noting the dead woman's body bobbed in the water several feet away. We treaded water.

"Are you okay?" Raven asked.

I spit out water. "I am." I motioned down with my finger. "We should go back."

"You think we'll find more bodies?"

"I've got a sickening feeling."

I refitted my face mask. When we reached the bottom, we grabbed hold of the jackline and an outer line, resuming our search pattern. Ahead of me and slightly off to my left, I caught a glimpse of a dark object resting on the bottom. When we reached it, I pinched the crab-trap line between two fingers. Three large Dungeness crabs writhed in the trap. We swam ten yards farther and I spied another crab trap, this one resting on a large rock. Dozens of crabs clambered over the rock and the trap.

Then I saw hair floating up from the rock. I jerked the jackline. Raven stopped. I jabbed his shoulder, then pointed. We let go of the lines and swam in that direction. When we got to the trap my stomach heaved. The crab trap lay atop the body of another young woman. She also had rocks tied to her, assuring that crabs would have their fill. I swallowed hard.

Crabs had eaten away the left side of her face, neck, and chest, exposing bone in places. She wore a thin blouse, shredded now, through which the crabs had ripped chunks of flesh from her left breast. Raven pulled a knife from his ankle sheath and flicked away the crabs. He moved the trap from the woman's chest. Then he tagged her body and yanked on a small cord, sending another marker balloon jetting to the surface.

I stared at the upper body of this woman, one side bone, the other side pale flesh. The disturbing image brought to mind a painting I'd seen of a beautiful young woman looking in the mirror at her reflection, which had become a skeleton. I shook my head. I saw a dark patch on the remaining skin of her chest. I brought my head in close. My face mask touched her flesh, and before my eyes a tattoo of the Virgin Mary came into focus.

When we reached the far end of the jackline, we moved it and the search lines ten feet to our right, then we swam back toward the boat along the lines. This meant I'd cover the same ground that Raven already had covered. But it also meant we wouldn't miss any bodies or evidence in our search. After two hours of searching we found nothing more. Raven tapped my shoulder and hiked his thumb upward.

We rose slowly through the cloudy green water. Once at the surface, we swam the short distance to the boat and hoisted ourselves onto the swim step. We sat there without speaking, reaching down to slip off our flippers. The fog had thinned in places, revealing dark green patches of trees along the shore. I don't think either of us knew what to say.

Suddenly, just as Raven pushed up from the swim step, about to stand, two loud pops broke the silence. Two bullets bit into the stern. Simultaneously, we both keeled over into the water. We grabbed our flippers from the swim step just as two more bullets dived between us with dull, watery zips.

"Move to the front of the boat," Raven said. "And stay there."

Raven had already slipped into his flippers. Before I could respond, he disappeared under the water. I worked myself forward along the side of the hull. I strained to see through the fog, but I couldn't locate Raven. I waited. And listened. I heard only the gentle rush of water against the shore. I treaded water for another ten minutes. No more gunshots came, but then neither did Raven. So I moved to the back of the boat and hoisted myself onto the swim step. I slipped off my flippers and dashed inside the cabin. I ripped the microphone from the side of the VHF radio to call the Coast Guard. But I hesitated.

If I got the Coast Guard involved, they'd claim jurisdiction, homeland security, and god knows what else, which would make it a lot harder for me to work this case. Raven might not be thrilled to see Coast Guard either. On the other hand, I could get the overworked Bellingham Police Department involved. They might make an obligatory call to the Coast Guard, but by the time all the bureaucratic wrangling over turf died down, maybe I'd know why a popular anchorage had suddenly become a gruesome killing ground.

I rummaged through my gear bag and wrestled my cell phone free. I brought up Ben Conrad's number. But before I could hit Send, the back of the boat tipped low. I ran outside. Raven sat slumped over on the swim step.

"I made it to the shore. Tried to work my way around the shooter.

He took off before I got there." Raven ran a hand down the side of his wetsuit. "Too heavy. Couldn't catch him in all this gear."

Raven breathed hard. I helped lift his tank from his shoulders.

"Did you see who took the shots?"

"No."

"See which way he ran?"

Raven shook his head. "Not a lot of ways to run. Probably took the trail up to Reed Lake."

"One gunman? Two?"

"Don't know. But I did get this."

Raven held a bullet between his thumb and index finger.

"Where?"

He pointed down. "Right underneath the boat."

"Someone didn't want their killing ground discovered," I said.

"Why use Eagle Harbor?" Raven asked. "It's not that deep. Boaters and crabbers are here year round. Last place I'd dump a body."

"Me too. . . . It doesn't make sense."

While Raven dressed, I called Ben Conrad. Ben sounded impatient.

"Can't talk. I'm in the middle of monitoring one of Janet's goddamn demonstrations."

"Then listen," I said. "We just dived at Eagle Harbor. There are at least two more bodies of young women down there. And when we came up someone fired a couple of shots at us from shore."

"Shit," Ben said. "What'd I do to deserve a day like this? Two more bodies in Eagle Harbor?"

"Uh huh. They're tagged and flagged. Maybe you should call the marine unit. Get them out here to raise the bodies before the crabs leave nothing for the medical examiner to examine."

"Maybe I should call the marine unit? . . . Fucking funny, Noble. I am the marine unit. You know that. Can you wait there?"

"How long?"

"Let's see . . . Eagle Harbor . . . Have to call the chief and get him to relieve me from monitoring this line of traffic . . . Get the police boat ready . . . Say two and a half to three hours?"

"I'll check with the fellow I'm diving with."

"Who's that?"

"Guy named Raven."

"Dan?"

"Raven."

"Native guy? Short? Muscular? Used to be a navy diver?"

"Uh huh. He used to be a SEAL."

"That's Dan. Dan Ravenheart Washington. Has a problem with authority. Minor run-ins with the law. But he knows the diving and salvage business. Tell him we could use his help recovering the bodies. We'll pay him of course."

"He said the Coast Guard hadn't cleared him for government work."

"Hell, if you don't tell the CG, I won't."

"I'll ask Raven."

I stepped outside and called to Raven.

"Can we sit tight until the police marine unit arrives? They want to hire you to help retrieve the bodies."

He leaned against the railing, looking forlornly out over the water. He didn't answer, so I tapped the railing lightly. He turned around. I asked again. He nodded slowly. I took that to mean yes.

"We'll be here when you get here," I said to Ben.

I snapped my cell phone closed and walked back out on deck. Raven turned to me. "Bad business, Noble. Many troubled spirits here in Eagle Harbor. Now two more souls need to find their way home."

I didn't need to ask. I stepped back into the cabin and grabbed the half-burned bundle of sage. A shiver rippled through me. I couldn't shed the image of that young woman's crab-eaten body. Something needed to be done, if not for the dead, then for the living. Raven already had his drum out by the time I returned. So for the second time in a few short hours, he drummed while I cleansed the air.

The fog had burned off by the time we completed this ritual. Behind us, two marker flags bounced gently in the water, aligned in a jagged row off our stern: one flag fifty yards away, the other double that distance. And beyond that, the park ranger's aluminum boat still sat between two old wooden pilings.

I touched Raven on the shoulder and pointed to the shore beyond the ranger's boat. "Take a walk with me."

We lifted the inflatable dinghy off the roof of Raven's boat and lowered it into the water. We pulled it around to the swim step. After we grabbed life vests and stepped into the inflatable, Raven popped the oars from their holders and rowed us toward a tiny beach on the far shore.

With his head bowed while he rowed, Raven reminded me of a monk passing contemplatively through sacred ground. We hadn't reached the beach yet when I grabbed an oar in the middle of a stroke. Raven cocked his head up and squinted, a bewildered but calm look on his face. I pointed to a small red-and-white crab-trap float we'd just glided past.

"Aren't crab-trap buoys supposed to be numbered?"

Raven nodded. I patted my pockets.

"Do you have a pen, pencil, something to write with?" I asked.

Raven patted his pockets. He shook his head. I pointed off our starboard side.

"Take us back to that buoy."

Raven dipped his right oar into the water and pulled hard. The dinghy spun around and he pulled with both oars. I leaned over the side and swung my arm out.

"Got it," I said.

Raven stopped rowing. I twirled the float around.

"3-4-7-4-2-8," I said.

Raven looked around the harbor.

"Lots of floats in here. You'd need a photographic memory for all the numbers."

"I don't have a photographic memory, but I do have a feeling."

"What feeling?"

I pointed. "Take us over to that one."

I grabbed the float when we got there and raised it from the water.

"This," I said. I held the float so Raven could see the number.

"Same number. Maybe all the floats belong to the same crabber," he said.

"Uh huh. Let's see."

We hopscotched around Eagle Harbor. Eight of the ten floats had the number "347428" scrawled on the white portion with an indelible marker.

"Do we need to go back to the boat so you can write that number down?" Raven asked.

"No. It's easy to remember."

Raven frowned. "How?"

"Three plus four is seven. Seven times four is twenty-eight."

"Strange mind, Noble."

I smiled. "Lucky for us."

Raven rowed us to the pocket beach. When our bow scraped the sand, I jumped out and pulled us in. A highly varnished wooden lap-strake dinghy lay tilted to one side at the top of the beach. Two long wooden oars were tucked partially beneath the center bench. A hand-carved plaque on the dinghy's stern read, "Dept. of Natural Resources." The ranger must have used it to ferry between the skiff and the shore. We hauled our dinghy next to it, then tied it off to a large piece of driftwood.

A rough-hewn road from Eagle Harbor led up to Reed Lake. Within half a mile, we must have climbed several hundred feet. To our left, the view looked east over Sinclair and Lummi Islands and Bellingham Bay, and beyond that to the snowcapped peak of Mount Baker and the bare tops of the Sisters poking into a dazzling blue sky. Dark green ebb waters racing south down Bellingham Channel swirled outside the entrance to Eagle Harbor, giving the sea a herringbone texture. A tug pulling two barges filled with wood chips made a sweeping turn just north of Sinclair Island.

"Brronk. Brronk. Brronk." A raven's deep, sonorous call echoed through the forest around us.

Raven scanned the trees, then raised his hands to his lips. He rounded his mouth. *"Brronk. Brronk. Brronk,"* he called. The raven answered his call, and he smiled.

About a mile up, the road leveled off, and several hundred yards from there, a group of signposts described in pictures and words the fauna and flora of Reed Lake for visitors who'd made it this far. In a clearing to the left of the signs, a pickup truck sat in front of a large building. Through dirty windows I could barely make out the shapes of heavy equipment—a dump truck and maybe an earthmover— housed behind the wide doors of the structure. A woodpile sat to one side of the building. Next to it, a woman wielding a chain saw worked her way through a large log. Chips and wood dust flew in all directions. The buzz of her saw competed with the rush of a nearby stream.

Suddenly, the saw stopped and the stream grew louder. The woman bent down and scooped up an armful of cut wood. She took a few steps toward the pickup. Then she saw us. She put the wood down and laid her gloves on top of the pile. She walked our way, smiling. She had a short, compact, and rounded body. Her arm muscles bulged under her T-shirt. She stopped a few feet before reaching us and stared at Raven. Then she squinted.

"I know you, don't I?" She closed her eyes and rubbed her forehead with her fingers. Then she opened her eyes and snapped her fingers. "Raven"—she pointed at him—"you dive. Five years ago you helped us secure the mooring buoys off Pelican Beach."

Raven nodded, the recognition apparently of little concern. The woman seemed nonplussed by his lack of enthusiasm. She turned to me and thrust her hand out. "Hi, I'm Carol. Carol Jenkins. But most people call me CJ."

I shook her hand. "Charles Noble. Most people call me Charlie. Do you work here?"

"Only when I have to." She chuckled and pointed to her T-shirt, where the large bold letters A-W-O-L followed the buxom contours of her chest. "No fancy uniform or Smokey Bear hat. But I'm the live-in ranger, park manager, trail whacker, mechanic, plumber—you name it—for the summer months. Come winter, look for me in Patagonia, the Yucatan, the Outback. Out in nature. Far away from people. Some-place interesting, exciting, challenging. What can I do for you, Mr. Noble?"

Out of the corner of my eye, I saw that Raven had wandered over to the signposts.

"A young woman was pulled from the bottom of Eagle Harbor by an anchor about a week ago," I said.

"It's horrible isn't it? It made me ill when I heard the news. Men treat women like disposable commodities. I see it all the time around the world. I see it here, too." CJ pointed down the hill toward Eagle Harbor. "They anchor their big party boats here. I've watched them with binoculars. Men with women young enough to be their daughters. It makes me think some guy got tired of this young woman and threw her overboard."

"Women," I said.

"Women?" CJ's head jerked. "I don't understand."

"Raven and I went diving this morning and found the bodies of two more women."

"No." CJ shook her head. "My god, this is terrible. The bodies of three women found here in Eagle Harbor?"

"Uh huh. Someone also took a few shots at us with a rifle."

"You're kidding?"

"I'm not. Did you see anyone else come this way?"

She pointed to the woodpile alongside the building. "I've been cutting wood most of the morning. People come and go all the time without me seeing or hearing them." She shrugged her shoulders. "You're the first people I've seen today. Who do you work for?" CJ asked. "The Coast Guard? FBI? Local police?"

"None of the above. I'm a private investigator." I flashed my license. "Any of those big party boats anchor in Eagle Harbor recently?"

CJ lowered her head, closed her eyes and rubbed them, then snapped her head back up. "About two weeks ago, a big boat, maybe eighty feet or so, pulled into Eagle Harbor. They partied through the night. I could hear them clear up here."

"Did you notice anything else about the boat, anything at all?"

"White. Sleek, modern design—I hate the way they look. Give me a boat with classic lines any day."

I smiled.

"The name," she said. "Something about the name seemed odd." CJ looked down again and pushed the gravel around with her foot. "I was on my way over to Anacortes for groceries in the park's boat, *Sea Shell*. I remember thinking. . . ." Her head popped up. "Big. . . . Long. . . . That's it. Long . . . Longhorn. The boat's name was *Longhorn*. It sounded so out of place here in the Pacific Northwest. It had the image of a steer with huge horns underneath the name. Do you think that the *Longhorn* may have had something to do with these women?"

"I don't know, but thanks for your help."

"Say, I really need to get back to work. I've got an intern coming in early July, but until then it's just me. Big windfall over the winter on the trail up to the airfield and Bradberry Lake. I've been clearing a little each day. You should take the hike up to the airfield."

"I've been up there," I said. "The view is great."

CJ nodded, then smiled knowingly. Raven walked up to us.

"What do you think of our interpretive signs?" CJ asked.

Raven shook his head. "Sad. People have to be told what to look for in nature."

"I know," CJ said. "But it's life in the modern world, where people are so removed from nature."

CJ turned to leave, revealing the back of her T-shirt, which read, "Adventure Without Limits." Now that gave a new meaning to AWOL.

six

Raven and I hiked back down the steep road. He rowed the dinghy out to his boat. We'd just pulled the inflatable up on the roof when Ben Conrad zoomed into Eagle Harbor at the helm of a black-and-green police boat. He tied up alongside us. Another man on Ben's boat already had his wetsuit on. Raven leaned over to chat with the other diver. Then Raven slipped on his wetsuit again.

Both boats bobbed in the water, swinging close, then bouncing off the fenders tied between them. The other diver stepped onto Raven's swim step and they helped each other saddle air tanks onto their backs.

Ben stood next to me on his boat. He nodded. "I'm glad Raven's here, or I'd have to go down with Oscar. I hate diving, especially on bodies. Those two know exactly what they're doing anyway."

I swung my legs over the rails of both boats to join Ben. We stood on the rear deck and watched Raven and Oscar slip under the water. Two black body bags attached to a yellow buoy bobbed in the ripples from their descent.

"Do you know anything about the boat that pulled up to the visitor's dock the other day, the *Longhorn*?" I asked.

"Why?"

"Park ranger says she saw it in here about two weeks ago with a big party going."

"Shit," Ben said.

"I take it that means you know something about the *Longhorn*."

"At least about the owner. This protest I just came from was against the development of Chuckanut Ridge. The man who owns the ridge property is a Texan named Dennis Kincaid."

"Let me guess. Mr. Kincaid owns an eighty-foot pleasure craft named *Longhorn*."

"Yep. And he's up here wining and dining politicians, bankers, and local business people on the boat so they'll throw their support behind his development plans. That's why Janet and her group staged their protest."

"And the protest was large enough to cause a traffic jam in Bellingham?"

Ben grimaced. "The protest *was* a traffic jam."

"I don't get it."

"Kincaid wants to put 800-plus homes on Chuckanut Ridge. The antidevelopment group estimates that would mean about 4,000 automobiles passing through Fairhaven and downtown Bellingham each day, from six in the morning to six at night. What's that, roughly 300 more cars an hour? So they got together a group of 150 drivers and had them drive a circuit between Fairhaven and downtown, keeping right at the speed limit."

"Smart folks."

"Damn effective. Janet's on the street corner next to her gallery in Fairhaven with a sign that reads, 'Is This the City You Want?'"

I chuckled. "Kinda drives the point home."

Ben winced.

Oscar spit out water as he surfaced. Ben lowered a hook attached to a thin steel cable over the side. Oscar grabbed the hook and swam back toward the body bags. The cable made a high-pitched wailing sound as it unwound from its spool.

After untying a body bag from the float, Oscar disappeared beneath the surface of the water with it. A moment later, he resurfaced without the bag. He swam toward us, and pushed himself onto the swim step of the police boat. Then Raven popped up, but he stayed in the water near the marker flag.

Oscar swung a stainless-steel arm out over one side of the police boat. He pushed a green button, and a winch whirred, slowly reeling in the steel cable and the body bag. Raven swam alongside the bag until it reached the boat. His lips moved as though talking to the bag.

Once Oscar had the body bag alongside the boat and out of the water, he let the sea drain from it before hoisting it onto the rear deck. Then he unhooked the cable, slipped on his face mask, and put his mouthpiece in. He jumped into the water. He and Raven swam with the cable toward the second marker flag, then disappeared beneath the water with another body bag.

"It'll probably take the medical examiner a couple of days to get to these women," Ben said. "You gonna wait to see what he says, or go after Kincaid right away?"

"Why wait?"

"How did I know you'd say that? That's what I love about you PI guys. Come and go as you please. Don't worry about probable cause or the chain of command. You're going up against power. If what Janet says is true, Kincaid's connected up the yin-yang. He may be from Texas, but he's got politicians in his pocket from Washington, D.C., to Washington State and all points in between."

"Connections can't place you beyond the law," I said.

"But they sure as hell can help you bend it."

Raven and Oscar brought up and drained the second body bag.

"Should we drag the harbor for more?" Ben asked.

I pointed to the body bags. "You've got probable cause that more are down there."

"Yeah. Let's see what the chief says. Now what about the shooter?"

"Somewhere along the shore, but the fog made it impossible to see him."

"And all the bullets are under the water."

"Not all of them," I said.

I dropped a spent bullet in Ben's outstretched hand. "Raven found it on the bottom."

"Damn. He found it on the sea floor?"

"Uh huh."

Ben shook his head in disbelief. "It's like the guy lives in an alternate universe and occasionally drops in to see how the rest of us are doing." Ben pulled a plastic bag from his pocket and dropped the bullet in. "I'll get ballistics to analyze it. Might match something in one of the databases."

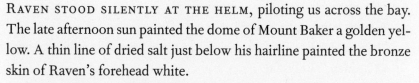

RAVEN STOOD SILENTLY AT THE HELM, piloting us across the bay. The late afternoon sun painted the dome of Mount Baker a golden yellow. A thin line of dried salt just below his hairline painted the bronze skin of Raven's forehead white.

"The police are paying you for your help, aren't they?" I asked.

He nodded.

"What do I owe you?"

He kept his gaze fixed out the windshield. "Nothing."

"You said you'd let me know after you saw what needed to be done."

"I just did."

"Nothing. Are you sure?"

"The police will pay me because I helped them raise the bodies of those women. I came with you because their souls needed to be set free. Even if you didn't know that when we left. That's a transaction of the spirit, for which there is no fee."

"Well, then at least accept my thanks."

Raven closed his eyes and nodded, then he went back to staring straight ahead. Halfway across the bay, he asked, "What happened?"

"With what?"

"The Coast Guard and you."

"I refused to obey an order I thought was illegal."

"Military doesn't like people who think for themselves."

"You know something about that?"

Raven nodded slowly, then resumed staring straight ahead.

After we rounded the breakwater at Squalicum Harbor, I had him take me to the *Noble Lady*. I shook my head as we passed the visitor's dock. *Longhorn* had already left.

I threw some fenders over the side and Raven pulled up next to the *Noble Lady*. I tied his boat off to mine so it wouldn't move while I transferred my gear.

Raven eyed the *Noble Lady*. "Your boat, Noble?"

"Uh huh. Designed by Bill Garden."

He pursed his lips and nodded. "You live aboard?"

"Uh huh."

"Doesn't go fast, does it?"

"Maybe eight knots flat out."

"Then you have to read the water."

"Wind. Weather. Currents. Tides. At eight knots, you always have to take them into account. You can't outrun a storm or plow through saltwater rapids at that speed."

"Good thing you don't need lettered signs to tell you what to look for on the water."

Raven scanned the length of the *Noble Lady*, then smiled. I think that meant he approved. After getting all my gear from his boat, I leaned out from the *Noble Lady*'s rear deck.

"You want to come aboard and have a beer?"

Raven looked straight at me, but his eyes suggested that he was gazing into a world far away. "I've been close to death and trapped souls today," he said. "I need to cleanse myself now." He reached up and untied his boat. He pushed off the *Noble Lady* and drifted a few feet away with his engine off.

"Hey, Noble," Raven said. "What's that number?"

I closed my eyes for a moment. I opened them and I pointed to Raven. "3-4-7-4-2-8."

Raven laughed. Then he started his engine. He made a sweeping turn and sped away.

I laid my wetsuit on the dock and rinsed it off with a hose. Then I walked over to the visitor's dock. All the slips on the shoreline side of the visitor's dock belonged to permanently moored boats. Vince Marcellis, a retired engineer, lived aboard *Misty Isle*, a thirty-six-foot Nonsuch sailboat, with his yellow Lab, Quark. I'd heard less than flattering talk about Vince's boat from crusty traditional sailors. Now, I'm not an experienced sailor, but I liked the Nonsuch. One sail, one sheet, and one halyard made it an extremely simple boat to handle. Its odd-looking "wishbone" mast reminded me of a bent hula hoop fitted over a pole. But with it, all you do is raise and lower the sail without much fuss.

Quark barked as I approached. Vince stuck his head from the cabin door. He wore a full beard and skullcap. I pointed to the other side of the dock.

"Eighty-foot boat, *Longhorn*, was moored here earlier today. Did you notice when she left?"

"More like eighty-four feet," Vince said. He pointed to the dock. "Each concrete dock slab is eight feet long. *Longhorn* took up ten and a half slabs. That makes eighty-four feet, give or take a few inches."

About what I'd expect from an engineer. "Did you talk to the owner or the crew?" I asked.

"Some. Kinda snooty folks. Never did meet the owner, only the captain and the first mate. Boat left at 1113 today. Headed into the San Juans, the captain said." Vince shook his head. "Not many anchorages for a big boat like that."

"Whaddya think? Sucia? Maybe Stuart?"

"Looked more like marina types to me."

"Friday Harbor? Roche?"

"Roche," Vince said.

"So they can cozy up next to all the other big boats with so few places to go," I said. Vince nodded.

I walked back to the *Noble Lady*, peeled my wetsuit from the dock, and stepped aboard. Roche Harbor is on San Juan Island. Standing in the galley, I flipped open my cell phone and called my friend Ed Sykes, the San Juan County sheriff. I caught Ed in a meeting. He said he'd call back. A few minutes later, my cell phone rang.

"You're quick."

"No, I'm Conrad. You expecting someone else?"

"Ed Sykes."

"Say hi to him for me. Listen, Janet wants to know if you and Kate want to have dinner with us tonight."

"Love to," I said. "Too bad that Kate can't join us. She's on a coast guard training cruise 24/7 for the next week or so. Where're we eating?"

"Janet said let's try that tapas bar."

"Topless bar?"

"Tapas bar. Tapas."

"Ah, you mean Flats, the restaurant in Fairhaven?"

"Yeah, she made reservations for us at seven."

"Good. I haven't eaten at Flats before."

I heard Ben mutter "topless" a few times then chuckle as he hung up.

A BLAZE OF ORANGE from the setting sun reflected off the large front windows of Flats. I walked into the restaurant early. The small space had tables packed tightly together on upper and lower floors. Outside, waiting diners lined the street. Inside, they crammed around the bar. Both good signs for a first-time patron.

Exposed brick walls gave Flats a cozy feeling. I made my way through the maze of tables and people to the bar. The bartender, a short man with dark hair and a bushy mustache, leaned over. "What'll ya have?"

"Got a local microbrew? Something dark?"

"Stout from Boundary Bay Brewery okay?"

I nodded. A black guy next to me swiveled around on his stool. He pointed to his glass. "I used to be a Guinness man until I tried one of these microbrews," he said.

Beneath an open-collar black shirt, he wore a gray T-shirt. The colors matched his mustache and beard. Looking at him, especially in his black Greek fisherman's hat, brought on a flash of recognition, followed by a flash of "What if I'm wrong?" I took a chance. "You're the author who lives aboard on Gate Six, aren't you?"

He had a great smile, and we shook hands. "Eugene Wendell," he said. "But most people call me Gene."

"Charles Noble," I said. "But most people call me Charlie. I'm a liveaboard on Gate Nine."

My beer arrived and I took a sip.

"I'm aboard a Shannon," Gene said.

"Nice boat. Tough boat. Forty-three-foot ketch?"

Gene's smile lit up the bar. "You know boats."

"I love them. All kinds. Mine's a deep-draft trawler. A 1969 thirty-six-foot Willard Aft Pilothouse."

Gene nodded. "In the late eighties, a Willard APH made a Pacific crossing from San Diego to Hawaii. Strapped fifty-five-gallon drums on the rear deck for more fuel if I remember."

"You're right," I said. "The owner was sixty-five years old, a former sailor who confessed to 'a serious love affair' with his Willard."

Gene laughed.

"Seems I'm not the only one who knows boats," I said.

I looked up from my next sip of beer to see Ben and Janet walking through the restaurant door. Janet wore a wraparound turquoise skirt and a sleeveless white blouse. A waitress ushered the pair to an empty window table.

I turned to Gene. "My friends just arrived. But stop by Gate Nine sometime. My boat's name is the *Noble Lady*."

"Likewise, next time you're over at Gate Six, you're welcome aboard *Wings of Freedom*."

"I never did ask what you write."

"Nautical thrillers," Gene said. "Set along the Inside Passage."

"Do they have copies at Village Books?"

"Always. And they're usually signed."

"My girlfriend and I are leaving for a three-week cruise soon. I'll have to bring one of your books with us."

I grabbed my microbrew and headed toward Janet and Ben.

"Hi, Charles," Janet said.

I winced. Her face reddened. I took the seat facing the window and Janet leaned my way.

"Sorry," she said. "I know how much you hate that name. . . . But it sounds so regal, so . . ." She hesitated. I knew exactly where she was headed.

"Noble?" I said.

"Yes. Prince Charles. King Charles. But Prince Charlie? King Charlie?"

I held up a finger. "That's what I like about Charlie," I said. "It sounds like a guy who'd pop the hatch on his engine room and be happy as a clam getting dirty working on his boat all day. Can you imagine a prince or a king doing that?"

"You have a point there," Janet said.

Ben grumbled. "Let's order."

I started for the menu, which rested on the table, but the setting sun caught my attention and held it. A few clouds had moved in over the western horizon. The dying rays of the sun turned the cloud bottoms salmon pink. Above the clouds, a thick band of violet faded to midnight blue, squeezing sunlight from the sky.

Finally, I turned away from the sunset to a young woman hovering over the table with a green pad and pencil. Since tapas are basically appetizers, I quickly scanned the menu and ordered three: grilled asparagus with mushrooms; scallops with cannellini beans; and a salad of grilled eggplant, roasted tomatoes, fava beans, and goat cheese. Ben and Janet also ordered.

"Was that nice?" Janet asked. "When we came in, I saw you talking with that black man at the bar. Isn't he the thriller author who lives aboard near *Big Ben*?"

"Gene Wendell," I said. "And it is nice seeing another black man who loves boats as much as I do."

Our waitress arrived with a basket of bread. Then Janet looked down at her wrist as though checking her watch, but she didn't have one on. "God, I'm so damned white. I need a tan. I just adore darker-skinned people."

Ben snapped. "Racial profiling."

Janet screwed her face up. "What?"

"Racial profiling," Ben said again. "You just generalized about, and assigned a value to, people based on their skin color. People do it all the time. But just let a police officer try it and the heat's on."

Janet huffed. "It's not even vaguely the same thing."

"I'm not saying you're using it for the same reason. I'm just trying to point out that the underlying sentiment is the same."

"No, it's not," Janet said. She turned to me. "Charlie, you're black, what do you think?"

I grinned, then pointed back and forth between them. "I think I know better than to step into the middle of an argument between you two. Sounds like you've got the makings of a great conflict. What do they say? The greater the argument, the more passionate the love when you make up."

Ben let out a belly laugh. Janet's face turned beet red.

"Maybe we'd better change the topic," she said to Ben.

He nodded.

"I heard you had a really intense day in Eagle Harbor," Janet said.

"When Raven and I—"

Janet blurted out, "Raven?"

"You know him?" I said.

"Know him? The yellow cedar masks that I have in the gallery, Raven carved them. People love them. I can barely keep enough in supply. He needs to carve more. This silver pendant"—she grasped the

piece dangling around her neck and held it over the table toward me—
"he made it. He's a great craftsman. Haida mother. Lummi father."

"A man of many hidden talents," I said.

"Fits his name," Janet said. "Listen to all the different calls a raven
makes. Raven's also the trickster and the shape-shifter of Northwest
coastal lore. You think Raven's this, and suddenly he changes into
that—something completely different. The elders say it's to remind
you never to take anything for granted—to always look beneath the
surface of things."

"Speaking of Eagle Harbor," Ben said, "you might need this."

He slid a small manila envelope across the table. I picked it up and
peeked inside.

"What's that?" Janet asked.

"A photograph I'm not sure you want to see before eating," I said.

"Especially if you intend to have a crab dish," Ben added.

Janet grimaced. She held up a hand. "You've convinced me. I won't
ask about it anymore."

Our waitress came back with a tray full of small plates. We had her
set them in the middle of our table for us to sort out and share. She also
poured glasses of wine for Janet and Ben. I stuck with my microbrew.
We toasted to friendship and beginning new relationships. Ben and
Janet kissed after the toast. It made me wish for Kate. After a few bites
of eggplant and goat cheese, I turned to Janet.

"Can you tell me more about Dennis Kincaid and the connections
he has to politicians and businesspeople here in the state?"

Janet finished chewing, then swallowed hard. She set down her
fork.

"That bastard," she said. "We have a lawyer investigating his background in Texas. Give me a day or two, and I'll know everything there
is to know about Mr. Kincaid."

"I bet you will," Ben said.

"Hey, buddy, you looking to pick another fight?" Janet said.

Ben smiled sheepishly. "No. I'm really looking to make up."

I pointed between them again. "Then maybe you two shouldn't order dessert."

"After a great dinner, miss dessert?" Janet said. She pointed at Ben. "First things first. Besides"—she turned to me—"I haven't told you about dating Bud Kincaid, Dennis Kincaid's darling playboy son."

"Bud?" I said.

"Bud," Janet said.

"Bud?" Ben said. "You dated him?"

"You know him?" Janet asked.

"No, but you never told me about him," Ben said.

"And you've told me about all the women you've ever dated?" Janet grinned. "Besides, it was a long time ago. Before my marriage. We were in college together. Here, at the university. Fast cars. Wild parties."

Ben blurted out. "You? A party animal?"

Janet smiled and waved a playful finger at Ben. "You mean you, Mr. Budweiser, weren't? Let's put it this way. If I sold sweatshirts for women in this town that read on the front, 'I Dated Bud Kincaid,' I'd make a bundle. Apparently Bud raised a little too much hell in Texas, and Daddy Kincaid sent him out of state for college. Daddy also bought property up here, including a fancy house for Bud to live in."

"So that's how Kincaid got his property, like the large parcel where you're fighting his development plans?"

"Yep. Kincaid kept buying property up here because it was so cheap, and after graduation Bud stayed around to manage Daddy's affairs."

"Still a playboy?"

"Far as I know."

Out of the corner of my eye, I noticed Ben squirming in his chair. He tapped Janet on the shoulder. "What would it say on the back?"

"What?"

"The sweatshirt. What would it say on the back?" He sounded impatient.

Janet paused, then smiled devilishly. "Don't Make the Same Mistake I Did."

Ben exhaled deeply.

"Charlie, did you meet the Wild Woman of Cypress Island?" Janet asked.

"Who?"

Janet ran a finger across her breasts. "Miss AWOL. CJ."

"Who don't you know?" I asked.

She winked. "Small town. Besides. . . . " She looked down into her wine glass. The atmosphere around the table suddenly grew thick with silence as dense as a fogbank that had blown in over the water. Ben's face contorted. He looked my way and raised his eyebrows. Janet took a long swallow of wine without making eye contact. She set her glass down and tapped it gently with her fingernail, setting off a few soft tings. She finally raised her head. Ben reached out for her. Janet brushed away tears.

seven

"Does it ever get easy?" she asked.

"Does what ever get easy?" Ben asked.

Janet looked at me. "Losing a loved one."

"I think so," I said. "But I'm not sure."

Ben sighed. "I'm sorry but I don't understand. This is about Thomas, but a moment ago I . . . I thought. . . . " A pained expression crossed his face. He turned my way. "I thought you two were talking about that woman ranger on Cypress."

Janet touched Ben's arm. "Years ago . . . before Thomas was murdered . . . CJ was his student at Huxley. One of his first grad students. She adored him . . . maybe a little too much."

"And he adored her back?" Ben asked.

"No," Janet said. "Female students were always attracted to Thomas. Hell, he was a handsome, smart, and passionate teacher. He flirted but he never crossed the line. It didn't matter that I was his wife. When Thomas invited CJ over to our house, she would eye me as though she wished I'd disappear. She got into fights with other female grad students."

"Over Thomas?" I asked.

"Not ostensibly, but Thomas knew the real reason. CJ hated it when other females got more attention from him than she did. Several grad students left the department because of her. Even after graduation, she found reasons to visit Thomas or call our home."

"Stalker," Ben said.

"She left the area for several years," Janet said. "Next thing I heard she'd gone to work for the Department of Natural Resources as a ranger on Cypress Island. A good job for her."

"Why's that?" I asked.

"She lacks appropriate interpersonal skills."

"She treated Raven and me appropriately today," I said.

"Just hope she doesn't decide to place you in her amorous crosshairs," Janet said.

"Kate would certainly have something to say about that, and I would not like to be in CJ's shoes when she did."

Janet laughed. Ben shook his head. We all returned to our dinners.

BACK AT THE *Noble Lady*, I checked my voice mail. A message from Ed Sykes said that a boat named *Longhorn* had pulled into Roche Harbor earlier in the day. I also checked the time: ten thirty at night. With Roche Harbor thirty-five nautical miles from here, that meant four or five hours on the water, depending on the currents.

I pulled a current atlas down from my bookshelf and looked up today's data. The currents up Hale Passage and down President Channel ran in my favor. If I left now, I'd get into Roche Harbor in the wee hours of the morning. But at least I'd be sure to intercept *Longhorn* so I could ask the crew a few questions. Like why they'd anchored in Eagle Harbor, and what they knew about the three dead women.

I turned to climb the steps up to the helm when someone knocked on the galley window. The boarding gate swung open. The *Noble Lady* curtsied to one side. Then the cabin door swung open, and Kate stepped inside.

"I thought—"

She held up her hand. "A young seaman came down with a bad case of food poisoning. The CO brought *Sea Eagle* back to port to get him to the hospital and have the food aboard inspected."

"You're all right?"

She ran her hands down the sides of her body and over her hips. "Fit." She smiled. "The CO gave us shore leave for the night. Most of the crew went out drinking. But I had other plans."

Kate's smile turned devilish. She closed the door, then undid a clip at the back of her head. She shook her head and her brunette hair cascaded softly over her shoulders. Kate walked over to me, wrapped her arms around my waist, and anchored a big kiss on my lips. I twisted slightly in her grip and slipped the current atlas onto the galley table. More urgent currents needed attention first. I ushered Kate down two steps into the master stateroom. Roche Harbor would have to wait until the morning.

After we slipped into the berth, Kate said, "I have to report for duty at 0500 hours."

"Great," I said. "I need to cast off at 0400 hours."

Kate squealed playfully. "Without me?"

"Only to Roche Harbor. Not exactly the *Noble Lady*'s preferred surroundings."

"Business?"

"Business."

"I don't want to know about it right now."

"I don't want to talk about it right now."

And we didn't.

THE FOLLOWING MORNING, I walked into the galley and peeked outside. A faint blue sky backlit the hills fringing the eastern edge of the city. Darkness still cloaked most of the bay. I put on a pot of coffee, then wandered back down into the stateroom, switched on a soft light, and nudged Kate.

"What time is it?" she asked.

"It's 0330 hours."

She rubbed her eyes. "Damn. You've got to leave, don't you?"

"I do."

She sniffed the air. "Coffee's on?"

"I thought you'd sworn off morning coffee in favor of healthful shakes with green stuff floating in them."

"It's not morning. It's oh-dark-thirty," she said. "I'll take mine black."

I slipped into my clothes while Kate hauled herself out of bed. I checked the *Noble Lady*'s water, oil, and fuel. Then I climbed up to the pilothouse and twisted the key in the ignition. I smiled when the engine fired right up and started to purr. Then I climbed back down and poured two cups of coffee. Engine vibrations created a tiny sea of ripples in each cup. Kate took a few sips, then set her cup down.

"I'll take it with me," she said, pointing to the cup. "You need to leave. Get up into the pilothouse. I'll cast you off."

After a kiss, I grabbed my coffee and climbed the pilothouse stairs. I pushed the side door open. Kate stood below me on the dock, steam rising from the cup next to her feet.

"Ready to cast off?" she asked.

"Ready."

She walked to the bow, where she undid one large dock line and tossed it aboard. Then she walked to the stern, where she loosened another line and placed it inside the fantail. She unwound both spring lines from their cleats, tossed one on the deck, and held onto the other while she walked the boat back out of the slip. All the while I looked down at her and thought, "Sharon would approve. You're with a woman who knows what to do around a boat."

Finally, Kate flipped the remaining spring line underneath the handrails and pushed the nose of the *Noble Lady* away from the dock so it would clear the large piling at the end. She waved. I waved back. Then she stooped down for her coffee cup.

My attention snapped back to the fifteen tons of fiberglass and metal underneath me. I cranked the wheel hard over to starboard. I eased the shifter into reverse, then gunned the engine. I slipped the gearshift into forward, and gunned the engine again. The *Noble Lady* spun like a top, and we glided down the fairway.

I looked back but I didn't see Kate. Then we passed the visitor's dock, where she stood with her coffee cup in hand. She waved, then threw me a kiss. And I thought, "Sharon would definitely approve."

Once clear of the breakwater, I pointed the *Noble Lady* just to the right of the green, flashing buoy at the entrance to the harbor. Technically, that placed me outside of the approved coast guard channel, but local boats frequently cut this corner, and doing so lined me up perfectly for the south tip of Portage Island.

Beyond the pulsing green light, calm, flat water ruled Bellingham Bay. I nudged the throttle lever forward and jiggled it until a low, thumping vibration settled throughout the boat. A chill still hung in the air, so I closed the pilothouse door. Then I pushed a button, which activated the autopilot, and stared at my radar to make sure I had a clear route. I leaned back into the helm seat, wrapped my hands around the warm cup, and took a generous sip of coffee.

The *Noble Lady* guided herself through the dark water. Ahead of me, the deep green hillside of Lummi Island slowly emerged from darkness. Behind me, the soft gurgle of the *Noble Lady*'s exhaust sounded. Overhead, a few seagulls cried. I savored another sip. For a boater, it doesn't get much better than this.

Approaching the south end of Portage, I fixed my gaze on my depth sounder. I set down my coffee cup and stood up with one hand over the autopilot, the other on the wheel, ready to reclaim control of the boat. The depth reading went from one hundred feet to fifteen feet within about a hundred yards. Funny, I feared that the depth would decrease even further, even though I knew that wouldn't happen.

I could have swung out farther toward the red buoy between Portage and Eliza Islands to stay in deeper water. But locals also cut in close to the tip of Portage. This shallow patch of water is a favorite for native Lummi crabbers. At times, it can be a minefield of red-and-white floats marking the location of crab traps sitting on the seafloor. Thankfully, only a few floats bobbed ahead of me. I took another long sip of coffee. I tried to fend it off, but the image of the crab trap sitting atop the body of that young woman rushed into my mind. I no longer wanted to discover what had happened to these women just for the sake of the Bayneses. I also needed to find out for me.

As I rounded Portage and entered Hale Passage heading north, the sea remained flat calm. But behind me, a thick wall of fog moved my way. I pushed the throttle forward, hoping the *Noble Lady* could out-run the fogbank. I hadn't made it halfway up the passage when wispy tendrils of mist began to swirl around the pilothouse windows and swoop over the foredeck. I pulled the throttle back. A moment later, a heavy white curtain descended and I lost sight of the *Noble Lady*'s bow.

Sudden fog is more frightening to me than high winds or steep seas. Sunlight played through the fog, lighting the smoky world outside with a luminous glow in all directions. I couldn't see where the water met the land, the air, or the *Noble Lady*. My head spun as I tried to regain my bearings. I couldn't continue peering through the pilothouse windows, or I'd run the *Noble Lady* aground. So I checked my compass heading, then turned my attention to the radar, forgetting the glowing white world that enveloped me and narrowing my attention down to the tiny, glowing green world on the radar screen.

Each sweep of the radar painted bright green landmasses on either side of the passage. Keeping an eye to the compass made it easy to steer away from these blobs that didn't move. I scanned the screen for blobs that did move—in particular, for one blob that should be moving ahead of me soon: the Lummi Island Ferry, transporting early-morning commuters to the mainland.

From a small depression on the left side of the screen, a green bulge protruded, then broke off, like a cell dividing under a microscope. The bulge headed toward the center of the radar screen, which meant the ferry was moving directly toward me.

I had to trust that the captain of that ferry had me on his radar, as he had to trust that I had him on mine. I didn't slow down or stop. Instead, I checked the compass, adjusted the throttle, and maintained a consistent course and speed. It's a way of telling that ferry captain, "This is who I am, and this is what I'm doing."

In good visibility, crossing paths with another vessel is not a problem. But in the fog it is like suddenly going blind, then being told you must cross a busy intersection with only a cane to guide you. Although I'd traveled this stretch of water many times, my hands gripped the wheel tightly.

The ferry maintained its course and speed. I maintained mine. The sound of the ferry's engine seemed to come at me from all directions in the fog. I fought the urge to look out the window and kept my eyes fixed on my instruments. We were an eighth of a mile away from each other, and the ferry was still coming directly at me.

This wasn't a game of chicken, so I pulled the throttle back and brought the engine to a stop. Two short blasts from the ferry's deep, throaty horn sounded, as if the ferry captain was saying "Thank you." I blasted my higher pitched horn twice to say "You're welcome." Then I brought the engine back up to speed.

Twenty minutes later, I popped out of the fog at the end of Hale Passage with a clear view to the early-morning horizon up the Strait of Georgia and the treed tops of the San Juan Islands gleaming in the sun against an aquamarine sky. I reached for my cup of coffee, but it had grown cold.

I piloted the *Noble Lady* across Rosario Strait, down President Channel, and around the east tip of Spieden Island. Roche Harbor has east and west entrances off of Spieden Channel, and a south entrance from Mosquito Pass. I headed for the narrower east entrance. Slightly after eight in the morning, I rounded Davison Head, about a mile from Roche.

I looked to port and counted three large motoryachts leaving through the western entrance. The sleek, aerodynamic shape of one seemed awfully familiar. I grabbed my binoculars from a shelf behind me and watched as *Longhorn* cruised out of Roche Harbor and into Spieden Channel.

With a top speed around eight knots, the *Noble Lady* would never catch up to *Longhorn,* which I'm sure could push eighteen to twenty knots with her throttles wide open. I whipped my VHF microphone from its holder and pressed the transmit button.

"Longhorn, Longhorn, Longhorn. This is Sea Sleuth, Sea Sleuth, Sea Sleuth on channel sixteen."

"Sea Sleuth, this is Longhorn."

"Longhorn, switch to Zero Niner."

"Zero Niner, Roger."

I pushed the arrow-down channel key on my VHF until the back-lit LED read 09.

"Sea Sleuth, this is Longhorn on Zero Niner."

I reached deep for a Texas drawl. "Longhorn, I'm just entering Roche and see that you're leaving. I heard you were in port and had hoped to catch up to my old friend Dennis Kincaid."

"Roger that." The male voice on the other end sounded relaxed, easygoing. "We're headed out the Strait of Juan de Fuca for Neah Bay, then up the BC coast to Port Alberni for some salmon fishing. Unfortunately, Mr. Kincaid isn't aboard. He'll be joining us at Neah Bay for the cruise north."

"That's too bad. I just missed him several days ago, too. I heard that *Longhorn* was in Eagle Harbor about the time that woman's body was discovered there. How awful to bring up a body on an anchor."

Silence followed.

Then finally, "Sea Sleuth, can I tell Mr. Kincaid who called?" Strain had replaced the relaxation in the man's voice.

"Martin Hunt, from Dallas."

"Mr. Hunt, where is *Sea Sleuth* right now?"

"Entering Roche from Mosquito Pass."

"Roger that. Mr. Hunt, we'll be sure to relay the message to Mr. Kincaid that you attempted to catch up with him. Longhorn out. Going to sixteen."

"Sea Sleuth out. Back to sixteen."

Longhorn executed a sharp turn and headed back into the west entrance of Roche Harbor. I also executed a sharp turn and headed back across Spieden Channel. Close by the east tip of Spieden Island, I looked behind me. Across the channel, *Longhorn* steamed out of Roche again. My VHF radio crackled.

"Sea Sleuth, Sea Sleuth, Sea Sleuth. Longhorn, Longhorn, Longhorn."

I didn't answer. *Longhorn* tried hailing me several times, the man's voice sounding more exasperated with each attempt. Finally he gave up. Funny how the mere mention of Eagle Harbor had caused *Longhorn* to change course.

I cruised back to Bellingham under a hot sun and blue skies. The fog in Hale Passage had burned away. I thought about tooting my horn when I crossed the ferry's path again, wondering if the captain would remember our morning encounter, but I didn't.

I turned the corner at the end of Portage Island into Bellingham Bay. Behind the hills surrounding the city, Mount Baker rose majestically, crowned with snow. I flipped open my cell phone and placed a call to Ben Conrad. I got him at his desk.

Ben grumbled. "I hate typing reports. You know, soon that's all cops'll do. Sit at a desk. Look at video monitors. Type up reports. Satellite imagery. Weaponized, small aerial drones. Robotic vehicles armed to the gills. They'll do all the police work."

"What about the investigative work?"

"You mean like asking questions and hunting down suspects?"

"Uh huh."

Ben chuckled. "Probably be handed out to smart-ass PIs like you."

"Got a question."

"See, I told you that's what'd happen."

"If I give you the number of a crab-trap float, can you get me the owner's name?"

"Trap from Eagle Harbor?"

"Uh huh."

"Shoot."

"3-4-7-4-2-8."

"I'll see what I can do." Ben hung up.

I made it back to port around noon. I'd just swung open the refrigerator door to rummage for lunch when my cell phone rang.

"Ray Bob," Ben said.

"Last name?"

Ben laughed. "Boy, you still got a lot to learn. This ain't like being down South where you get guys with a name like Billy Bob Thompson. This is the Northwest and Ray's a Native American fellow. Lives out on the reservation, and that is his name, first and last. Raymond Bob."

"Got it."

"He's got a record, too. DUI several years ago. Arrest for possession of drugs with intent to sell. Another for domestic abuse."

"So Ray likes to get drunk, sell drugs, and slap women around?"

"All qualities of a fine citizen."

After I hung up with Ben, I called Raven.

"Know a guy who lives on the reservation, named Ray Bob?"

"Yes."

"Know how I can find him?"

"Maybe."

"How?"

"You had lunch yet?"

"No."

"You like fish sandwiches?"

"Maybe."

"Pick me up in ten minutes," Raven said. "We'll grab something to eat."

"Where?"

"On the rez."

"At the casino?"

"No. At a little stand in front of the college."

"And this is how we'll find Ray Bob?"

"It is."

eight

The road out to the Lummi reservation worked around the northern edge of Bellingham Bay before dipping inland near the airport. Across a small bridge over the Nooksack River, a sign with a red, yellow, and white image of a salmon read, "You Are Entering the Lummi Nation."

Raven nodded toward the sign as we passed by. "Sovereign nation. It's why there's so much conflict between landowners and Indians on the rez," he said.

"Landowners? I thought the land belonged to the tribe."

"It does, but not all of it. Some of the best shoreline spots are owned privately."

"But it's a reservation."

"Uh huh. Decades ago, those waterfront parcels were taken from Indians in backroom deals."

"So, on the reservation not all of the land is part of the reservation. Sounds complicated."

Raven smiled. "But the Lummis still own all the water rights."

"And the landowners probably don't like that, because it means the tribe is in control of a critical service."

"Uh huh."

"Sounds even more complicated. Landowners and the tribe working anything out?"

Raven chuckled. "Some. Mostly it's in the courts."

"Sounds like the only people who will win are the lawyers."

"It's the price you pay when egos and emotions run high."

We came to an island of trees, which split the road into a confusion of arteries. In the center of the island, a purple sign with painted gold letters read, "No Excuse for Abuse."

We drove around the island to a road on the other side. Not far down that road we pulled to a stop in front of the Northwest Indian College. Across the road, a large painted carving of three figures in a dugout canoe sat on the grounds of Saint Joachim's Catholic Church. The figure in the middle of the canoe wore a priest's skullcap and carried a Bible close to his chest. The carving seemed to depict a missionary being carried into Indian lands by willing converts.

When we exited the car, I turned and pointed to the carving. "That when the problems began?"

Raven didn't answer. He turned and stared across the road.

"By transporting that priest, it seems like they're unwittingly introducing the seeds of their own undoing," I said.

Raven shook his head slowly. "You don't understand Lummi ways. Many years before the priests came, our people received a great prophecy: 'When the men dressed like loons arrive, have mercy on them.'" He pointed. "That priest isn't in control, those paddlers are."

He sighed, then walked toward a pink travel trailer on our side of the road. I followed him. The trailer, attached to a pickup truck, had been turned into a mobile lunch stand. A pink awning stretching out from the trailer's roof provided meager shelter for customers waiting to order. When our turn came, a rotund man with a short ponytail stuck his head out from the movable café. A dirty pink apron hung around his neck. He looked at me, but spoke to Raven.

"Ain't seen you for a long time, bro."

Raven reached in and gave the man a clasped-thumbs handshake.

"You want some food?" the man asked.

Raven turned to me. "Fish sandwich okay?"

I turned to look at the menu board. "Let's see, what're my choices?"

Raven jabbed me in the ribs.

"Great. I guess I'll have a fish sandwich."

The sandwich came on a bun, and the sauce tasted as good as the fish. We stood under the awning, eating. When Raven finished his sandwich, he stuck his head back into the trailer.

"Have you seen RB?"

The man handed a sandwich to the next customer in line. "He fishes some. Mostly he works out of his home."

"Dealing?" Raven asked.

The man stuck his head out and eyed me again. "Why, you suddenly working with the law?"

"Know where we could find him?" Raven asked.

"At his home."

"Which is where?"

The man grimaced. "Bro, you hardly ever come around. And when you do, you come asking questions. I sell lunch, not information. . . . Next."

The man went back to his customers. Raven tapped me on the arm. "Come," he said. "Lunch is over."

We walked through the rest of the lunchtime crowd back toward the car. Someone tugged my shirtsleeve. I turned to look down into the eyes of an older woman. Her salt-and-pepper hair framed a pleasant, bronze-skinned face, though sadness dulled her hazel eyes.

"Ray Bob lives off Smokehouse Road," she said. "First street on the left after you turn off Haxton." She squeezed my arm tighter. "I hope you are the law. We need to clean up the rez. And we'd do well starting with him."

She took a bite of her fish sandwich. Then she pivoted and walked away.

Turning onto Smokehouse Road afforded a tree-lined vista clear across the reservation to Bellingham Bay and beyond it, to a regal view of Mount Baker framed perfectly by the trees. From this vantage, the mountain shimmered and hovered above the city and the bay, twice as large as it appeared closer up.

Old-time mariners called this phenomenon "looming." From a distance, many a frightened seaman mistook a native canoe with only three paddlers for a three-masted man-o'-war headed their way. At the Coast Guard Academy, we learned that cold air beneath warmer air deflects light down, magnifying objects behind it and displacing them upward.

A pickup truck emerged from this mirage, speeding down Smokehouse Road. It turned in front of us, onto the road where Ray Bob lived.

"You get the feeling that our good names have preceded us?" I asked.

"Maybe Carl doesn't sell information, but he gives it away to his friends," Raven said.

I turned onto the unnamed road. Up ahead, the pickup screeched to a stop. Its doors flew open and three men jumped out. They raced to a rectangular, prefabricated house. I stopped behind the pickup. I reached under the seat and grabbed my pistol. Then I tucked it into the small of my back. The men stood shoulder to shoulder at the front steps of the light gray house. Raven and I stepped from the car. I pulled my T-shirt down over my jeans and the handle of my gun.

"Somehow I don't think they're delivering fish sandwiches to Ray Bob," I said.

Raven stepped in front of me. He walked up to the men.

"RB home?" he asked.

The man in the middle of the trio shook his head. "Nope."

He folded his thick arms across his chest. With his gut spilling over his belt, he reminded me of a sumo wrestler.

"If you haven't been inside, how do you know Ray Bob's not home?" I asked. I walked up beside Raven.

"'Cause he ain't," the man to one side of Mr. Sumo said. This fellow wore a cut-off T-shirt that exposed skull-and-crossbones tattoos on both arms.

"Why don't you tell RB that a friend of his wants to see him?" Raven asked Mr. Sumo.

"Told you, RB ain't home."

"Then you won't mind if we leave him a note?" Raven said.

I took a step closer to the stairs. The three men stiffened.

"Won't mind if you leave, bro," Sumo said.

The third man eyed us silently. Thin and wiry, the same height as Raven, he looked like a real scrapper. A thick, angry scar curved from his left ear down to the corner of his lips. He stepped to one side. I watched him from the corner of my eye while I spoke to Sumo.

"We only want to ask RB about his crab traps. It's not worth any of you getting hurt over."

Raven moved toward the stairs. The man with the tattoos stepped in front of him. He threw a left hand at Raven. Raven leaned to one side, dropped down, and caught the man with a swift, powerful round-house kick. The cracking sound recalled stepping on fallen leaves. The man groaned, then fell to the ground clutching his side. Raven jumped in front of the big man. I spun around to the scar-faced man. He reached behind his back and pulled out a knife. He took another step closer. I threw up my hands. He stopped.

"Whoa," I said.

Then I quickly reached behind and pulled out my gun. "Bullet trumps blade," I said. "Now why don't you pick up your friend and take him to the emergency room. I think he's going to need his ribs taped."

Sumo glowered. Scarface sneered, but he put his knife away. Raven and I stepped back. The two men dragged their friend off.

"Nice kick," I said to Raven.

"Courtesy of the United States Navy," Raven said.

"SEAL training?"

Raven nodded.

"You wanna knock? Give me a minute. I'll go around the back, just in case RB doesn't feel like company," I said.

I crouched below the height of the windows and worked my way to the back of the house. A red pickup truck parked there had stacks of crab traps in its bed. I stood beside the back door, pressed up against the house. Raven knocked.

"RB, it's Raven."

A moment later, RB crashed through the back door. I raised a leg and caught his shins, which sent him sprawling in the dirt on his stomach. I pounced on his back and rammed the muzzle of my pistol into the soft spot at the base of his skull. Then I patted him down and pulled a knife from an ankle holder, which I tossed into the nearby brush.

I turned RB over. Raven stood at my side. RB sat up. He tried to stand, but I shoved him back down. He had a pretty-boy look. Tall. Clean-shaven. Boyish features. He'd slicked his black hair back, then turned it forward, under and around his ears.

"What the fuck you want, Raven? Come bustin' onto the rez askin' questions 'bout me. And who's this?" He pointed to me.

"Man with the questions," Raven said. "You dealing?"

RB nodded toward me. "Thought Sherlock Holmes here was the one with the questions."

"Decided I'd ask one of my own first. You dealing?"

"Is that what this's all about? Drugs? You still angry about Richie's death? Bro, you got to let go of the past if you ever gonna get on with the future."

Raven thrust the flat of his palm into RB's face. RB toppled back and blood spurted from his nose. I put out a hand and held Raven back. Given what I'd seen before, I knew Raven had already reined himself in. I'm sure the ex-SEAL could have easily driven RB's nasal bone into his brain. RB grimaced. He shook his head.

"Fucking broke my nose."

I reached into my pocket and threw RB a handkerchief. He wadded it and stuffed it up his nostrils.

"We're not here to settle old scores," I said to Raven.

"Then what the fuck are you here for?" RB said.

The bloodstained handkerchief in RB's nose gave his voice a muffled, nasal sound. Behind me, Raven sighed.

"Your crab traps were in Eagle Harbor," I said.

"What of it? Some're still there."

"The bodies of three young women were found weighted down under the water. One of your crab traps sat on top of one of the corpses."

"Hell, I stopped using young women for crab bait a long time ago."

I raised my gun. "Smart ass. If Raven didn't break your nose, I will."

"What the fuck do you want me to say? I killed three women to attract the crabs?"

"No. I want to know when you dropped your traps in Eagle Harbor."

RB sneered. "I've been dropping them and picking them up there every two or three days for the last several weeks."

I pulled the picture that Ben had given me from my shirt pocket and flashed it at RB. "Have you seen this woman?"

He turned away without looking. "No."

I slapped the muzzle of my pistol against his head, not hard but enough to hurt. RB winced.

"Look at her, dammit," I said.

He gave the young woman's photo a quick glance. His head twitched. He squeezed his eyes closed. "No. Like I said, I ain't seen her."

"Have you seen the *Longhorn* in Eagle Harbor?"

"Could have. Lots of boats in there this time of year."

"I didn't say the *Longhorn* was a boat."

RB winced. He rubbed his head. "Yeah, well other than boats, what else would I see in Eagle Harbor?"

"What else have you seen?"

"Look, I didn't see those women. I didn't kill those women. And I didn't see anyone dump their bodies."

"Then why'd you have your goon squad here to keep us from asking a few questions?"

"Because I heard Raven was coming, and he's touchy around me because of his little brother."

Raven stood with his back to me, looking out toward the bay and the mountain. "You ready to go?" I asked him. He didn't hear me. So I went over and tapped him on the shoulder. "Let's go."

We walked toward the car. RB called out.

"Hey, Holmes."

I spun around.

"Next time you come on the rez, leave Mr. Watson behind."

I pointed at RB. "You'd better hope we don't have to come back on the rez looking for you."

We drove down Smokehouse. Mount Baker grew smaller the closer we got to the bay. Raven said nothing. He just stared straight ahead.

"What was that all about?" I asked.

No reply. I turned off Smokehouse and onto Marine Drive, heading back to the marina. A turkey vulture circled overhead before landing in a tree with other vultures. Then, as if I'd just asked the question, when, in fact, several minutes had passed, Raven said, "My little brother died of a drug overdose on the rez during the time I served in Desert Storm. The police botched the investigation."

"And when you got back you investigated on your own?"

"Uh huh."

"RB was implicated?"

"He sold Richie the drugs."

I placed a hand on Raven's shoulder. "I'm really sorry."

Raven stared out the window. "Yeah, so am I."

We drove the next twenty minutes in silence. I pulled up to Gate Five. Raven took off his seatbelt and placed his hand on the door lever without opening the door.

"You think he's telling the truth?" Raven asked.

"RB? Hard to know if it was the pain talking or whether he recognized the woman in the photo. When I asked about *Longhorn* he answered quickly, as though the name rang a bell, but it could have been the pain talking there, too. You want to come by the *Noble Lady*?"

Raven shook his head. "No. I need to sit quietly with my anger." He opened the door and walked down the ramp toward his boat. I drove around the harbor to Gate Nine.

When I got to the *Noble Lady*, I found that the zipper on the rear enclosure had been pulled up and the boarding gate left partially open. I slid my gun out from behind my back, then stepped aboard. A woman sitting on the fantail jumped up suddenly. I flinched.

"Sorry to startle you," she said.

I slipped my gun into my pocket. She could not have been more than five feet tall. About forty years old. I looked down on her round face, short, dark gray hair, sunbaked brown skin, and intense, dark eyes.

"Are you Charles Noble?" she asked.

"I am."

"Maria Delarosa," she said. "I know the women you found in Eagle Harbor."

"Maybe you'd better step into my office," I said.

I unlocked the cabin door and held it open while Maria Delarosa stepped inside.

nine

On second thought, "barreled inside" might better describe Maria. She lowered her head and moved quickly, reminding me of a little bull. I stepped inside and closed the door.

"Can I offer you anything to eat?"

She didn't answer. Instead, she whipped out three photographs and slapped them down on the galley table like a poker player revealing a winning hand.

"Juanita Gutierrez, eighteen. Melinda Corazon, sixteen. Carmela Rodriguez, twenty-one. All Mexicanas." She rolled the *r*'s in the women's names.

All lovely, smiling women. I recognized Melinda from the morgue photo Ben had given me, and the other two as the women Raven and I had found when we dived.

"You must find out who has done this," Maria said. It sounded like an order. "You must find them and bring them to justice."

"Have a seat, please," I said.

Maria reluctantly sat.

"First, how did you even know I was investigating this case?"

"Janet Paulsen."

"Yes, and. . . ." I urged her on with a roll of my hand in the air.

"Is this necessary? We need to talk about the women, not about me."

"Please, indulge me."

Maria huffed. "All right. I'm an activist. A labor organizer for migrant farm workers in Whatcom and Skagit counties. Janet's an environmental activist here in Bellingham. I saw her yesterday at a meeting of groups opposed to the development of Chuckanut Ridge."

"Pardon me if I don't get the connection between developing Chuckanut Ridge and migrant farm workers."

Maria shook her head. "You're obviously not an activist."

"Obviously I'm not."

"Housing," she said. "Supporting the development of medium- and high-income homes on the ridge pulls precious resources away from low-income housing. Those migrant laborers who manage to get visas and stay, who manage to work their way off the farms, need decent places to live here, as do many people who can't afford the high price of real estate here." Maria spoke in rapid-fire English.

"Got it."

"But beyond that, Janet usually supports farm-worker issues, so I support the environmental issues she's concerned about."

"An activist's quid pro quo."

Maria winced. "Something like that."

I pulled a pen and pad from underneath a stack of books. I looked at Maria. "Notes," I said. "Now tell me about these three women."

"Each young woman is the daughter of a migrant family. Each went missing about three weeks ago."

"Missing? Did the families report this to the police?"

Maria lowered her head and shook it. "You don't know much about migrant labor either, do you?"

"Obviously not."

"First, these women were not living with their families. Second, my families don't trust the police and they don't go to the police . . . for anything. Period. Third, some of them are undocumented. Going to the police risks deportation. So they suffer mistreatment and abuse in silence."

"If their daughters weren't living with them, how did the families know they were missing?"

"The migrant worker community is close, well-knit. News travels fast."

"What news?"

Maria frowned. "You're frustrating."

"I've been told that."

"I don't know what news. Whatever news alerted them to the fact that their daughters were missing."

"Are any of the families of these three women illegal immigrants?"

Maria shrugged. "Some I'm sure are. Maybe all. I have a 'don't ask, don't tell' policy on the farms."

"What else do you know about these women?"

"All three had mothers and fathers who came here first and worked hard in the fields for several years to send money home for their children to come and join them."

"Let me guess. That money wasn't for the services of an immigration lawyer?"

Maria let go a small laugh. "Maybe you do know something after all. That money was to pay the coyotes. Five to ten thousand dollars, maybe even more. That's what a coyote charges to smuggle a person out of Mexico or South America into the States." She sneered. "Most families cannot save anywhere near that amount. So they give the coyotes their life savings and work the rest of their lives to pay the bastards off."

"Only some of that work is less than dignified."

Maria cut her eyes at me. "Most of the work migrant laborers do is less than dignified, but some young women are forced into prostitution to pay off the coyotes."

"Like these three women?"

"A family usually says their daughter works in the 'hospitality industry.'" Tears formed at the corners of Maria's eyes. "But everyone knows it's a polite way of saying she works as a prostitute."

"Works where?"

Maria sighed. "I organize farm workers, not sex-trade workers," she said. "But I've heard they work in communities near the farms. Maybe here in Bellingham as well."

"They must have pimps, places they stay when they're not working, ways of contacting their families on the farm."

Maria sucked her teeth. "I organize. You investigate. If I knew all of this I wouldn't be here talking with you now."

"Is it possible that the families of any of the three women would allow me to question them?"

Maria nodded. "Maybe. That's all I can say. Maybe if they know you are not the police and that you are trying to bring those responsible for the death of their daughter to justice. Maybe I can convince a family to speak with you."

I reached for the pictures of the young women, but Maria grabbed my wrist.

"Only if you promise not to show these pictures to the police and not to speak a word of this to any authorities."

"You know it's possible the police could make the search for the women's killers a lot easier."

Maria gathered the photos from the table with a sweep of her hand and stood up. "Then I will find someone willing to respect the lives of the poor people I work with." She reached for the doorknob.

"Hold on," I said. "I promise not to go to the authorities with this."

Maria spun around, grinning. "You're easy."

I held up a finger. "On one condition."

Her grin dissolved into an intense stare. "Maybe not so easy," she said.

"That you promise to find a family of one of the dead women that will talk to me."

"I said, 'Maybe.'"

"Not good enough," I said. "I need your promise that you *will* find me a family."

Maria smiled. "I like you." She extended her hand and we shook. "You've got a deal. I promise." She slapped the photos on the table.

She reached for the door again, then twirled around with a twinkle in her eyes. "If you ever get tired of being an investigator, I'll get you a job as a labor negotiator."

I winked. "Don't know that I'm as tough as you."

"Tough? You want tough, try negotiating with a Dutch farmer from Skagit Valley or Lynden."

Maria handed me her business card. She walked out the cabin door and stepped off the boat. I slipped her card into my wallet. When I opened the refrigerator door, I just held it, staring. I didn't have the energy to fix myself food. So I pushed it closed and snapped open my cell phone. I called my favorite Thai restaurant and ordered garlic shrimps in black bean sauce to go.

Every community, like every person, harbors a dark side—a shadow part that most would prefer to keep hidden. The dark side of larger cities is often flaunted in displays of neon and flesh. In smaller towns, the dark side isn't always as visible. I had yet to venture into the shadows of Bellingham, though it looked like that's where this investigation would lead me. Buddhists say that within the light one finds darkness, and within the darkness one finds light. I had a pretty good idea where to find the dark side of this city. But once I found it, would I also manage to find the light?

LATE THAT NIGHT, I sat alone, sipping a cup of coffee at a booth in the Horseshoe Café. Opened in 1886, the café boasts that it's one of the oldest continuously operating eateries west of the Mississippi. If you listen closely, you can still hear the tinny sounds of an out-of-tune piano, where a guy with a handlebar moustache, wearing a bowler hat and a white shirt with black armbands, plays cowboy medleys from the 1800s. If you squint, you can still see the twirling, puffy white petticoat of a dance-hall madam hustling drunk cowboys into the saddles of her fillies upstairs.

The truth is that the Horseshoe Café serves good food, has Internet access, and best of all it's open 24/7. It's also just around the corner from Railroad Avenue, which is Bellingham's street of darkness and light.

Along the avenue during the day, people sip lattes at Starbucks, eat bagels at the Bagelry, and sweat their way to perfect bodies at the hot yoga studio.

At night, after the curtain drops on the legitimate businesses along the avenue, it rises on a new cast of characters, who deal drugs from doorways, begin brawls at bars, and sell sex from the street. The avenue's the perfect place to step through the looking glass into the topsy-turvy world of Bellingham's underbelly.

I finished my coffee near midnight and sauntered out the door of the Horseshoe Café. I took a left at Railroad Avenue and strolled down the street past Wonderland Herbs & Spices, Avenue Bread, the Bagelry, and Avellino.

I'd started across Magnolia Street when a tall woman coming my way bumped into me and stumbled partway to the ground. I reached down to help her up.

"Excuse me," she said.

She smiled, and a hint of her fruity perfume drifted my way. She held onto my arm as she regained her balance. Then she leaned into me and whispered in a low, sultry voice, "Would you like a companion tonight?"

I flashed a smile. "I would."

"Hi, I'm Monique."

Monique, if that was really her name, hooked her arm in mine. She pivoted around and walked with me across the street.

"If you have a car nearby, we can go there," she said. "If you want more privacy, I have a room we can use. That'll cost you extra. Do you need a menu, or do you already know what you want?"

"Maybe you can tell me about your specials," I said.

Monique hit my arm playfully. "A man with a sense of humor. I like that."

"My car's in the middle of the next block," I said.

"A man who's prepared, no less."

She squeezed my arm tightly and leaned her head on my shoulder. Then she placed her hand on my back and rubbed me. Her hand wandered over my shoulder blades, dropping to my waist and below, before she hooked her arm in mine again. Smart woman. Forget the soft touch of seduction. Monique had just frisked me for weapons.

When we got to my car, I opened the passenger door. Monique turned to me. Her face registered surprise. "And a gentleman, too," she said.

Her short, dark skirt rode up high on her bare white thighs as she slowly and deliberately slipped one leg inside the car, then the other. She pulled the cascading tresses of her blonde hair out of the way as I closed the door. I walked around to the driver's side.

Across the street, in front of the bus depot, a plain white van glowed orange under the sodium streetlamps. Damn. That van had "police stakeout" written all over it. Once behind the wheel, I turned to see Monique looking over her shoulder at the van. She turned back to me.

"Honey, let's get this over with now. You're not packing. You're not nervous. And you treat me like a lady instead of a whore." She motioned with her head over her shoulder toward the van. "So what is it? Fuck me or arrest me?"

"Guys in the van, police?"

"Here once or twice a week."

"Vice or drugs?"

"The word is it's drugs. You're not with 'em?"

"If I was would I be asking you to drive with me?"

"Are you asking me?"

"I am."

"Let's drive," she said.

"Got a favorite place?" I asked.

"Small parking lot between the railroad crossings down by the old Georgia-Pacific plant. It's quiet, private, and you can look out on the bay."

I started my car and reached down under my seat as we drove to check that my pistol still lay where I'd left it. Several blocks later, I pulled into the shadowed gravel parking lot, stopped the engine, and turned off the lights.

Starlight illuminated the dark waters of the bay and silhouetted the jagged tops of rotting wooden pilings. To our right, the marina lights cast an orange glow over a large freighter at dock. In the confined space of the car, Monique's perfume mixed with the smell of cigarette smoke that emanated from her hair. She pulled her legs up under her on the car seat and looked around the car.

"Kind of cramped in here," she said. "But we can manage." Then she leaned into me and whispered. "What'll it be? Oral's easy, and I take you for an oral guy. Am I right?"

"No," I said. "I want something else."

Monique chuckled. "You weren't kidding about my specials." She leaned away from me. "Okay, here they are. Anal. Breasts. Like I said, it's tight in here, but I've done tighter. Kinky's fine. Feet. Underwear. Underarms. If smelling them gets you off, no problem. Nothing risky. Bondage. Inserting foreign objects. Don't do that. You want that rocket in your pocket in my silo, you've got to wear protection. I've got condoms on me. Now, for the prices—"

I unrolled a wad of bills from my shirt pocket. Monique stopped talking.

"Information," I said.

She shrieked. "Information? You bastard. You lied. You're a cop."

Monique shouldered her door open and sprang from the car, storming away in her high heels, headed back toward Railroad Avenue. I started my car and pulled out of the parking lot. I drove on the wrong side of the street. Monique cast a glance at me and sped up. I sped up to match her. She slowed down. So did I. We danced this way along the darkened street, past the hulking behemoth buildings that had once processed paper. I rolled down my window and shouted.

"Three Mexican women were found at the bottom of Eagle Harbor. They may have been working the street. Do you know anything about them?"

"Fuck you," Monique said. She kept walking.

"I'm not a cop. I'm a private investigator working for the families of the victims. They want to know what happened to their daughters. Regardless of how you made a living, if I'd brought you up from the bottom of the ocean, maybe someone who loved you would want to know who did it, and why."

Monique stopped suddenly. She turned to me and sneered. "What makes you think anyone would care about a hooker like me?" Then she marched off.

Several blocks ahead of us, a black van turned the corner and headed our way. Its headlights flashed twice. Monique's head snapped up. She ran around to the passenger's side of my car and banged on the window. I slowed to a crawl. She walked in the street alongside me.

"Please, mister. Please, open the door and let me in."

I stopped my car, rolled down the window slightly, and raised my head toward the oncoming car. "Your pimp?"

Monique's body shook. Her voice now sounded like a child's. "Please, let me in. Danny'll kill me."

ten

Danny's car came closer.

"Tell me what you know," I said.

Monique banged on the window. "You gotta let me in."

"Three young women were murdered. If you know anything, I need it."

Danny had come to within half a block. His headlights illuminated the terror in Monique's eyes. She looked at Danny, then at me. She closed her eyes. "Okay. I'll tell you." I hit a switch and the door locks clicked. Monique whipped the door open just as Danny pulled up in his black van.

Danny rolled down the window and stuck his head out. He looked to be a man in his late twenties, with long dark hair tied into a ponytail. He rested his elbow on the window frame with his bulging biceps in plain view beneath the sleeves of his T-shirt, rolled up to display a scorpion tattoo. A cigarette dangled from his lips.

"Yo, Monique, everything all right over there?"

Monique flashed Danny a smile. "Fine," she said. That seductive, saccharine ring had returned. "Just a little preemptive negotiation."

Danny smiled. He shined a flashlight through the open window into my eyes. I bit my tongue and gave Danny a two-fingered salute. After he drove off, I turned to Monique and chuckled.

"Preemptive negotiation?"

Her body still shook. "Wrong words?" she asked.

"Maybe closer to the truth than you realize."

"Look, if I don't return with money for Danny I'll be on the streets tomorrow with a black eye and bruises. Can we drive back to the parking lot? I'll use my mouth however you want me to, but you have to pay me for my time."

I drove back over the first set of railroad tracks into the parking lot by the water. I opened the glove compartment and a vanity light came on. I laid out the three photographs on the glove compartment's small door.

"Have you ever seen these women?"

Monique lowered her head. I studied her facial expression. She looked from picture to picture. The lines around her eyes and the corners of her mouth tightened.

"It's hard to say if I've ever seen them. You know, I see a lot of people in my line of work."

I grabbed her left arm. "Don't bullshit me."

Her right arm moved toward her bag. I grabbed that arm too. She struggled with me. "What do you pack? A blade? A small-caliber pistol?"

She lowered her head to bite me. Her teeth brushed my skin. I thrust her forearm up and into her throat hard. She gagged, then struggled for a breath. I ratcheted up the pressure, and she quickly gave up the fight.

Monique whispered in a hoarse voice, "Maybe I know something."

I let her arm down, then pulled her purse from her side. I popped it open and took out a "ladies' special"—a tiny .22 caliber pistol.

I pointed the weapon at Monique. "Honey, this is what you use for preemptive negotiating," I said. Then I slipped it into my pocket.

"Look, two or three weeks ago, I'm just starting my shift at ten thirty at night. After my first trick, I see these three chiquitas working my part of the Ave." Monique dropped her seductive voice in favor of a street-hardened one. "So I called Danny and asked him what the fuck happened. Had he suddenly gone south of the border on me or some-thing? Danny went ballistic. He told me to disappear for a few hours and then show up for work again. When I came back after midnight, the chiquitas were gone, and I never saw them again. That's all I know. That's all I have to tell."

"Any of these pictures look like the women you saw that night?"

"Let's say they bear a strong resemblance to the chiquitas that tried to cut in on my business."

"Thanks," I said. I handed Monique her purse, then I peeled five twenty-dollar bills from the roll in my pocket. "That enough?"

She managed a weak smile. "You want change?"

"No. Consider it a tip for great lip service."

"Can you drive me back to the Ave?"

"That's where I was headed. Sounds like I need to have a little talk with Danny the Pimp."

Monique's body stiffened. She grabbed my arm. "Look, mister, Danny'll kill me if he finds out that I told you about him and the chiquitas."

I took her arm from mine and squeezed it. "Danny won't find out."

"Shit. My first trick tonight turned out to be some old geezer who only wanted to watch me get off. Then you come along. I shouldn't have worked tonight."

"Maybe you should find another line of work altogether."

"Easy for you to say, mister. And do what?"

"Get a job?"

"Already got one. Make more money in one night than most people make in one week."

"And how much of that goes to Danny?"

"Business overhead. Besides, I'm still young. I'll work a few years. Sock away some cash, then get out."

"How many times do you think a woman just beginning her career on the streets has said that? Then at forty she's still trying to turn tricks, only her Danny has long since moved on to younger women who fetch him more money?"

"What the fuck do you know?"

I stopped the car around the corner from the Horseshoe Café, and Monique stepped out. She leaned back inside with her hand out. I slapped her pistol in her hand. "Just so you know. I took the bullets out."

She snatched the pistol from me. "Fuck you." Then she pulled her head from the car. Before she closed the door she peeked in and said in a loud voice filled with born-again seduction. "Baby, that was so good. Come back and visit Monique soon." She brushed her skirt down over her behind, then strutted into the night.

When I worked for the Coast Guard Investigative Service, we unraveled a base prostitution ring run by a rear admiral. Junior female officers, some even married, had worked as prostitutes. Johns included enlisted men and other officers. I remember a young ensign we interviewed before she went to the brig.

"I did it for the thrill, the excitement, and the money at first," she said. Then her head dropped. "I wanted to stop but I was told I'd never receive a promotion unless I continued to take on the men assigned to me. That's when I knew I was trapped."

Denial is as powerful an urge as sex.

I swung around the block and parked uphill from Railroad Avenue. Then I switched the lights off. With an unobstructed view of the street corner just up from the Horseshoe Café, in less than half an hour I watched four drug deals go down and six prostitutes pick up johns. Every so often a police car cruised by slowly, and the prostitutes and dealers vanished into cars or slunk into the shadows of alleys. But the moment the cruiser left, the avenue's nightlife reemerged. This well-choreographed dance of law and disorder reminded me of a streetwise version of peekaboo.

An hour into my surveillance, the black van I'd been hoping for pulled up to the corner. It stopped, but Danny kept the engine running. Monique and two other women sashayed over to the van. The side door slid open. The women stepped inside. Suddenly, Monique came flying out as though shot from a cannon. She landed on her ass. Monique buried her head in her hands for a moment before picking herself up and scurrying away, holding the side of her face. Danny had apparently reasserted himself as the preeminent preemptive negotiator.

The other women left the van twenty minutes later. Their walk reminded me of how I must look making my way from the stern to the bow of the *Noble Lady* when she's rolling in beam seas. An hour later, Danny's van crawled around the corner again. Two different women sidled up to the side door, then stepped in, emerging later with that same wobbly walk. Danny must have given these women a little something to help take the edge off of their work. What a considerate employer, concerned about the well-being of his workforce.

When Danny's van pulled away from the corner, I drove down a block and parked my car under a darkened streetlamp across the avenue and slightly down from where he met his girls. I looked both ways along Railroad Avenue, but I didn't see the white police van. Perhaps they'd tired of watching these late-night reruns of crime drama.

Like clockwork, an hour later, Danny's black van materialized from the shadows at the far end of Railroad Avenue. I pulled my Browning from beneath my seat and pumped the action once to make certain I'd chambered a round. I clicked the safety off.

Danny swung his van into the corner and stopped. I pushed my door open quietly and stepped from my car. In the middle of the block, two women pivoted around, then strolled arm in arm toward the van. One wore a skirt so short it could have doubled for a wide belt. The other had on pink boots and a pink cowgirl hat. I crossed the avenue and trailed them to the van. When the women reached the back of the van, the side door slid open. I raced in front of the women, leapt into the van, and slammed the door closed.

I caught Danny's neck in the crook of my arm. I tightened my fist and jerked his head back against the front seat. I buried the muzzle of my pistol deep into the base of his skull. He squirmed and tried to turn around. I flexed my arm tighter. Then I whispered in Danny's ear.

"Two hands on the wheel, sweetheart. If they leave it, you're dead."

Danny mumbled, "Who the hell are you?"

"Your trick for the night," I said. "Now drive, and remember, if I don't see both hands on the wheel at all times, the last sound you'll hear is the click of this trigger."

Danny coughed and struggled to breathe. "Where to?"

"How about the parking lot between the railroad crossings, near the old Georgia-Pacific plant?"

"Don't know it," Danny said.

"Sure you do." I slapped the barrel of my pistol across the back of Danny's head, hard. His body stiffened and he reached for his head. I flexed my arm tighter around his neck. "Two hands on the wheel, remember?"

"Okay. Okay," Danny said in a breathless voice. "The parking lot between the tracks. What, are you unhappy with what you got from one of my girls? Tell me who. Man, I'll give you your money back and a free ride with someone new the next time."

I whipped my pistol across the other side of Danny's head. His body rippled with a spasm of pain. I whispered in his ear again. "Hands on the wheel. Drive."

I kept my arm locked firmly around Danny's neck and his head pulled back against the front seat. It forced him to drive stiff-armed down Railroad Avenue. When the avenue came to an end, we turned right, and a block later we turned left. We passed a train yard where an Amtrak train minus its engine slept.

On the other side of the street, a thin steam cloud, turned orange by sodium lights, rose from a stack of the power plant that now occupied the former Georgia-Pacific site. After crossing the first track, Danny pulled into the parking lot that Monique had taken me to. He turned the engine off. I clamped down on his neck with my arm.

"Both hands on the dashboard," I said.

When he placed them there, I pulled back even harder on his neck, which brought his head back over the seat. He gurgled, struggling to breathe. I slid the side door open. Then I reached outside the van and raised the door handle to open the driver's door. I kicked it further open. I snapped Danny's head back again, just to make sure he didn't try to go for the pistol or knife I'm sure he had somewhere nearby. Danny coughed.

"Get out. Hands behind your head. Lie face down on the ground," I said.

I helped him along by shoving his head toward the open door then grabbing him under the shoulder and yanking him out of the van. He rubbed his neck and turned to face me.

"Hands behind your head and on the ground."

I motioned down with my pistol. When Danny placed his cupped hands behind his head, he winced.

"I'm hurt."

"From the look of things, so was Monique."

Danny started to kneel, then rose to face me. "Hey, you're the black guy that Monique took down here a little while ago. Something go wrong, pal?"

I pointed to the ground, and he dropped to his knees.

"On your face," I said.

"You the police?"

Danny fell spread-eagle in the gravel of the parking lot. I dropped on top of his back. With one knee on his neck, I frisked him, pulling a large Bowie knife from a sheath at the small of his back. I threw it near the front wheel of the van. Then I patted down his legs.

"A lot went wrong," I said. "For starters, I have this crazy belief that women—all women—should be treated with respect. When I see a man hit a woman, my gut churns."

I found nothing on him other than the knife.

"Hey, Monique can handle it. Fact is, I think she likes the physical contact. Lets her know how much I care."

"Get up," I said. "Keep your hands behind your head."

Danny rose, and I spun him around to face me. I let the back of my hand crash into his cheek. My hand buzzed from the impact. In the faint glow of the lights from the power plant, I saw a trickle of blood ooze from the corner of Danny's mouth. He licked it.

"Feels good to know how much I care, doesn't it?"

Danny sneered. "You bastard. I've had enough of your—"

He dived for his knife, but he only made it partway there. He lay sprawled in the gravel, his arm and fingers stretched out toward the weapon. I grabbed his ponytail and lifted his head. He got up onto his knees. I shoved my pistol into his temple and dragged him by the hair, crawling, to the front of his van.

He didn't move quickly enough for me, so I bounced his head off the front bumper. The bumper flexed as he hit. Danny groaned. I held onto his ponytail.

"Three young Mexican women worked Railroad Avenue a couple of weeks ago. Suddenly they disappeared. What do you know about that?"

"You like that brown coochie, huh? Thought a black guy like you would go for white pussy like Monique."

I pulled back on Danny's head and let it fly into the bumper again. He squeezed his eyes closed and shook his head rapidly, as though trying to throw off the pain.

"Wrong answer. Want to try again?"

"Fuck you. What, did Monique tell you that I knew something about some chiquitas?"

"No. Someone who knew the women said they may have worked as pros."

"Well, there's your answer. Maybe they did. They sure weren't mine."

I sailed Danny's forehead into the bumper a third time.

"Another wrong answer. You're quickly losing the few brain cells that you have. Think hard before you answer again."

"Shoot me," he said.

I wrapped my hand around Danny's hair, ready to send his head back into the bumper. I thought about slapping him with the pistol again, but I glimpsed the Bowie knife off to one side. I recalled the tale of Samson and Delilah. I tucked my gun into the waistband at the small of my back. I dragged Danny to the front wheel, where I reached down for his knife.

"Hey, what are you fucking doing?" he shouted.

I slashed through his hair just above my fist, which still left his ponytail almost shoulder length.

"Giving you a trim," I said.

"Okay. Okay," Danny said. "About two weeks ago, Monique calls me and tells me that chiquitas are working the avenue."

Apparently, Danny's hair was also the source of his strength, and just like Samson, he didn't want to lose it.

Danny continued. "So I came down and had a little talk with them."

"Bullshit."

I pulled what remained of his hair taut.

"Okay. Okay. So I came down and roughed them up a little. Hell, the bitches didn't speak English. How else could I get my message across?"

"Then what did you do with them?"

"Whaddya mean, what did I do with them?"

I jerked on his hair.

"I left them at my house and called for them to be picked up."

It only took a slight pull of Danny's hair.

"Okay. Okay. I called a guy named Frank. . . . Only guy around I know who runs Mexican broads. . . . Thought they mighta belonged to him."

I had to pull harder this time. Danny huffed between words.

"Okay. Okay. A Lebanese guy. . . . Frank Abadi. . . . Owns a strip club. . . . Runs his women out of there. . . . Off I-5 as you enter Mount Vernon."

"Club's name?"

"Two Lips or something like that. Shit. Mount Vernon ain't that goddamn big and it's the only one in town. . . . What happened, some-one kill those girls?"

"What makes you say that?"

"Frank nearly killed 'em when he picked 'em up."

I yanked on Danny's hair one more time, harder than before. "Man, please don't cut off any more of my hair. The bitches love it long."

I put the knife to his hair and wanted to give him a crew cut. Instead, I flung the knife as far as I could. It splashed into the bay.

"If I find out you're lying to me . . . or if I find out you've hit Monique again . . . I'll come after you and I'll toss you in the bay with a bald head."

I dragged Danny by the hair up to his feet, pointed him in the direction of the road beyond the railroad tracks, and waved him on. "Start walking," I said.

Danny rubbed his head and shuffled off. Just before the tracks, he turned around. "Hey, what are you gonna do with my van?"

"Give myself a ride back into town."

I left Danny's van on Railroad Avenue, but tossed his keys down a sewer where he belonged. I drove back to the marina in my car. I checked the dashboard clock. The lighted blue display read 3:35. I thought about turning around and driving down to Mount Vernon, but Frederico Oller's voice popped into my head: "Don't rush into a piece too quickly. Study it. Sight-read it first. Then, when your hands touch the strings, they will be ready."

eleven

A Bach fugue playing on my cell phone woke me from the depths of a dream about diving, in which I discovered a woman's body underwater. I turned the lifeless body over, expecting to see a young Mexican woman, but instead I saw my late wife, Sharon.

I don't remember answering my cell phone, but a man on the other end chortled, then said, "Walked on the wild side last night, eh, buddy?" I recognized Ben's voice.

"You saw the reruns?"

"Late night TV."

"The department's into reality prostitution shows?"

"Actually, crystal meth is the crime du jour. We're recording some of the meth dealers we're building a case against. DA'll use the footage in his prosecution, but don't worry, your dirty little secret's safe with me"—he laughed—"and most of the police force."

"How much did your guys record?"

"Just the pickup. At least you've got good taste in hookers. This have something to do with the three dead young women being in the same line of work?"

"Maybe."

"After Legs gets into your car and the two of you drive away, 'maybe' is all you've got? You're talking to a twenty-year veteran of the force. You got something on our three dead women or not?"

"Something, but I'm not at liberty to say."

"Protecting a source?"

"I am."

"You're not a news reporter, you're a PI."

"I know that."

"We've got you on tape committing a crime. DA could charge you as a john."

"And you'd show the tape to him?"

"I said 'could.' Frankly, I was thinking that we got about a five-minute gap in last night's recording just about the time you showed up. A problem with our equipment or something."

"Thanks."

"Look, you need to protect sources, fine. But watch your back out there. You're dealing with hard-core criminals, many of whom have migrated from big urban centers to sleepy little Bellingham."

"Like Danny the Pimp?"

Ben chuckled. "So you ran into Danny Escobar, did you?"

"Long hair, ponytail, likes to slap his women around."

"Danny Escobar."

"He's Hispanic?"

"You sound surprised. Hispanics are the largest minority group in the country, and in the state. Washington's an equal opportunity state, which means equal opportunity for crime. Escobar's from Colombia or Argentina. I can't remember."

"And Frank Abadi?"

"Look who's asking about this region's most upstanding citizens. Abadi runs a strip club outside of Mount Vernon. Hispanic women, mostly Mexican, work his poles. Men stick dollars into G-strings out front, and stick other things into other places in private rooms in back. Even hear that Frank has one night set aside as ladies' night. Men do the stripping, and women do the sticking. Skagit County vice has raided the place more than a few times. So I'm putting two and two together and coming up with three. Three dead young women who worked at Abadi's place. Would I be right in assuming that?"

"It's something I can't confirm."

"Can't or won't?"

"Can't."

"But when and if you can confirm this, you'll let me know?"

"If I can."

Ben chuckled. "Loyal son of a bitch. Client's lucky to have you on the case. You need someone to watch your back, you let me know."

"I will."

After getting off the cell phone with Ben, I called Kate, even though the *Sea Eagle* had not returned from her training maneuvers. I left my callback number. A moment later, Kate called back. I sat down at the galley table.

"I'm in the women's head with my head stuck out the window to get better reception. I shouldn't be calling you," she said. "But I couldn't resist. . . . Are you calling to say you miss me?"

"Yes and no. I wanted you to hear this from me before you heard it from someone else."

"This sounds serious. Do I need to sit down?"

"I paid for the services of a prostitute last night."

"I *need* to sit down." She paused. "I'm assuming this is part of your investigation?"

"It is."

"And how much of this prostitute did you investigate?"

"Little or nothing."

"And how much of you did she investigate?"

"Little or nothing."

"Then why call me?"

"Because a police undercover unit filmed her picking me up. Ben's seen the tape. I'm sure Janet will hear about it. The story might get back to you."

"Oops. Caught in the act. And that's why you called?"

"It is."

"I'm flattered."

"Flattered?"

"That you care enough to want me to hear this directly from you."

"I'll also be at a strip club later tonight."

"The kind where they do lap dances in G-strings?"

"Uh huh."

"Also part of the investigation?"

"Uh huh."

"Are you planning on investigating beyond the G-string?"

"Nope."

"Then I'm flattered again. Hey, do I need to ask for an immediate shore leave?"

"Why?"

Kate laughed seductively. "To hold my own against the prostitutes and the G-strings."

"I think I can wait."

"But now I'm not sure I can."

In the background, I heard a loudspeaker blare an indecipherable order.

"Gotta go," Kate said.

"I do," I said.

"Do what?"

"Miss you," I said.

"That's nice," she said. "But now my body's trembling and I have to go back to work."

I folded the cell phone closed. When I stood and walked toward the refrigerator, my body trembled too.

In Kate's honor, I made a healthful protein smoothie and downed it before pulling out my guitar and the *English Suite*. My guitar lesson with Frederico Oller loomed less than two hours away. I'd gotten a jaunty rhythm back in the Prelude, but the second movement, Duarte's classical adaptation of a Castilian folksong in a minor key, sounded heavy, grave, and stilted. I practiced the first eight lines several times.

Afterward, I thought about taking a shower aboard the *Noble Lady*, but that meant using water from my tank and dumping gray water into the harbor. So I threw clothes and soap in a bag and hustled up to the pay-showers at the top of Gate Nine.

FREDERICO OLLER'S BASEMENT STUDIO always managed to stay cool, even on a warm day like today. Soft light filtered into the room from the large picture window that looked out on a small grove of fir trees. Señor Oller wore his usual dark suit, white shirt, and thin tie. He closed his eyes as I played the Prelude to the *English Suite*, humming along with me. When I finished he opened his eyes, nodded, and smiled.

"Good. Very good," he said. He pointed to the picture of him playing with Segovia. "El Maestro would be proud."

I launched into the second movement, but Señor Oller stopped me after two measures. "Slow down," he said. "You're jumping in too quickly. Step back. Here"—he pointed to the first four measures— "read and hum. Read and hum. Read and hum."

Señor Oller took my guitar from me. I read and hummed the first four measures several times before he handed it back.

"Now play," he said.

I did, and this time the folk song still sounded heavy and grave, but it flowed like billowy white clouds moving slowly across a dark blue sky.

Señor Oller tapped on the music and nodded. "Read and hum. Read and hum. Read and hum, before you play. Then the music comes from here"—he pointed to his heart—"not from here"—he pointed to his head.

I hummed the beginning of the second movement several more times. Then I played it. The first sixteen measures flowed effortlessly. But I ran into a brick wall, and I backed up. I tried playing beyond this first part several times but I couldn't. I sighed and placed my guitar across my lap. I turned to Señor Oller. He rubbed his chin.

"Played this before?" he asked.

"Yes."

"Played well?"

"Yes."

His face lit up. "You must let go of remembering how well you once played. Approach it with a beginner's mind, a beginner's heart, a beginner's hands. Then you may discover that you will learn to play it in a way you have never played it before." He chuckled. "You might enjoy your playing even more."

Señor Oller touched my arm. He pointed to the picture of Segovia, then to the *English Suite*. "Duarte wrote this for El Maestro's second wedding," he said. "El Maestro married Emilia, one of his prized, young pupils, at the age of sixty-eight. He fathered a child at seventy-seven. Love knows no age or condition; no beginning or end. Love is. And love asks only for a beginner's mind, heart, and hands. It gives hope to us all. Yes?"

I looked into Señor Oller's sparkling eyes and touched his shoulder. "Yes."

DANNY THE PIMP HAD ONE THING RIGHT: Finding the only strip club near Mount Vernon proved easy. The neon sign atop the tall post in front read, "The Tulip Patch. Where Our Flowers Are Always in Bloom." Okay, so Frank Abadi had a sense of humor, giving the club a name that dripped with local satire. Skagit County prides itself on its annual Tulip Festival, where every spring, fields awash in color draw thousands to this valley nestled between the mountains and the sea. Considering Danny's business, it's no wonder he recalled the club's name as Two Lips.

The Tulip Patch took up two storefronts in a rundown strip mall on the outskirts of Mount Vernon. I got to the club just before midnight. Pickup trucks crammed the parking lot. In one of the windows, a miniature version of the lighted displays used in sports stadiums and arenas alternately flashed "Girls! Girls! Girls!" then a digital image of a tulip opening to reveal a nude woman. What did the display show on ladies' night?

I pulled into a space and shut down the engine. I switched off the headlights and sat in my darkened car, watching. Men wandered into the club, in groups or alone.

One man leaving the club caught my attention. He strolled toward his car with his back toward me. I popped the glove compartment door and reached for the small pair of binoculars I kept there and raised them to my eyes, focusing them in the dim light. I couldn't see his face, but I could see his hair pulled back and down, turning forward under his ear. He stepped into a red pickup truck piled high with crab traps. So Ray Bob not only liked snaring crabs but also liked snaring tulips.

I circumnavigated the building on foot before I entered. Bricks filled in most windows. Heavy chains secured exit doors. Apparently, fire marshals hadn't visited the Tulip Patch recently. Several cars sat behind the club. A rear door opened, and a woman in a flowing silk robe stepped out. She took a long drag from her cigarette, then blew out a thin stream of smoke that curled upward like a shimmering ghost under the green glow of overhead security lights.

I patted my pockets to make sure I'd left my gun in the car. Then I walked to the front door and pulled the large, tubular Lucite handle toward me. The cloying smell of floral air freshener mixed with alcohol assaulted me. A big, bald man in black slacks and a black T-shirt greeted me at the door with a gap-toothed smile. He motioned for me to raise my hands, then frisked me quickly and waved me in.

Fake smoke blew across a large stage at the front of the club, where three women danced with shining silver poles. Red and blue lights cut paths through the smoke as they followed the women's undulating bodies. A sultry saxophone played in the background. Tables sat in concentric half circles around the stage. A brass bar separated patrons from dancers. Men waving bills leaned over the bar. Dancers wiggled toward the excited sea of hands, stopping short then thrusting their pelvises forward to receive the phallic currency inserted into their G-strings.

I took a table at the rear of the club, but I didn't go unnoticed. A blonde woman in net stockings and a tight outfit that reminded me of a Playboy bunny costume got to my table nearly at the same time that I did. She shook her cleavage in my face. Don't get me wrong, I'm a lover of the female form, but somehow all this display of flesh for the sake of making money didn't titillate or excite me. It actually made me sad.

The waitress cooed. "Must be your first time here, taking a seat so far away from all the action. Want a drink to help you relax?"

I ordered a beer, and the waitress threw a hip my way before sashaying off to the bar. At the front of the club, a man in a dark blue business suit with an open-collar white shirt and a loosened red tie hopped up onstage. He lunged for one of the dancers, who twirled around a pole just out of his grasp. Suddenly, two burly men pushed through the crowd and carted him out of the club on their shoulders.

My beer came with a petite brunette waitress who also showed ample cleavage. I got the feeling this was all part of the game—checking me out to see what kind of woman I responded to.

The brunette smiled, then she said in a faux southern drawl, "Should we run a tab?"

"I'll pay for the beer now," I said.

She set a glass down and bent over provocatively as she poured the beer. The head rose quickly to the top of the glass without spilling over. She played her fingers up and down the glass. "I love sipping head." She pouted and winked. Then she tapped my bill onto the table. I broke out laughing. Pouty Lips twirled around and also gave me a hip snap as she left.

So far, the Tulip Patch reminded me of Comedy Central. I took a sip of beer then looked at the bill. I didn't laugh then. For the price of one beer I could have bought a twelve-pack.

I'd only taken a few sips of beer when another woman in a skimpy outfit strolled up to my table. I imagined that somewhere in the club a man sat behind a one-way mirror, or maybe in front of a bank of video monitors, dispatching girls to lone patrons.

"May I sit?" the young woman asked.

"Yes," I said.

I suppose I shouldn't have been surprised when she wriggled herself between the table and me to sit in my lap. She draped her arm around me and whispered in my ear, "Lap dances are only fifty dollars for five minutes. Can I swing my legs around and give you one?"

I took a sip of beer and said, "I was hoping for a lap dance in a more private place. I was also hoping for a Mexican dancer."

The woman didn't miss a beat. "Honey, I'll be right back. We aim to please our men."

Now I imagined this woman strutting into that backroom like a waitress walking into the kitchen with an order. When the door closed, she'd yell, "One Mexican. Table 37."

Sure enough, a young Mexican woman appeared from a corner of the club and walked my way. She wore a thong bikini that begged for a beach in the bright sun of Puerto Vallarta or Acapulco, but seemed out of place in the fake smoke of this darkened club. She stopped at my table and turned on a weak smile.

"Señor, this is Alex"—she patted her chest—"I may sit?" Alex spoke in a soft voice. She struggled with her English.

"*Sí, señorita, por favor.*" Her smile brightened as I struggled with my Spanish.

Under normal circumstances I'd be thrilled for this beautiful young woman to ask for my lap. But as Alex lowered her firm, round flesh onto my legs and turned so her barely covered breasts poked into my chest, a wave of nausea swept over me.

Atop her burgeoning brown beauty, my mind superimposed images of the corpses that Raven and I had found at the bottom of Eagle Harbor: fed on by crabs, a breast and one side of her face now bone, and a small crab scurrying from between her lips. I closed my eyes and shook my head. When I opened my eyes I didn't see beauty and youth sitting on my lap, I saw only death. I reached for my beer again.

Alex put a hand on my shoulder. "The señor, he is okay?"

I patted her knee. "Yes."

"The señor, he wishes for a private lap dance?"

"No."

Alex gasped. "The señor, he is not pleased with Alex?"

"No. The señor is very pleased with Alex."

She narrowed her eyes and shook her head. She struggled for words. I pointed to the seat across from me.

"Please have a seat there."

Alex stood up and pulled out the chair. Simultaneously, a door in the shadows of the club creaked open and slammed shut. Alex had barely managed to sit when a short man dressed in a blue-and-white Hawaiian shirt strutted up behind her. He tapped her on the shoulder. She stood and quickly disappeared into the shadows. The man took her seat. He looked toward the front of the club and snapped his fingers over his head. Then he looked at me.

"Frank Abadi," he said.

The first waitress I'd had appeared at the table. Abadi looked at my drink.

"Another beer for Mr. . . . . ?"

"Campbell," I said.

"A beer for Mr. Campbell. Whiskey for me."

Abadi stared hard at me. Lights from the stage glistened in the sweat on his head, visible through his thinning hair. He adjusted the gold chain around his neck.

"You're not from here, are ya?"

"Western sales manager for Mitsubishi, based out of San Diego."

"San Diego, huh?" He nodded knowingly. "Got it. Developed a thing for Mexican girls, huh?"

The waitress slapped down a glass of beer in front of me and a shot glass in front of Abadi. Then she removed my half-finished glass. No seductive pouring or making a wisecrack about sipping the head this time. She turned and left promptly.

"You here long?" Abadi asked.

"Three days."

"Something wrong with Alex? Too old. Too young. Meat in the wrong places? You want Mex for sex, I can get 'em."

I took a sip of beer. "Alex is just what I'm after."

"She say something wrong to you?"

"Not at all."

"We got private rooms in the back. And a menu to suit your budget and your tastes."

"I'm looking for something more," I said.

A sly smile broke out over Abadi's face. "Twosome? Threesome? We can do that too."

"No."

Abadi's smile petered out.

"I want Alex for the entire night in my motel room."

Abadi's eyes flashed wide. "That how it's done in San Diego?"

"That's how it's done."

"Only been asked for that a couple of times up here." The cash register in his eyes went *kha-ching, kha-ching*. "Where ya staying?" he asked.

"I'll call and tell you tomorrow."

Abadi leaned his head back and threw the entire shot glass of whiskey down his throat. He swallowed hard. He laughed. "Here I thought you were a newbie when you walked in. I can see you've done this before. Don't want Alex at the same place the company's paying for, huh?"

I smiled and pointed at Abadi. "Smart guy."

"Okay, here's how it works. Eight hours. Twelve hundred dollars. You pay in advance. I'll have Alex delivered to your door at ten P.M. tomorrow night and picked up at six A.M. the next morning."

I took a swallow of beer. "One hundred now. One hundred when Alex shows up. A grand when she leaves."

"No way."

"Thanks for the beer." I slid back from the table and stood up. I'd only walked a few paces when Abadi called out.

"Mr. Campbell, not so fast. Have a seat."

I turned around and walked back but I didn't take a seat. Abadi stood up to meet me. He rose only to the top of my chest. He looked up. "Two hundred. Five hundred. Five hundred."

"One hundred for the seat. One hundred for the leading lady's appearance. A thousand for her performance."

Abadi took a deep breath. "Western sales manager, huh? They should make you the fucking CEO of Mitsubishi. All cash?"

"All cash."

I pulled out a wad of twenties and peeled off five for Abadi. He handed me a card.

"When you know where you'll be, call this number. I'll have Alex there at ten." He wagged the bills in my face. "Just remember one thing. You screw around with me and you'll be pushing up daisies instead of my tulips."

twelve

I awoke the next morning and lay in bed as the *Noble Lady* rocked gently, and a lone cloud moved slowly back and forth across the skylight.

Stepping over the line into the shadows of Bellingham frightened me less than watching my own shadow emerge. The part of me that enjoyed ramming Danny the Pimp's head into his bumper I usually manage to keep in check. But something about a man who sells a woman's body tips me over.

I tumbled out of bed, then pulled Maria Delarosa's card from my wallet. I called her cell phone. She answered with the sounds of heavy equipment whining and grinding in the background.

"I need you to translate for me."

"I'm a labor negotiator and human rights activist, not a translator. You can hire them from the yellow pages."

"It's a human rights issue. A young Mexican woman whom I'd rather not see at the bottom of the ocean floor."

"When?"

"Nine tonight at a motel near Mount Vernon. I'll call when I have the exact location."

"I'll be there."

I also called Raven.

"Can you meet me in Mount Vernon this evening?"

"Where?"

"Don't know yet."

"When?"

"I'll call later and tell you."

"Why?"

"To talk a young woman out of winding up at the bottom of Eagle Harbor."

"Hmmm. . . . Spirit called your name again."

"Do you have a weapon?"

"Call me later," Raven said.

I took that to mean yes, though I decided not to ask if he also had a permit.

I fell to the floor for a round of push-ups, sit-ups, and some stretching. Okay, so I didn't raise the heat on the *Noble Lady* to 105 degrees like Kate's hot yoga studio; still my body felt refreshed. I mixed a protein smoothie and, while sipping it, I read and hummed the first lines of the second movement of the *English Suite*. Afterward, I played them over several times on my guitar.

When I'd finished my morning rituals I popped the engine access cover, checking fluids and vital signs. Finally, I climbed up to the pilothouse and cranked the ignition key. The engine fired up and the *Noble Lady* purred.

I don't like being shot at. Especially when I don't know the shooter. Some things had bugged me ever since Raven and I took gunfire while diving in Eagle Harbor. How did the gunman get onto the island? And how did he escape from Eagle Harbor? Why hadn't the park ranger run into him, when we so easily ran into her? Had I missed a trail? Had she not told us all she knew? Could Cypress Island yield evidence that we'd overlooked?

The wonderful thing about Cypress is that it's only accessible by boat. So, satisfying my curiosity meant cruising there in the *Noble Lady*. A real sacrifice since I probably wouldn't have time to cruise back to

Bellingham and then drive down to Mount Vernon to rendezvous with Alex. What a hardship. I'd have to cruise the *Noble Lady* from Cypress to La Conner and tie up at one of my favorite docks.

With the *Noble Lady* ready, I unraveled the lines tethering me to land and pushed the boat back into the fairway. I hopped aboard and scrambled into the pilothouse. On our way out of the harbor, we slipped quietly past finger piers normally crammed with boats but now peppered with empty spaces. Boating season fast approached its crescendo in late July.

I rounded the breakwater and passed the green entrance buoy. I brought the *Noble Lady* up to speed, then set her on course. I clicked on the autopilot. The sun dazzled in a cloudless blue sky. Little wind blew across Bellingham Bay. Far in the distance, the clear weather treated me to a rare sight. I blinked my eyes, then pulled out my binoculars. No, the clouds hadn't played a trick.

To the left of the saw-toothed, snowcapped peaks of the Olympic Mountains, the massive snowy dome of Mount Rainier stood tall behind the dark shadows of the low-lying islands that fringed the rippled waters of the bay.

When a coast guard assignment had first brought me to the Northwest years ago, I'd read a book on Mount Rainier. Tahoma, "the Mountain that was God," the first inhabitants here called volcanic Mount Rainier. She stood across the water and apart from the "Home of the Gods," as the Greeks knew Olympus—the fiery local god looking askance at the presence of stranger-gods bent on staying.

Tahoma disappeared behind the tallest part of Fidalgo Island. I turned my attention to the dark green hills south of Bellingham and several ridges in from the bay. A developer wanted to populate this landscape with hundreds of homes. And the fiery local residents looked askance at the presence of strangers bent on staying.

A swift ebb carried me through Devil's Playground. I never did ask Raven what the natives called this stretch of water. Past Viti Rocks, the ebb whipped me like a slingshot pellet toward the Cone Islands. From there I headed into Eagle Harbor, where I counted fifteen boats on mooring buoys and at anchor—another sign of boating season under way, and diminished fears of more dead bodies. I didn't share the same optimism of these boaters at Eagle Harbor.

A gleaming white Bayliner zoomed out of Eagle Harbor, headed my way. Water topped with foam curled from the boat's bow. I slowed down as *Wake Up* sped past me with the captain waving and smiling as if to say, "See me in my pretty boat."

I spun the wheel hard left, and a moment later *Wake Up*'s wake crashed into the *Noble Lady*, sending her rocking and reeling as though we'd just ventured into four-foot seas. Dishes rattled in the sink below me. Behind me, books jumped over guardrails and hit the floor. I slid the pilothouse door back and watched as *Wake Up* sped merrily along, oblivious to the havoc in her wake.

Now, I have nothing against going fast in boats. But I bet every captain of a sailboat or a slower trawler like mine would love to have the captain of a fast boat like *Wake Up* aboard just once to experience the broken dishes, lost meals, and bone-jarring crunch from a fast boat's wake. Maybe then the captains of these seagoing rockets would slow down when they met us on the water.

I anchored at the mouth of Eagle Harbor in fifty feet of water. Behind me, toward the shore, sun glinted off the windshield of the park ranger's boat tied to the two pilings, which leaned at angles and oozed tar from their pores as though suffering the withering effects of old age.

I lowered my dinghy and rowed a couple of hundred yards into the small beach where the park ranger had pulled her dinghy above the sand and rocks. The tide still ebbed, so I let my dinghy float in the water and tied a long line from it around a large piece of driftwood on the beach.

I had remembered my hiking boots. I slipped into them and left my sandals near the park ranger's dinghy. Half a mile up the trail, a raven's cluck emanated from the forest to my left, followed by the rhythmic swooshing of air as the big bird flew overhead.

I liked Raven. I've known men who'd spent many years embarking on dangerous missions, witnessing horrors, and committing unspeakable acts, all in the line of duty. They often appeared aloof as a means of self-preservation, a way of keeping distance between the outside world and the demons they battled within. I wondered how much of Raven's seeming aloofness lay in his obvious spirituality, and how much resulted from the inner battles he fought.

Not much farther along the main road, a trail led off to my right. I *had* overlooked another way a gunman could have escaped. Grass had overgrown most of the trail, but fresh tire marks cut two narrow lanes through the growth.

It took me half an hour to reach the buildings where the park ranger lived and worked, at the edge of Reed Lake. No sounds of life emanated from the compound. I called out several times. No one replied. I knocked on the garage door. No one came. I climbed up a high stairway to a white door that looked like it might open into the ranger's private residence. I knocked on the door pane. No one answered. I tested the handle. Locked.

Water from a fast-moving stream rushed behind the building. I turned to walk down the steep stairs when a loud buzz came at me. A hummingbird hovered a few inches in front of my face. We watched each other for several seconds before the bird buzzed away. Maybe it liked my bright orange T-shirt.

The throaty whine of a diesel broke the stillness of the day. It approached the compound from below, on the road I had walked to get here. I climbed down the stairs and took a seat at a picnic table near the interpretive signboards. Moments later, the park ranger bounced to a stop. I stood up. The ranger bounded out of the truck and over to me. She had a big smile.

"Mr. Noble, what brings you back?"

"It's funny," I said. "What I remember most about you is AWOL. But I've forgotten your name."

She laughed. "At least you remembered what's most important about me. Adventure without limits. Carol. Carol Jenkins."

I snapped my fingers and pointed to her. "That's right. CJ."

"Just out for a cruise and a hike?"

"No, I came to ask you a few questions."

Her smile dissolved. "About the women?"

"About the shots that were fired."

"I told you all that I knew."

"It's more about the trails on the island."

She squinted, then screwed up her face, accentuating the network of lines already there. "Trails?"

"Yes, that trail off to the right as you're coming up here, where does it lead?"

"Oh, it connects to the Lake Loop, but most people don't walk that way because it's overgrown. I just came over it a few minutes ago. Lake Loop goes to Duck Lake, with turnoffs for Pelican Beach and Eagle Cliff. Beyond Duck Lake, the trail leads to Smuggler's Cove."

"On the west side of the island?"

"Yes."

"On the day we were shot at, no one came up this way?"

"I told you before, no one as far as I know."

"So whoever shot at us could have taken the cut-off to Duck Lake."

"Could have." CJ hiked her thumb over her shoulder toward the pickup truck. "Can you walk me back to the truck? I need to unload cut wood from a tree that fell on the Duck Lake trail."

"I'll help."

She frowned and shook her head. "It's what I get paid to do. Besides, you're not insured."

"Well in that case," I said, "I think I'll take a walk over to Smuggler's Cove."

"Hope you packed a lunch. It's a good five or six miles there and back to Eagle Harbor."

I winked. "For breakfast I had a protein smoothie with all manner of healthy ingredients."

CJ shook her head and frowned. "Never cared for that stuff."

"It grows on you," I said.

I started back down the trail when I caught a glimpse of a rifle shell casing in the dirt. I walked over to the side of the road and bent down to pick it up. A Remington 30-06. I turned and called to CJ, who was unloading wood from her pickup.

"Spent rifle shell." I waved it at her. "Do you own a rifle?"

She called back. "Hunters. The island's open to deer hunting in the fall."

I examined the shell further. It looked too new to have weathered the winter. I slipped the casing in my pocket and continued on to Smuggler's Cove.

At first the trail paralleled Eagle Harbor, giving me a bird's-eye view of the boats, most of which were sailboats or fast, sleek Bayliner types. But one boat caught my attention: a tugboat with a green and gray hull that stood proud among the boats around it. I couldn't make out the boat's name from this distance, but it looked like a Lord Nelson Victory Tug. A classic boat not unlike the *Noble Lady*.

At the head of Eagle Harbor, the trail cut through tall grass then headed inland past huge stumps of old-growth cedar. From some of the stumps, new cedar trees had sprouted and grown, wrapping their roots around the stump like a spider weaving a web around a fly, intent on sucking life from its host.

I reached the juncture of the Duck Lake trail and the trail to Pelican Beach. Ahead of me, two women were walking in my direction, engaged in an intense conversation. I didn't think they noticed me.

I called out so as not to surprise them. "Hello."

The heads of both women snapped up. "Ahoy," the older woman said. She'd tucked her gray hair under a black Greek fisherman's cap.

We stopped upon reaching one another.

"Are you on a boat?" the younger woman asked.

"Willard 36 Aft Pilothouse moored at the entrance to Eagle Harbor."

The older woman nodded. "Bill Garden classic," she said. "Don't see many of them on the water."

"You know boats."

"We own a Victory Tug."

"Gray and green? Anchored in the harbor?" I asked.

"That one," the younger woman said.

"Out cruising the San Juans?"

"Hell," the older woman said. "We ought to be in Prince Rupert by now, but we got a damn late start this summer. One of our cats got sick, and we had to leave him in a veterinary hospital for a month. It kind of set us back."

The younger woman smiled. Her blue eyes sparkled. "But he's okay now," she said. "And ready to cruise north."

"First time north?" I asked.

The women looked at each other and burst out laughing. "Twentieth summer to Alaska," the older woman said.

"Oops."

"Have you taken your Willard to Alaska?" she asked.

"Been to Alaska on a large boat, but only as far as Desolation Sound on my own boat."

Both women shook their heads. In unison, they said, "You've gotta go north."

"I intend to."

"At least north of Caution," the older woman said.

"Cape Caution?"

"Yep," she said. "North of Caution. That's where the cruising's at its best."

"We planned to cruise up to the Broughtons this summer," I said.

"Nice," the younger woman said.

"If you get that far, go a little farther, through Nakwakto Rapids and back into Belize Inlet," the older woman said. "Our friend Charlie shares a float home in Strachan Bay with a fellow named Buck. If you do go, please tell him Helen and Denise said 'hi.'"

I extended my hand to both women. "Charlie's my name too. Charlie Noble."

Helen, the older woman, laughed. "Named after the galley stovepipe, huh?"

"My dad cooked on a merchant marine boat."

"Guess you were fated to be a mariner."

"We need to get back to *Kaddis*," Denise said. "To check on our cats."

"*Kaddis*? Interesting name for a boat."

"*Kaddis* is a Nubian word," Denise said, "which means cat."

"Nice to meet you, Charlie," Helen said. "And don't forget. North of Caution. That's where the real excitement starts."

We parted ways, and I continued walking toward Smuggler's Cove. Helen's voice played over again in my mind. North of Caution? Forget cruising the Inside Passage. North of Caution seemed my destination tonight.

The trail to Smuggler's Cove wove down through cedar and fir forests to the west side of Cypress Island. The remnants of an old cabin stood up from the shore.

A plaque in front of the crumbling remains told the story of Zoe Hardy, who early in the twentieth century rowed a boat out to Cypress Island and homesteaded this small bay, eking her survival from the land and the sea. She must have been one strong woman. Reading about her life brought to mind CJ, Kate, Janet, Helen and Denise, and the many other strong women who still cruised these seas.

I stumbled over rocks, making my way down to the water's edge. From the number of crushed shells, it appeared that Native Americans long ago had also used this beach. I stooped down to pick up a broken clamshell.

Sharon loved to beachcomb. She'd spend hours walking the shoreline, picking up shells, lamenting that they were broken, placing them back where she'd found them, then continuing to look for more. I liked to walk with her to experience her joy upon finding a perfect shell or piece of glass with worn, rounded edges. We'd make up a story about the age of the glass, where the fragment came from, and the route by which it got to the beach where we had found it.

Sunlight flashed off a metallic object in the grass near the remains of Zoe Hardy's cabin. It looked like the metal leader from someone's lost fishing tackle. I walked over to it and pushed away a layer of finely

broken shells with my foot. Then I reached down to pick up the rem-
nants of a necklace. I cleared small strands of seaweed from the tiny silver links. The seaweed hid a small charm, which now dangled from
the chain. I turned the charm over in my hand and squinted. A halo of
light surrounded an image of the Virgin Mary's hooded face, which
bore a beatific smile.

A cold shiver worked its way through my body. I'd seen this same
image before, tattooed on the upper chest of the second woman that
Raven and I had found underwater at Eagle Harbor. I tucked the necklace into my pocket next to the rifle shell.

When I checked my watch I realized I needed to get back to the
Noble Lady and down to Mount Vernon to prepare for tonight's rendezvous with Alex.

thirteen

When I got back to my dinghy, I met CJ pushing her dinghy into the water.

"Leaving home?" I asked.

She laughed, then pointed out toward the water. "Going to town," she said.

"Friends?"

"Supplies."

"It must get pretty lonely out here."

She sucked her teeth. "Lonely I can handle. Dating scene I can't. Like men who. . . ." She shook her head. "Sorry, that's more about my life than you probably care to know."

And apparently more than she cared to tell.

CJ got into her dinghy and I pushed her off the beach. My dinghy floated in a rising tide. I pulled it to shore, untied the tether, and hopped in. Then I headed back to the *Noble Lady*.

The course from Cypress Island to La Conner took me back up toward Bellingham Bay, then away from the bay toward Strawberry Island and Anacortes. A coast guard patrol boat hovered close to a large oil tanker that was lumbering away from the refinery docks at March Point. Past the point, I lined up between the red-and-green buoys marking the only safe route through narrow, shallow Swinomish Channel. The dredged channel flows like a swift river, and this afternoon it flowed with me, which made the cruise down to La Conner short.

When I reached the marina, I executed a wide, sweeping turn to approach the dock heading upstream. I'd learned my lesson the hard way the first time Sharon and I had tried docking a boat at La Conner. That day, we had come in with the current and nearly wiped out the back end of an expensive motoryacht. Today I worked against the ebb, which gently pushed the *Noble Lady* toward the dock. With the engine in forward at its lowest speed, I made just enough headway against the current to hold the *Noble Lady* in place against the dock.

Another boater stood on the dock, waiting to catch my lines. I pushed the pilothouse door open, stepped out on deck, and tossed him a midship line, which he whipped around a cleat. Then I shut the engine down and stepped off to tie the other lines.

With the *Noble Lady* secure, I called a motel near Mount Vernon whose sign along the freeway I remembered because of its slogan, Sweet Suites for Tired Travelers. A pleasant man answered my call.

"I need two adjoining suites, one for myself and one for my assistant, Mr. Edward Barnes. My name is Campbell. George Campbell. We'll be staying for only one night."

"Mr. Campbell, you can take room 209; Mr. Barnes, room 207," the attendant said.

I gave the man my credit card number. Afterward, I called Raven.

"Meet me at the marina in La Conner about seven."

"Armed?"

"Armed."

I also called Maria Delarosa.

"The Executive Motel, just off I-5 in Mount Vernon. Room 207 at nine."

"Do you need me to bring anything for this young woman?"

"A change of clothes."

"Did you happen to get her size?"

"Eighteen- to twenty-year-old, medium."

"Medium? A lot of help that does. You're an investigator. Aren't investigators supposed to be observant?"

"Maritime investigations. Maritime security. Women's dress sizes still remain a mystery to me."

Maria chuckled. "I'll figure something out."

Finally, I took Frank Abadi's card from my wallet and called the cell phone number on it.

"The Executive Motel in Mount Vernon. Room 209 at ten o'clock," I said.

"A man will knock on the door, and you will pay him one hundred dollars. Then he will send Alex to your room. When he picks her up in the morning you will pay him one thousand dollars. Any questions?"

"No."

"One more thing. The guy who's delivering Alex has simple instructions: No money, no girl. Anything seems funny, he does whatever it takes to collect what you owe me. That understood?"

"Clear. Nice doing business with you."

"Nice? Alex is nice. Business is business." He hung up.

I took a shower and changed into fresh clothes. Raven picked me up in La Conner at seven. We discussed the evening's plans over dinner at a restaurant on the main street, which overlooks the channel. At eight thirty, we left for the Executive Motel.

I picked up the card keys from the front desk and handed the one for room 207 to Raven. The front windows of both rooms faced the motel's main parking lot. When I opened room 209 it smelled like freshly made linen, which made me wonder if motels, like large bakeries, have a spray they use to trick the senses of their guests. I knocked on the metal door to the adjoining room. Raven knocked back. I turned the latch on my side. He turned the one on his. We both opened our doors and— voilà!—we stood facing each other.

"I'll wait here for Maria to arrive?" Raven asked.

"Yes. Turn the television up and keep your conversation down."

"You'll knock when you're ready?"

"Three times."

"Think we can pull this off?" Raven asked.

"What do you think?"

Raven patted the bulge beneath his armpit. "We've got one helluva backup plan."

I smiled, then swung the door closed and locked it. Raven did the same.

I checked that I'd chambered a round before slipping my pistol into a drawer of the television stand. Then I kicked off my shoes, turned on the radio, and fiddled with the dial until I found a classical station. Violins, a viola, and a cello lamented, playing long, foreboding passages in a minor key. I didn't recognize the piece. When it finished, the program's host named the last several selections that she'd played. I'd listened to the String Quartet No. 14 in D Minor by Franz Schubert, written near the end of the composer's life.

At nine o'clock, someone knocked on Raven's door. I heard him usher Maria in and explain our plan to her.

At five minutes to ten, I pulled back an edge of the curtain. A layer of clouds now covered the stars. In the parking lot, a black Lexus came to a stop. A man exited from the passenger door, which probably meant that Abadi had a backup plan as well—more muscle. Soon the man knocked on the room door. My throat tightened. I undid the chain and swung the door open. I recognized the heavyset man as one of the bouncers who had escorted the rowdy customer from the Tulip Patch. A whiff of cigarette smoke and alcohol came off the man. He held out his hand.

"One hundred dollars."

I plucked a wad of bills from my shirt pocket and thumbed off five twenties, which I handed to him. He smiled fiendishly. "Alex'll be right up. Sweet dreams. I'll see you at six in the morning."

I turned the music down. High heels clicked on the stone steps leading up to the second floor. Alex tapped lightly on my door. When I opened it, I sucked in a breath. She wore a tight black strapless dress, with a black and red silk shawl wrapped around her shoulders. She'd rolled her hair into a bun, which she supported with a large wooden comb. Her lips glowed with ruby lipstick. Silver pendants hung from her earlobes. Alex looked every bit a saucy Mexican dancer, and not a hooker working for a small-time hustler like Frank Abadi. In fact, she reminded me of photographs of a young Frida Kahlo.

She smiled and brushed her hand down the side of her dress. "The señor is pleased?"

"The señor is very pleased," I said.

She stepped into my room and closed the door behind her. I checked out the window. The black Lexus sat in the parking lot with its lights off. Alex sat in a chair next to the desk, with her legs crossed. Her gaze darted around the room. I pulled the drapes tight and dimmed the room lights. Then I knocked three times on the adjacent door. Raven knocked back. We both undid the door latches and swung our doors open.

I beckoned with my hand toward Alex. "*Señorita, por favor,* please come with me."

Maria Delarosa stuck her head into my room. She spoke in rapid-fire Spanish to Alex and waved her forward. Alex's eyes grew big. She looked between Maria and me. Then she looked at the door. She said something to Maria. Maria spoke to me.

"She's scared that Mr. Abadi's men will come to harm her," Maria said.

"Tell her that I will not let that happen. That we're here to take her away from Mr. Abadi for good."

The two women conversed in Spanish.

"She said that Mr. Abadi told her if she did not appear at six o'clock in the morning he would hold her parents responsible and expect them to pay all the money owed for transporting her out of Mexico. If they cannot pay, Mr. Abadi will send his men to harm her parents."

"Can you find out her real name and where her parents are?"

"Probably," Maria said. "But I need some time. Let me try to get her into this room first."

"Tell her that I will not let anything happen to her parents," I said.

Maria spoke to Alex again and reached a hand out for her. Alex pulled away. Maria stepped forward and placed an arm around Alex's shoulder, then whispered in her ear. Alex began to cry. Maria helped her up from the chair. I pulled my gun from the nightstand drawer and accompanied the women into room 207. Raven quickly swapped rooms with me, and we locked both doors.

I stood with my back against the door adjoining room 209. "What did you tell her?" I asked Maria.

"That she is too young and too beautiful to sell her body for the likes of any man."

I nodded. "Take her into the bedroom, and please don't make any noise. Turn on the television if she continues to cry."

Alex sobbed on Maria's shoulder as Maria shepherded her into the bedroom. I picked up the telephone and called Raven in room 209.

"Show time," I said. "The men are in a black Lexus."

I hung up and placed my ear to the door as Raven made a call to 911.

"My name is George Campbell. I'm at the Executive Motel in Mount Vernon," he said to the 911 operator. "Two men have been acting suspiciously outside the motel. I don't believe they're guests, but they've prowled the rooms and now they're sitting in a car outside. . . . Yes. . . . I'm in room 209. . . . Wait a minute. . . . They're in a black Lexus down in the parking lot in front of my room. . . . Thank you. . . . Yes, I started to go to bed but I couldn't sleep so I called. . . . Yes, please have the police knock on my door."

Raven hung up. The telephone in room 207 rang. I picked it up.

"You get an Oscar," I said.

"It's not over yet," Raven said.

"I'll be waiting."

I hung up.

Five minutes later, a red light pulsed in the parking lot. I peered out the window. A police officer shined a light in the Lexus and asked both men to step out. They pointed up to room 209. One officer stayed with the men, while the other officer hiked the stairs to Raven's room. He knocked on the door and Raven opened it.

"Mr. Campbell, may I have permission to search this suite?"

"Why?"

"Both men said they believed a woman was being held against her wishes in this room. They said they were investigating the matter for the woman's family."

Raven went ballistic. "What? Bullshit. I'm here on business from Seattle. There's no one in this suite except me."

"Please, Sir, it would help greatly if you would agree to let me search the room."

"Damn. I can't believe this, when I'm the one who made the call. . . . All right, but please make it quick."

"Thank you, Sir. This won't take a minute."

The police officer entered Raven's room and the door slammed behind him. Closet doors opened and shut, as did the bedroom and bathroom doors. A few minutes later, the officer radioed his partner.

"Sam, they're bullshitting us. Room's clean. No one's here other than Mr. Campbell. I say we take them into the station and question them further. . . . Right. . . . I'm coming down now."

Next the officer spoke to Raven. "Mr. Campbell, thank you. I'm sorry to have intruded on your privacy. Have a restful night. I won't need anything further. We'll be taking these men with us and they won't bother you again."

I watched as the police car pulled away with both of Frank Abadi's men. Raven knocked on the door between us. We unlocked the doors and he stepped in. I opened the bedroom door. Tearstains smeared Alex's makeup. She sat on the edge of the bed. Maria knelt before her, holding her hand, whispering in Spanish.

"Time to go," I said to Maria.

She stood and helped Alex up from the bed. Alex stared at me with swollen, red eyes. She shook her head and then turned to utter something in Spanish to Maria.

"She says she does not know whether to bless you or to curse you," Maria said to me.

"Tell her I'm not sure either."

Maria conveyed the message to Alex, who managed a weak smile.

"Can you stay with Alex tonight?" I asked Maria.

She turned to Alex and patted her hand. "Of course."

"Then take her in your car. Follow Raven and me to my boat at the La Conner Marina."

I heard Raven's footsteps outside the rooms. I peeked my head back inside 209 to make sure we hadn't left anything there. Raven stepped back into 209 as well, holding his pistol. It looked like a lightweight Glock.

"No one's around. Time to go now," Raven said.

He took the lead, and I brought up the rear. We ushered the women down the steps to Maria's car. Then Raven and I slipped into his car, and we headed to the La Conner Marina. When we got to the marina, I stepped from Raven's car and walked toward Maria's. Raven called out.

"Noble."

I turned around. He drove closer.

Through his open window, he said, "She's a beautiful girl."

"She is."

"We're not letting her wind up at the bottom of Eagle Harbor."

"We're not."

He pointed to me. "You did a good thing back there."

I pointed to him then to myself. "We did a good thing back there."

"Your plan."

"Your acting."

"We pulled it off."

"We did."

Raven rolled up his window and sped away. I escorted Maria and Alex to the boat.

Inside the *Noble Lady,* I turned down the sheets on my bed in the master stateroom.

"Alex can sleep here," I said. "Maria, there's a smaller berth at the bow for you."

Alex shook her head vigorously. *"No, señora, por favor."* She patted the bed.

"I'll sleep with her," Maria said.

With the women settled, I checked the *Noble Lady*'s vitals. After the engine warmed up, I cast off the dock lines and headed us out into the dark waters of Swinomish Channel. On a clear day, I'd cruise from La Conner to Bellingham without using radar or GPS. But on an overcast night like tonight, I brought up radar, GPS, and my navigational computer.

With the blue vessel icon lined up to follow a dashed yellow line on the computer screen, I hit the autopilot button and scanned the darkness for the green and red lights of other boats.

When Prometheus stole fire, he raced from angry gods who eventually caught him. Zeus chained him to a rock, where an eagle daily ate out his liver only for it to grow back and be eaten the next day. Stealing light from darkness is how I'd describe taking Alex away from Abadi. And while Abadi bore no resemblance to Zeus, I was sure he'd relish the opportunity to mete out Prometheus's punishment to me.

We'd just passed Strawberry Island when I heard someone climbing up the pilothouse steps. Maria sat down on the bench behind the helm. She said nothing for several minutes.

"The soft instrument lights. The glow from the computer screen. The darkness outside. It feels like a sanctuary in here," Maria said.

"Sometimes it is."

"That darling girl is sleeping. She's been so traumatized by her experience since leaving Mexico that she's afraid to trust anyone. But she did tell me as she drifted off that her name is not Alex. It's Eliana. Eliana Morales. She said she doesn't know where her parents work, but she believes it's somewhere in Skagit Valley. She's right, you know."

"About what?"

"Freeing her is as much a curse as it is a blessing. They'll come after her family as a way of exacting their revenge for her escape."

"Can you find them?"

"Her family?"

"Yes. Can you find out where they stay?"

"I think so."

My fingers fumbled along the top of the instrument panel until they found their way over the small links of the broken silver chain I had found at Smuggler's Cove. I stepped away from the helm briefly and switched on a light above Maria's head. I handed the necklace to her.

"Do you know what this is?" I asked.

She turned it over in her hand once. "Where did you get this?"

"On a beach on the other side of Cypress Island from where the three young women were found. It's a necklace of some sort."

"No," Maria said. "Not a necklace. It's an ankle bracelet. Probably a present to mark a young girl's First Communion."

fourteen

I didn't feel the *Noble Lady* tip when Raven stepped aboard. He knocked on the pilothouse door. I sat up, blinked my eyes, and shook my head, trying to wake up. Raven stood on deck, looking through the window. I opened the door. His hair shone as though he'd washed it. He'd threaded his ponytail through a hand-tooled silver ring, which I guessed he'd made.

"Thought you might have slept up in the pilothouse last night."

"The women slept down in the stateroom," I said.

I crawled downstairs and opened the cabin door. Raven stepped inside. I got some coffee going. I yawned.

"You're up bright and early after a late night," I said.

"Thought Alex might need a chaperone," Raven said.

"Eliana. Her real name's Eliana Morales."

"Still might need a chaperone."

The steps leading to the stateroom creaked. Maria walked into the galley. I poured three cups of coffee, handed one to her and the other to Raven. She took a sip, then set the cup down on the table. "If I'm going to locate her parents, I need to leave now." She nodded toward the stateroom. "My *poquita* is still sleeping. Can I trust you both to keep her safe?"

Raven reached into his pocket, pulled out his Glock, and slapped it down on the table next to Maria's coffee cup.

"Call me the moment you find them," I said.

When Maria left, I tiptoed into the stateroom and grabbed some clean clothes without disturbing Eliana. Raven stopped me as I walked out the cabin door.

"I have one too," he said.

"One what?"

"A daughter. Nineteen years old. She lives with her mother in Port Hardy."

"Do you get to see her much?"

"I haven't seen her since the divorce."

"How long ago?"

"Seven years."

"That long? Port Hardy's not that far away. Why haven't you gone to see her?"

Raven stared off into space. When he didn't respond, I gathered my clothes and my toiletry bag. I pulled the cabin door open.

"Noble," Raven said.

I turned around.

Raven sighed. "I don't know why."

I nodded.

"If Eliana wants to take a shower have her use the one on the boat," I said. "It'll be safer."

Raven nodded.

I took a shower and dressed in the washrooms near the harbor office at the top of Gate Nine. I thought about riding my bicycle to the police station. I needed the exercise. But it was already nine o'clock, and a thick layer of clouds still hovered over the bay. The wind blew in from the south. I slipped behind the wheel of my car just as a few raindrops pattered the windshield.

Three young Mexican women were at the bottom of Eagle Harbor. Someone shot at Raven and me after we found two of the bodies. The women were probably undocumented immigrants brought into this country by coyotes, and forced to work as prostitutes. I found a spent rifle shell on Cypress, as well as a religious charm that Mexican girls are given at First Communion. We found a native crabber's traps at Eagle Harbor. The crabber later showed up at a strip club where the owner pimps Mexican women. All coincidence? Human trafficking gone awry? Or rich boys on big boats partying with what they regarded as throwaway women, and then actually throwing them away?

I tapped on the steering wheel. After asking Ben about the bullet that Raven had retrieved from the bottom of Eagle Harbor, I also needed to have a talk with Bellingham playboy Bud Kincaid.

I sat in the parking lot and called the Bellingham Police Department. The receptionist informed me that Ben was out on patrol. I left my callback number. A couple of minutes later, Ben called me back.

"Don't want to hear anything about the three women found in Eagle Harbor."

"Why?"

"Chief is trying to unload the case on the Coast Guard."

"Why?"

"Chief hates marine investigations. Says our boats just sit at the dock and eat up maintenance funds."

I laughed. "He doesn't know what the letters B-O-A-T stand for."

"Bring On Another Thousand."

"Have you seen a ballistics report on the slug that Raven pulled from the water?"

"I have."

"Would it happen to be a 30-06?"

"Damn, Noble, are you psychic? . . . Yeah, it's a 30-06."

"Could you also pull up what you have on Ray Bob again?"

"Can't right now, but if you tell me what you want maybe I can get it for you later."

"That domestic abuse charge. I want to know more about the woman involved."

"I'll see what I can dig up."

"Thanks. How's Janet?"

"Happy. Thinks they've got a deal with Kincaid to buy that property he wants to develop. I hope they do, so she can stop being a tree hugger for a while."

"Yeah, but you love it."

"Don't know about that. Maybe I love her."

"What'd I hear you just say?"

"Gotta go. I'm on the department's time. Talk to you later."

Ben hung up. I smiled. I called Janet's art gallery next. A young man named Kenneth answered.

"Ms. Paulsen's busy at the moment."

"Tell Ms. Paulsen that Mr. Noble's on the line."

"Sir, I'll have her get back to you."

"Son, I'll hold until I hear directly from her that she can't take my call."

Kenneth huffed. A moment later Janet picked up.

"Did I interrupt you?"

"No," Janet said. "What makes you say that?"

"Kenneth."

"Oh, he thinks it's cool to project an image that we're always busy."

"You need a new receptionist," I said.

"Are you kidding? Kenneth's an art student at the university. He brings a younger generation into the gallery. It's good for business."

"Yeah, but he puts off an older generation with money . . . bad for business."

"I thought you were a private eye, not a business consultant. A 'fish-eye,' if I remember."

Janet laughed. I joined her.

"Do you know where Bud Kincaid lives?" I asked.

Janet stopped laughing. "What the hell do you want with him?"

"Fish-eye business."

"Has to do with the three young women?"

"Confidential."

"Did Maria talk with you?"

"She did."

"So you're helping her?"

I paused. Janet jumped in. "Also confidential?"

"Yes."

"Good. She's a capable woman and now I know she's in capable hands."

"She's also feisty. Now how about Bud Kincaid?"

Janet sighed. "I remember the house only too well. He lives at 2500 Chuckanut Crest Drive. A house at the top of the mountain. Misty-fjord-green color with a great view of the bay."

"Misty-fjord-green?"

"What do you expect? I'm an art gallery owner."

"Misty Fjord sounds more like a place I should go with the *Noble Lady*."

South of Fairhaven, Chuckanut Drive twisted and turned past home after home where red-and-white yard signs read, "No Development of Chuckanut Ridge." Just before the drive opened up into an expansive view of Chuckanut Bay, I took a small road veering off to the left. Chuckanut Crest Drive wove—hairpin after hairpin—past exclusive luxury homes. Even these yards had signs against development—ironic, since these homeowners had reaped the benefits of developing these lush green hills. What's that called? I snapped my fingers. NIMBY. Not In My Back Yard.

The higher the drive went, the further I climbed into the clouds. Fog blanketed the roadway ahead. I slowed to a crawl to avoid driving off the mountain, and I wished my car had radar like the *Noble Lady*.

Suddenly, a wrought-iron gate spanned my side of the road ahead. I slammed on the brakes. No gate crossed the other side of the road, leading down from the mountain, but a line of tire spikes like the metal teeth of an asphalt monster dared any driver to venture the wrong way on that side. I pulled up to the kiosk beside the gate and pressed the button marked 2500. A rapid-fire succession of touch-tones sounded through the speaker grille beneath the keypad. A moment later, someone picked up a telephone on the other end.

"Hello," the male voice said.

"Mr. Kincaid," I said. "George Campbell, private investigator. I wonder if I could ask you a few questions about that matter at Eagle Harbor."

"My father sent you?" the man said.

"He didn't give me the gate code."

"It's 5-2-3-9-2," the man said.

"I'll be right up."

I chuckled to myself, then punched in the code. The wrought-iron gate rumbled back, and I drove through.

Chuckanut Crest Drive continued to wind its way upward through switchbacks and through fog. I held my breath and swallowed hard to clear one ear that had filled from the elevation gain.

Finally, the asphalt road became a dirt and gravel road, which after one more switchback dead-ended at a house that looked, well, on a day like today, misty-fjord-green. I must have risen above the layer of clouds. The fog now hovered close to the ground, and above me treetops reached into a clear blue sky.

I parked in front of the detached four-car garage and stepped quickly through the mist to the covered walkway leading to the front door. The large pillars at the front of the massive house reminded me of a modern-day version of a southern plantation. I rang the doorbell and waited, half expecting a maid or manservant to answer. When the door swung open, a blond-haired man with a boyish face and a dimpled chin stood before me.

"Mr. . . . ?"

"Campbell," I said. "George Campbell." My father's first name, my mother's maiden name. The alias had grown on me.

"William Kincaid." He extended his hand and we shook. "Please, come in," Kincaid said. "I wasn't expecting you. Father didn't call to say you'd be here."

"You can never predict where an investigation might lead," I said.

I stepped into the foyer. Kincaid closed the door behind me. I sucked in a breath and held it as I stared at the view out the window, which took up most of the front room wall. I looked out and down over an infinite expanse of billowy gray and white clouds. Every so often, the deep green summits of an island poked through.

"Lummi. Orcas. Cypress." I whispered the names.

"You know your islands, Mr. Campbell," Kincaid said.

Kincaid looked like he'd just gotten out of bed or the shower. He wore a misty-fjord-green terrycloth bathrobe and matching terrycloth slippers.

"It's a shoes-off house," Kincaid said.

I slipped off my shoes and walked across the oiled cherrywood floors into the living room. I continued to stare out the window.

"Stunning view," I said.

"Yes it is," Kincaid said. "Care for a seat?"

I followed Kincaid into the living room and sank into a plush, white couch. It reminded me of a first-class seat in an airplane high above the clouds. I pulled out a pad and pencil, mostly for the effect. I turned to Kincaid.

"Within the past two weeks, the bodies of three women were pulled up from Eagle Harbor."

Kincaid sighed and shook his head. "I'd heard about one woman. I didn't know about the other two. That's tragic."

"*Longhorn* was seen in Eagle Harbor about the same time."

Kincaid shrugged and raised his hands palms up. "And your point is?"

"No point. Just that the police are investigating the connection between the boat and the women, and—"

"And you're the private investigator Father hired to collect enough information so we can make sure nothing taints the Kincaid name." His accent crossed a sleepy southern drawl with a patronizing prep-school twang.

"Telling me what you know would certainly help."

"To the best of my recollection, Eagle Harbor is a small cove on the east side of Cypress Island."

"It is."

"Mr. . . . Mr. . . . ?"

"Campbell."

"Yes, Campbell. . . . It's not the kind of place Father or I would take the boat. I don't know where you heard that *Longhorn* entered Eagle Harbor, but whoever said that was obviously mistaken." The sleepy southern drawl won out with this last sentence.

"Well, then, I don't suppose—"

"Bud, where are you? Are you coming back to bed?"

The dreamy, high-pitched female voice floated down from above. I turned and looked up over my shoulder. A woman clad in a very short, misty-fjord-green terrycloth bathrobe leaned over the tubular railing of the second floor. She held a glass of wine in one hand, and swayed enough to concern me.

Kincaid frowned. "Tiffany, I'm talking to this person."

"Oops," Tiffany said. She placed her hand over her mouth, then disappeared from the railing.

"Now where were we, Mr. Campbell?" Kincaid tapped the side of his head as if trying to fix my name in his brain.

"Where's *Longhorn* now?"

Kincaid stood up. So did I, but I had about four inches of height over him. He narrowed his eyes.

"When's the last time you spoke with my father?"

"It's been a while."

"And he hired you?"

"I'm investigating the deaths of these women and their connection to *Longhorn*."

Kincaid shook his head. "I don't believe my father hired you. Who are you, a reporter looking for a story?"

I flashed my license. "An investigator. I—"

Kincaid came at me, pushing me back, out of the living room. "Whoever you are, get the hell out of my house."

I grabbed his arm, spun him around, and twisted his arm up and behind his back. "Didn't they teach you some manners growing up?"

I threw Kincaid up against one of the posts supporting the second floor. "What was *Longhorn* doing in Eagle Harbor?"

He gritted his teeth. I pushed his arm up harder. "None of your damn business."

"So it has been in Eagle Harbor?"

Kincaid struggled against me. "I didn't say that, and if you don't let me go I'll go to the police and have you arrested for assault and battery."

I ratcheted his arm higher. "I'm sure the police would love to talk with you about those three women found at the bottom of Eagle Harbor."

Sweat broke out over Kincaid's face. "I told you"—his voice sounded strained, breathy—"we don't take the boat to Eagle Harbor."

"Well then, maybe you can tell me why someone saw *Longhorn* at Smuggler's Cove?"

"Who? I don't know a Smuggler's Cove."

"Other side of the island from Eagle Harbor."

"Why would *Longhorn* be there?"

"That's the question."

"We go to places with more accommodations than a small bay without any protection from the wind."

I released Kincaid's arm and pushed him toward the couch. He stumbled up against it, then turned around and wagged his finger at me.

"I'll call my father and you'll be history, Mr. Campbell, or whoever the hell you are."

"I'll see myself out," I said.

I slipped on my shoes and walked through the front door, then under the covered walkway to my car. Small bay. No protection from the wind. Bud Kincaid obviously knew enough to describe the characteristics of Smuggler's Cove. And as far as calling his father, that's exactly what I hoped he would do. Then maybe I'd catch Daddy Kincaid in the midst of trying something foolish that would help me understand how and why three young women had ended up at the bottom of Eagle Harbor.

I drove down Chuckanut Crest Drive and passed the right way over the tire spikes at the gate. I'd almost made it to Chuckanut Drive when my cell phone rang. I reached into the glove compartment and fumbled for the phone, but by the time I flipped it open the caller had hung up. I checked recent messages. Raven had called me seven times. I pressed Send, and my cell phone dialed him back.

"She's gone," Raven said. "Eliana's gone."

fifteen

I raced back to the marina. When I got to the *Noble Lady,* Raven
stepped from the fantail onto the dock to meet me. He didn't make
eye contact, and I didn't see the pride I'd seen in his face when he
arrived to guard Eliana. My throat tightened. I wanted to yell. But I
also don't believe in kicking someone when they're down.

"What happened?"

Raven pointed to the large, open hatch on the foredeck. The hatch
vented the forward part of the boat, and also provided a means of escape. I already had a good idea what had gone wrong.

"About a half hour ago, Eliana said she needed to shower and to
dress," Raven said. "I hung a blanket over the opening into the stateroom so she'd have some privacy. She turned the shower on, and the
boat rocked as she moved around. The shower stayed on too long, and
when I checked, the forward hatch was open and she was gone."

"Did you check the marina restrooms?"

"Men's and women's as well as both showers."

"Check the boats on the dock? She could have jumped aboard one
and hidden there."

"Walked every dock on this gate. . . . Nothing."

Raven slumped. He spoke to the ground. "I let her down. I let you down. I'm sorry."

I grabbed Raven's shoulder. "The only letting down will be if we don't find her."

I leaped aboard the *Noble Lady* and checked inside. Eliana had left behind the clothes she'd worn to the motel, which meant she'd dressed in the jeans, T-shirt, and tennis shoes that Maria had brought her. I locked up the boat and jumped off onto the dock. Raven hadn't moved.

"Come on," I said. "We have a young woman to find."

Raven murmured. "And too many places to look."

"We'll head downtown first," I said.

Raven jogged over to his car. I pulled out of the parking lot and raced down Roeder Avenue. I turned left on F Street, then right on Holly. I flew past Maritime Heritage Park. But a moment later, I stomped on the brakes and swung into the parking lot of Tamales Mexican Restaurant. Raven pulled into a space next to me and bolted from his car.

"She doesn't speak English well, but she does speak Spanish," I said.

I yanked open the restaurant's door and stepped inside, nearly running over a waitress with a tray in her hands. But she smiled.

"Be with you shortly," she said. "Two for lunch?"

"We can't wait."

The waitress frowned. Raven stepped past her on his way to the bar. He launched into an exchange with a native fellow who sat nursing a beer. I followed the waitress. She placed her tray down on an empty table.

"A young, attractive Mexican woman, dark hair, about this tall"— I raised my hand to my chest—"may have stopped in here to ask directions. She doesn't speak English well. Have you seen her?"

The waitress ignored me, instead lifting a plate of chicken enchiladas from her tray and setting it down in front of a young couple who looked as though they were sharing the dish. The spicy aroma wafted my way. My stomach growled. The waitress must have heard me. She chuckled low while continuing to set down a bowl of rice and a plate of refried beans.

Finally, she lifted her head. "You sure you don't want to eat?"

I raised my hand again. "Mexican woman—"

The waitress shook her head. "No. I haven't seen her but it gets busy in here. Ask the owner. Maybe he knows." She pointed toward the bar.

By now, Raven had worked his way down a few seats. I walked up behind him.

"Owner's behind the bar," Raven said. "Said he hasn't seen Eliana come in. None of the other customers I talked to had seen her either."

"At least we know where to ask."

"The other Mexican restaurants downtown," Raven said.

"Familiar food. People who speak your language. I'll take Taco Bandito and Taco Grande," I said.

"Leaves me with Taco del Sol and Mi Casa, Su Casa," Raven said.

I jumped into my car and wove my way through downtown Bellingham to Taco Bandito. I parked near the Federal Building, where a gathering was assembled with placards that read, "U.S. Out of the Middle East" and "Stop the Development of Chuckanut Ridge." Police had erected barricades.

I walked down an alleyway to get to Taco Bandito. The young woman behind the counter sported a crew cut and a pleasant smile. She had pierced ears, a pierced lip, a nose ring, and a pierced tongue.

"Like, would you like to have a seat?" she said.

I started to say, "Sorry, like I don't speak like that dialect of English." Instead, I pushed my way out the door and headed back up the alleyway to Taco Grande.

Taco Grande had seats spread out onto the sidewalk. Noise from the protest across the street grew. My cell phone rang. I whipped it from my pocket and stepped away from the restaurant.

"Nothing at Taco del Sol," Raven said. "I'm off to Mi Casa, Su Casa."

"Nothing at Taco Bandito either," I said. "I'm in front of Taco Grande."

I closed my cell phone and sidestepped a waiter to get inside Taco Grande. An older man with gray hair and bushy gray eyebrows rang up a sale on the cash register. He squinted as I approached him. Then he turned on a wide smile.

"A table for one?" he asked.

"Did an attractive young woman who doesn't speak much English come in here within the last half hour?"

"And you are, Señor?"

I pulled out my wallet and flashed my license. "A private investigator looking into her disappearance."

The man's hand flew to his head. He shook his head and mumbled something in staccato Spanish.

"She asked to make a call," he said. "I asked if it was local. She didn't understand what I meant. I asked where she was calling. She didn't know. I asked whom she was calling. She wouldn't say. She gave me the number and I dialed it. It wasn't local. An intercept said I needed to use the area code. She spoke in broken English to someone. I couldn't hear her well."

"Thanks," I said. I turned to leave.

"Wait," the man said. "After she hung up she asked me for directions to Railroad Avenue."

"Did she say where on the avenue?"

"No."

I raced to my car and got in. I started the engine but then realized I couldn't drive straight ahead because the protest was now spilling into the street, and the police had cordoned off the intersection in front of me. I called Raven.

"She's somewhere on Railroad," I said. "She made a call out of the area."

"To Skagit?"

"Probably to ask Abadi to pick her up, and he gave her the meeting place. You're almost at the north end, so drive slowly south. I'll head to the south end and drive slowly north. We've got to find her before Abadi or his thugs do."

I snapped the phone closed and made a sharp U-turn. To get to the south end of Railroad Avenue, I threaded my way through downtown Bellingham's maddening labyrinth of one-way streets that became two-way, and two-way streets that became one-way.

A center island ran the length of Railroad Avenue—a remnant of the railroad tracks, I guessed. I cruised along slowly, peering into store-fronts and between parked cars. I hadn't gotten far when a car horn blew. I checked my rearview mirror. A line of cars had formed behind me. So I pulled over into an empty space and fed a meter. Then I set out to cover the rest of the avenue on foot.

Across Railroad Avenue from where I'd parked, patrons sipping coffee sat in black wrought-iron chairs around small wrought-iron tables under a large, green Starbucks awning. On my side of the avenue, the marquee of a nearby nightclub announced the coming of The Motown Cruisers, a local 60s group.

After crossing an intersection, I looked through the store window of a gift shop I came to, but I didn't see Eliana. Past the gift shop, I reached a seedier part of Railroad Avenue.

A man looked furtively in both directions after stepping from an adult store. Not the boutique sex-toy shops you find in suburban strip malls, but a magazine and peep-show joint that conjured up images of flashers in trench coats. The adult store had no windows. I made a mental note that Frank Abadi might have friends in other areas of the flesh business, friends who might shelter Eliana until he could arrange for her transport.

I walked farther down Railroad. Across the avenue, Raven also moved on foot, but in the opposite direction. We exchanged glances, then continued our separate ways. In the middle of the block, my cell phone rang. Maria Delarosa sounded cheery. A knot tightened in my stomach.

"I found Eliana's parents," she said. "They're working on a farm in central Skagit County. They're anxious to see Eliana. Can I bring them to the boat this evening about nine?"

I sighed. "Yes," I said.

"What's wrong?"

"Eliana slipped away from Raven."

"What?" Maria's voice soared to shrill heights. "I left her in your safekeeping and now you've lost her?"

"Don't worry, we'll have her back on the *Noble Lady* at eight."

"You'd better." Maria hung up.

I hurried across Magnolia Street to the bus station. I ducked into the waiting room. A group of kids, dressed completely in black and with dyed black hair and piercings everywhere, huddled in a corner. They glared menacingly at me as I scanned the room. I ran out of the station and almost knocked over a police officer about to enter. He held me by the shoulders to keep me from falling.

"Sir, is there a problem?"

"No."

"Are you here waiting for a bus?"

"No."

"May I see some form of identification?"

My hand went to my back pocket. His hand went to his gun.

"Hold on, cowboy," I said. "I'm reaching for my identification."

His glare reminded me of the kids in black. I handed him my PI license. He perused it carefully.

"Can I ask what you're doing in here?"

"Looking for someone."

"Do you have a description?"

"Yes."

"Which is?"

"I don't have the time."

"Sir, I—"

I started walking away. "Look, detain me or let me go." It sounded like a line Monique might use. "But before you detain me call Detective Sergeant Ben Conrad and explain to him why."

He called out. "You know Ben?"

"I do."

The officer said nothing more.

I crossed back over Magnolia. Raven stood in front of a feed store. "Nothing," he said.

"Did you check the Horseshoe Café?" I asked.

"No."

"I didn't go into the adult shop."

"Food or flesh?" Raven asked.

"Food."

We walked a block down then crossed over to the other side of Railroad Avenue, the corner where later this evening Danny the Pimp's women would stumble into and out of his black van. Raven entered the Horseshoe Café first. I stepped inside behind him and whispered in his ear.

"Far end of the counter."

Just at that moment, Eliana turned around. Her eyes flashed wide. She bolted from her stool into the kitchen. Raven ran after her. I raced outside and headed down the alley next to the café. Eliana never came my way. I caught up to Raven and we jogged to the street at the far end of the alley. I looked both ways but I didn't see Eliana. I pushed Raven off to the right. I went left. When I got to the next corner, I saw the back of a young woman in blue jeans and a white T-shirt, with long dark hair swaying as she headed for a nearby crowd.

I called back to Raven. "She's headed for the protest at the Federal Building." I ran in that direction.

Several hundred demonstrators against U.S. foreign policy in the Middle East, and against unrestrained local development, milled in front of the Federal Building. They spilled into the street. On the opposite side of the police barricades, only a few counter-demonstrators held signs reading, "Terrorism Is Being Told What I Can and Can't Do

With My Land" and "Support Our Troops, Let Them Buy New Homes on Chuckanut Ridge."

One lone man stood in the middle of the intersection waving a sign that read, "Against the War, For the Development, Let's Find Common Ground." Judging by the number of people around him, I'd say that guy really had an uphill struggle. A line of police officers separated the two demonstrations—some officers on foot, some straddling motorcycles, some in cars, and some no doubt in plainclothes mixed in with both sets of demonstrators. I didn't see Ben.

I waited at the edge of the main demonstration for Raven, who jogged across the street to meet me. He was breathing hard.

"I still think she's meeting someone back on Railroad," I said. "I'll go into this crowd and try to flush her out. You hold back and pick her up if she comes out."

Raven nodded and backpedaled from the demonstration. I twisted my head in both directions, standing on tiptoes to get a better view. I waded into the thick of the crowd, where heat rose amid all the bodies. Sweat oozed from my pores. Elbows and hips pressed close to one another. I had little room to move, even less to see around me. Suddenly, an arm reached to grab mine. A woman pulled me onto the sidewalk.

Janet Paulsen had a huge grin. "Thanks for joining us," she said.

"I'm looking for a young Mexican woman who disappeared into the crowd. Have you seen her?"

"You're working?" Janet asked.

"To save her life."

Janet shook her head. "Oh no. You think—"

"I don't have time to talk," I said.

I moved with Janet farther back from the street, closer to the entrance to the Federal Building. I climbed atop the heavy black railing that fronted the building and scanned over the heads of demonstrators, between the waving signs. I caught a glimpse of a woman in blue jeans and a white T-shirt headed for the alley next to Taco Grande. I jumped down and elbowed my way through the crowd. I ducked under a police barricade. An officer yelled, "Hey, you." I didn't turn around.

I sprinted toward the alley. When I got there, Eliana stood halfway down the narrow passage, transfixed, looking my way like a doe caught in the glare of headlights.

"Eliana, stop," I said.

She turned and ran. I started after her. Suddenly a car's wheels squealed and the afternoon sun reflected off the hood of a black Lexus lurching down the alley, trapping Eliana between the car and me.

sixteen

Eliana froze. The Lexus slowed to a crawl thirty yards away from her. She stood at least that distance from me. The windshield of the Lexus framed an image of two men. I recognized the driver as the man who'd delivered Eliana to the motel.

I instinctively reached to the small of my back, feeling for my pistol. The driver glared at me. I stared back without flinching, even though my heart sped. I'd left my pistol on the boat. I kept my hand behind me anyway. The passenger door of the Lexus swung open and a beefy guy with a crew cut stepped out. He stood tall enough to lean his elbow on the car's roof.

Eliana looked at me, then to the Lexus, then back to me. I waved her toward me.

"Walk slowly back to me," I said.

Eliana turned in my direction.

"*Aquí. Aquí,*" the big man yelled.

She turned back to him.

"*Aquí,*" he said. He pointed to the car.

Eliana shook her head. The man slammed his fist on the roof of the car. Eliana flinched. He whipped his index finger at her.

"*Aquí.*"

It appeared to be the only Spanish this guy knew.

"Eliana, *aquí*," I said. Okay, so I didn't have a large Spanish vocabulary either, but at least I could use her real name and speak softly.

She turned toward me again, but she shook her head.

"Bitch, get your ass over here," the big man said. "Mr. Abadi knows where your parents live, and if you don't come back with us, we'll pay them a visit next."

"No," Eliana yelled. She shook her head violently from side to side. "Not my parents." She patted her chest.

Apparently Eliana knew more English than she let on.

"Eliana, your parents know that we have you," I said. "We're bringing them to see you tonight. Come."

Eliana turned to me and yelled. "No. Not my parents."

She thrust her palm toward me, then walked to the Lexus. The big man stepped away from the door. He lunged for Eliana's arm, grabbed her, and bundled her through the passenger door. Then he yanked the rear door open and jumped in. The moment the door slammed closed, the driver gunned the accelerator. The Lexus took off like a black bullet, headed right at me.

I had no time to turn and run. Malicious satisfaction beamed from the driver's eyes, while Eliana's eyes held sheer terror. "Flatten yourself against the wall," I heard my mind say.

The Lexus sped closer. But before I could even move, I saw Eliana lean over and lock her teeth on the driver's hand. He tried to shake her off. The Lexus swerved. I dived for the ground on the other side. Fiberglass crunched, and metal scraped along the brick wall. The Lexus came to a stop about twenty feet from me. The passenger door flew open. So did the rear door.

Inside the car, a man moaned, "My head. Fuck. My head."

Eliana tumbled out onto the ground near me. Starting to my feet, I looked up into the muzzle of a semiautomatic pistol that the big man was aiming at me.

A moment later, two arms came out of nowhere and wrapped themselves around the big man's neck. Raven put him into a chokehold,

bending the big man back and down and squeezing tighter, like an ana-
conda coiling around its prey. I jumped to my feet, grabbed the big
man's gun arm, and brought his wrist down hard against my raised
knee. The gun fell and I scooped it up from the ground. I reached for
Eliana and pulled her to her feet.

The big man's face reddened under the chokehold. Raven twisted
the man's neck slightly, then jerked hard. The man groaned, and when
Raven let go the man crumpled to the ground.

Raven waved me away. "Get her out of here," he said.

I tossed him the gun. "One still in the car, probably injured," I said.

"I'll take care of him," Raven said. He waved me away again. "Just
get Eliana away from here."

I grabbed Eliana's arm, and we headed out of the alley.

ELIANA SAT AT THE GALLEY TABLE, her lips trembling like a survivor
plucked from icy waters. Tears ran down her cheeks. Dinnertime
hadn't arrived yet, so I pulled a bag of tortilla chips from a cabinet
above the sink.

"You don't have to go back to Frank Abadi," I said.

Eliana closed her eyes, but she said nothing. I reached into the
refrigerator for a package of cheese.

"Maria will be here this evening with your parents."

Eliana sighed. Her eyes closed. Her head dropped.

I found a jar of salsa hiding at the back of another cabinet. I grated
the cheese, then dumped everything in three separate bowls. I pushed
the salsa in front of Eliana. She stared at the bowl, then pushed it back
toward me.

"Sorry. I'm not a good enough cook to make my own salsa."

The *Noble Lady* shuddered. Someone stepped aboard. Eliana sucked
in a breath and pushed back against the seat. I held up one hand while
pulling the blind back with the other.

"Don't worry," I said. "It's Raven."

The cabin door opened, and Raven stepped in. We stared at each other without speaking.

I once commanded a coast guard lifeboat called out to rescue a thirty-foot sailboat that had lost its mast in storm-force winds and forty-foot seas. I put a swimmer, Seaman Eric Whitman, in the water with a line. We managed to get the shaken couple from the sailboat back to our boat. Eric stayed in the water to help them climb aboard.

My crew hauled them in, then hustled them below for medical attention. Only I stood on deck as Eric climbed aboard. A huge gust of wind blew him from the rungs of the ladder without his line. I don't remember thinking twice before donning a wetsuit and jumping in after Eric while I could still see him. We didn't say much afterward. But each year at Christmas, I get a card from Eric, which reads only, "Thanks."

Raven reached for a chip and scooped up some salsa. "Good salsa," he said.

I put a hand on his shoulder. "Thanks," I said.

Raven nodded, then he walked over to Eliana.

"Are you all right?" he asked. She took his hand and squeezed it. Raven nodded again.

I dipped a chip in the salsa, then sprinkled some cheese on top. I hoped that rescuing Eliana from Frank Abadi's clutches proved the right thing to do. I didn't want her to be the fourth body beneath the waters of Eagle Harbor. I popped the chip in my mouth. The dead women were daughters of Mexican farm workers, who may have been illegal immigrants. The women appeared to have been trapped into prostitution as a way to repay the men who had smuggled them out of Mexico. Maybe Eliana could shed some light on their murders.

My cell phone rang. Maria sounded frantic. She spoke rapidly in Spanish, and I couldn't understand her.

"Calm down," I said. "We've got her."

She didn't calm down, but she did switch to English. "It's not Eliana I'm worried about," she said. "Abadi's men have surrounded the camp where her parents live. I'm just outside the gates. I'm afraid to go in."

"Stay put. I'm leaving right now."

I snapped the cell phone closed.

"Trouble," Raven said.

"Trouble. Think you can keep Eliana here this time?"

"I won't let her out of my sight for anything. . . . Not even to use the head."

Eliana sat at the galley table staring into space, expressionless.

I made sure to grab my gun this time. I raced up the Gate Nine ramp to my car. At a stoplight before the freeway entrance, I called Maria for directions. I drove down the freeway like a maniac, weaving in and out of cars and trucks along the way. I raced to help Eliana's parents, but deep down it felt like I also raced from my guilt at placing them in jeopardy to begin with.

At an exit for an outlet mall, I swung off the freeway into the dying evening sun. The cloverleaf I followed looped back over the freeway, heading east toward shadowed foothills awash in a soft, orange glow. Several miles past the signs for Gucci, Tommy Hilfiger, and DKNY, the asphalt road turned to gravel.

A mile later, I made a right turn at a huge power-line tower. The gravel road turned to dirt. Acres of farmland stretched as far as I could see on either side of the road. A mile down the dirt road, next to a small stand of cedar trees, I stopped my car behind another parked car. The door of the other car swung open and Maria Delarosa jumped out. I pushed my door open and stepped out to meet her. She tugged on my arm.

"This way," she said.

I reached back in the car for my gun. Maria dragged me off the road behind a tree. Two buildings stood in a field half a mile beyond the trees. Maria pointed.

"The long one is the dormitory," she said. "The small one, the latrines and the washrooms."

I pointed to the dark green SUV parked to the side of the dormitory. "And that must be Frank Abadi's men."

"Yes," she said. "I was there, outside the dormitory, when they pulled up. They asked me if I knew Miguel and Naida Morales. I spoke in broken English and told them I worked for the archdiocese, but I would ask around for Miguel and Naida Morales. They laughed, and in English called me a 'stupid little fucking nun.' I bit my tongue and told them I needed to be with a very ill migrant worker in another camp. Then I left and parked here, behind the trees, where they would not see me."

"Eliana's parents aren't at the camp yet?"

"No." Maria checked her watch. "With this much light, at this time of the year, they are probably just getting off work."

"How will they arrive?"

"By truck."

"Then we'll stay here and intercept the truck before it gets to the camp."

"If only it were that easy," Maria said. She pointed toward the foothills in the distance, beyond the camp. "They'll be coming from fields over there."

I took a deep breath. "That doesn't leave much time, or many options. Stay here." I exhaled and slipped past the trees.

"Señor," Maria called out. "What may I do?"

"If I don't return with Miguel and Naida, call the Bellingham Police Department and ask to speak with Detective Sergeant Ben Conrad."

I tucked my gun into the small of my back, then set out, making a wide, sweeping arc away from the camp. I followed a large overhead power line. I sank up to my ankles in the soft dirt of recently plowed fields. The sickening smell of manure grew stronger as I walked. A gentle buzz emanated from the power lines. A subtle charge of current coursed throughout my body, giving me a slight headache. Walking through this field reminded me of fighting forward through a snow-bank. I stumbled, pulling my leg out of the fetid earth. I brushed dirt from my jeans, my shirt, and my forehead, but I succeeded only in mixing manure with my sweat.

Finally, I turned at a point where the dormitory stood between the

SUV and me. I slogged through the dirt toward the buildings as the orange glow in the sky faded to dark blue. Joyous sounds of children's laughter floated through the field. Neon lights flickered on around the camp. The children played on squeaky swings and a rusting teeter-totter in a small playground close to the latrine building.

An older child saw me. He squealed, then pedaled a bike furiously my way. A group of kids ran behind him. I flipped my shirttail over the handle of my gun. The boy came to a screeching stop in front of me, throwing dirt from his tires as he braked.

He sniffed the air, then wrinkled his face. He turned and called back to the other children in Spanish. They let out a collective laugh. I put a finger to my lips. I didn't know the word for silence in Spanish, but I gave it a shot.

I said quietly, *"Silencia, por favor."* I pointed beyond the dormitory, then put my finger to my lips again. *"Silencia."*

The children grew silent. I walked past the latrines. The children swarmed behind me, following me as if I were a Pied Piper. The boy on the bicycle showed off in front of the others, zooming ahead, then circling the group. When I walked past the latrine building, he got off the bicycle. He pointed to me, then he pointed to the latrines. He said something in Spanish and laughter erupted again from the group.

"Silencia," I said.

Perhaps the children thought it a game. They joined in shouting, *"Silencia,"* picking up my plea as a chant. We neared the dormitory and their chanting grew louder. Across the field, a small dust cloud moved toward the camp. I pushed my back against the side of the dormitory and slid along the outside wall, past windows covered with nothing more than cut-out sections of burlap bags. Close to the edge of the dormitory, I heard one of Abadi's men call out.

"They're coming. Go back there and shut up those fucking kids."

A dozen kids still hovered around me, chanting, *"Silencia."* The door of the SUV opened, then closed. I looked around. I couldn't make it to the latrine. The chanting of the children droned in my ears. I backpedaled along the wall and dived through a burlap-covered window. The kids crowded around the window, chanting, *"Silencia."* Through the weave of the burlap, I strained to see outside. Abadi's man swaggered around the corner. He waved his gun.

"Hey, what are you kids doing over there?"

Several kids turned toward the burlap and pointed. *"Silencia,"* they chanted.

"What's in there?" he said.

"Silencia," they answered in unison.

He muttered to himself, "Maybe I'd better have a look." Then he walked toward the window.

seventeen

I looked around the dormitory. Sheets hanging from two-by-four crossbeams cordoned off the large area into smaller spaces. Several thin mattresses covered the floor nearby. Beside me, a burned candle rested on an altar, where a rosary lay in front of a framed picture of the Virgin Mary. I peeked through the burlap again. The man came closer.

Suddenly, the boy on the bicycle thrust his way in front of the other children.

"*Silencio,*" he said. He put a finger to his lips. He pointed at the burlap. I held my breath. "Tomás is sick. He's sleeping inside."

"Kid, you speak good English," the man said. "If he's sleeping, then why are you all yelling outside his window?"

"When he's well, he's a bully. Now he's sick, so the others bully him."

"Hah," the man said. "Guess the little shit had it coming."

Abadi's man walked away. The other children began chanting again.

"*Silencio,*" the boy called out.

The chanting stopped. Finally, I got it. I'd been off by a vowel with my Spanish. The boy gestured for me to climb back out the window.

The truck with the workers rumbled into camp. Once outside, I leaned over to the boy on the bike. I pointed to the truck.

"I need to find Naida and Miguel Morales before those men do. I must get them away from the camp or they will be hurt."

The boy with the bike stood tall. He patted his chest. "Not to worry, Señor, Alonzo will help."

Alonzo huddled with the children like a coach with his team. He spoke in hushed Spanish, pointing to several kids. The truck's brakes squealed. People filed over a gate at the back of the truck. The children ran toward them. I walked to the edge of the dormitory. Abadi's men waited by their SUV. Alonzo walked his bike behind the swarm of children. He looked back once in my direction, winking, then subtly patting down the air with his palm.

Farm workers trudged toward the dormitory. Abadi's men pushed off from the SUV. "Naida and Miguel Morales," they shouted.

No one responded. The children played in and out of the adults.

"Naida and Miguel Morales," Abadi's men called out.

A man and woman just stepping off the truck raised their heads.

"There," one of Abadi's men said. He pointed to the couple.

"Naida and Miguel Morales?"

The men drew their guns. The couple climbed back into the truck.

Suddenly, Alonzo shouted in Spanish and the children turned, running toward Abadi's men, swarming them and jumping on top of them. Alonzo waved me forward. The men fought to throw the children off their backs. Some workers ran to help the children.

"Take the truck, Señor. The truck," Alonzo said.

I ran for the truck. I yanked open the driver's door and a man with wide eyes held up his hands and moved out quickly from behind the wheel. In the back, a couple cowered. I cranked the ignition key. The couple moved toward the rear, ready to jump off. I turned to them.

"No, por favor," I patted my chest. "Eliana is with me. Eliana."

One of Abadi's men fired a shot in the air. Miguel had a leg over the rear gate. I started driving. Alonzo rode up on his bike. He shouted to

Miguel in Spanish and Miguel pulled his leg in. In the rearview mirror, I saw him wrap his arm around his wife. They hunkered down in a corner. A bullet shattered the passenger's side window. I rammed the gearshift into second.

Dusk made finding the road a challenge. Abadi's men needed only to jump into their SUV to catch us in this old rig. I frantically searched the dashboard with my fingers, pulling each lever I came to. The wipers turned on. The defroster whirred. Finally, the headlights lit the dirt road leading away from the camp. I jammed the shifter into third.

When I looked back from my sideview mirror, I saw Abadi's men jump into their SUV. Then I thrust my head out the window. Alonzo pedaled frantically, in a vain attempt to catch up with the truck. He dangled something from his fingers as he rode.

"The keys," he yelled. "The keys, Señor." He patted his chest. "Alonzo has the keys to the SUV."

I honked my horn twice. Alonzo broke off his pursuit.

When I got to the dirt road, Maria had her car idling. She ran to the back of the truck. After a hurried exchange in Spanish, the Morales couple climbed down. Maria led them to her car, where she opened a rear door and waved them in.

I sprang from the truck. Maria ran to me. "Take them directly to my boat at the marina," I said.

She sniffed the air. "God, you stink."

Then she leaned in and kissed me on the cheek before running back to her car.

FROM THE MARINA PARKING LOT, I called Raven on my cell phone.

"Maria's here with Miguel and Naida," he said.

"You want to bring me some soap and a change of clothes?" I said.

Raven chuckled. "Shitty job, but someone had to do it, huh?"

"Just bring them to me," I said.

After a shower, I walked back to the *Noble Lady*. Raven opened the back door as I stepped on. He held one hand low and out of sight, behind his back.

"Eliana and her parents are inside," he said.

I walked through the door. Everyone gathered around the galley table. Naida clutched her daughter. Miguel sat next to his wife with his legs crossed, facing away from his family, a stern look on his face. Maria sat on the other side of Eliana. She said something to Miguel. He didn't answer. Maria looked at me. Her eyes dropped. She shook her head.

I spoke to Maria. "Tell them they can use the stateroom if they want to be alone with Eliana."

Maria spoke to Naida then pointed to the stateroom. Naida extended her hand to Eliana but Eliana did not reach back. Instead, she followed her mother into the stateroom like a dutiful daughter. Miguel stood up. I guessed his height at five-foot-eight. He wore a short-sleeved white shirt, stained with dirt, jeans frayed at the knees, and dust-covered tennis shoes. He slid from behind the table and stood with his back against the cabin door. He looked down at the floor, then around at the ceiling and the walls.

"Tell him he can have a seat," I said to Maria.

She spoke a few words to Miguel. He shook his head and refused to move. I slid into the bench behind the galley table, next to Maria. Raven slid in next to me. Murmurs and muted sobbing wafted in from the stateroom. Miguel turned and looked out the window onto the dark rear deck.

I turned to Maria. "What's going on?"

"Shame. Guilt. Embarrassment. Anger. On everyone's part," Maria said. "Miguel and Naida are devout Catholics. Their daughter is living in the worst kind of sin. Eliana knows she's disgraced her parents."

"But it's not her fault," I said. "They paid coyotes to bring her out of Mexico."

Maria nodded. "Which only deepens their shame."

"So they'll just disown her? She's their daughter."

"It's sad. The few women who do manage to leave forced prostitution aren't always welcomed home. Like I said, they're devout Catholics. They feel tainted."

"If they're so devout, haven't they heard about forgiveness?"

"Perhaps her mother could forgive her. But her father has too much pride."

"Pride? His daughter's been forced to sell her body, and he's worried about his pride?"

"I'm not saying it's right," Maria said. "But given his life, he doesn't have much else other than his pride."

"So what becomes of Eliana?"

"If we can keep her away from the streets, there's a program she can enter with other young women like her. Education. English. Help with immigration. It's not easy, but some make it."

I pounded my fist on the table. Maria and Raven jumped.

"You should tell them to read their Bible more closely," I said.

Maria frowned. "What?"

"Especially, the part about Mary Magdalene in the New Testament," I said.

Raven leaned in to our conversation for the first time. "Who?" he asked.

"The prostitute who washed the feet of Jesus," Maria said.

"Will they at least tell us what happened after they paid the coyotes?" I asked.

Maria touched my thigh softly. "I know you want to help," she said. "Let me see what I can do." She slid from the bench and spoke to Miguel. He would not turn to face her. He answered in a voice muted by the cabin door. Maria patted him on the shoulder before walking into the stateroom.

The voices of the three women wove into and out of each other. Maria's crisp and sharp. Eliana's and Naida's flat and dull. After several minutes, Maria emerged with a half smile.

"I told them that truth is the first step to redemption. And I took your advice. I reminded them of Santa Maria Magdalena. Miguel, I'm not sure about. Eliana either. But Naida said she would tell us what she knew."

Naida and Eliana emerged from the stateroom arm in arm, with tear-strewn faces. Mother and daughter had the same dark eyes. The same angular cheekbones. The same thick, long hair, though Naida's now had wide swaths of gray, and she'd wrapped it into a bun. The same beauty shone through their pain and suffering. Eliana still wore the jeans that Maria had given her. Naida wore a blue denim skirt caked with dirt.

Raven and I got up from the table. Naida and Eliana slid into our places. Miguel still refused to turn away from the darkness outside the door. Eliana sat between her mother and Maria. Naida spoke while Maria translated.

"Miguel and I have been married for twenty-five years," Naida said. "We've known each other since we were children." Naida smiled for the first time. She spoke to me as she talked. Even though I could not understand her words directly, her eye contact conveyed her anguish, her pain.

"Miguel wanted to become an engineer," Naida said. "I wanted to be a mother and a teacher." She turned away from me and spoke directly to her husband, who muttered to the window in Spanish.

"She said she will always love him no matter what," Maria said. "She asked him to come be with his wife and daughter as a family, even if it means overcoming his pride. He said it wasn't his pride but his honor. Without honor what does a man have? he asked."

"Tell him that honor in the eyes of others means nothing when compared to honor in the eyes of the person he sees when he looks in the mirror," I said.

Maria spoke. Miguel mumbled back. "He asks how would you know about such things?"

"Tell him I was an officer in the Coast Guard for twenty years, but I disgraced myself in the eyes of my superior officers because I refused to lie when asked to. Tell him that's why I'm no longer wearing a coast guard uniform; I wanted to be able to salute the person I saw in the mirror each morning."

Maria spoke to Miguel again and he answered to the darkness.

"He says that was a very noble thing to do."

I laughed. So did Raven. Maria frowned. Miguel started to turn around, then caught himself. He spoke to Maria.

"Why do they laugh at my dishonor?"

"Not your dishonor, Señor. We laugh at my last name, which is Noble," I said.

Miguel laughed before Maria could translate my words. Then he turned to me and said in halting English, "Maybe . . . had . . . no . . . choice."

"Of course I had a choice," I said. "Just like you do." I patted the table. "*Aquí*, Señor Morales."

Miguel looked between me and his wife and Eliana. Tears welled in his eyes. Tension mounted uncomfortably in the galley. Finally, he took a step in my direction, then another. Maria slid from the bench and Miguel took her place next to his daughter.

"Papa," Eliana said.

He pulled her toward him, and kissed her on the forehead. The Morales family sobbed together.

Naida reached for a napkin and dabbed her eyes. She stretched across Eliana and patted her husband's arm. Then she continued to speak. Maria took a seat beside Miguel on the crowded bench. She continued with her translation.

"We wanted more than what our poor village offered," Naida said. "So we worked in the fields and nursed our dreams at night in our bed. Then this beautiful child came along. When she was thirteen, Miguel said to me, 'We must do something with our lives so that Eliana and her children can have a better life.' That's when we decided to cross the border. We paid a coyote."

Miguel broke into the conversation in Spanish. Maria also translated for him.

"But they weren't as vicious in those days as they are now," Miguel said. "We paid them to take us across the desert. They were sly and resourceful. They knew which border guards on both sides to bribe. They had water and food prepositioned in the desert. They helped us much like Robin Hood helped the poor people of his day. We made our way as far from Mexico as we could. That's how we arrived in the Skagit Valley. We heard there were jobs for crop pickers here."

Naida sighed. "But the coyotes would not take children across the desert," she said. "So we had to leave Eliana with other family members. We promised her we would send money for her to join us. We lived very simply so we could send money back to Mexico."

Miguel joined the conversation through Maria. "But times changed," he said. "And the coyotes joined forces with the narcotics traffickers. They wanted upwards of ten thousand U.S. dollars to bring Eliana across the border. We never dealt directly with the coyotes. Always with someone who knew someone who knew someone who knew the coyotes."

"And they made us a deal," Naida said. "They said we could pay them two thousand dollars as a down payment. When Eliana arrived she would work for their associates for a certain period of time to repay them for the service of bringing her out of Mexico."

Miguel pounded the table. "We knew we were taking a risk," he said. "They never told us they would treat Eliana like a slave. We tried to find out about her. But each time we asked, we were told to be silent because one word to the American immigration authorities would send us back to Mexico and we would never see our daughter again."

Finally, Eliana spoke. "I made no money," she said without Maria's assistance. "All the money went to my clothes, my food, my—how to say it?—my lodge . . . ing." She continued in Spanish. "No money went even to repay the debt my parents owed to the coyotes."

"Can we back up?" I asked Eliana. "What happened once the coyotes picked you up in Mexico? How did they bring you here?"

Her head dropped and she started to cry. Eliana gazed at the table. Naida looked lovingly at her daughter. Miguel sighed, before setting his jaw and staring ahead with grim determination. Raven stood in the doorway to the stateroom, his eyes closed but his lips moving as if uttering a prayer. Maria awaited Eliana's words with her lips poised half open.

I reached my hand out toward Eliana and gently tamped down the air. "Go as slowly as you need to," I said. "But please don't leave out any details, no matter how insignificant you think they are."

Eliana began her story through Maria.

eighteen

"We met the coyote's men at a bar. We had to leave that night, they said. All of us. About two dozen or so. We could not go home again. We could not contact our families. They took away cell phones, watches, radios. They stripped and searched us. The man searching me laughed at me as I stood before him naked. Then he touched me everywhere, poked his fingers everywhere. He claimed he needed to check for money or drugs."

Miguel's jaw flexed. Naida squeezed her eyes closed. She also squeezed Eliana's arm.

"They split us up into two groups," Eliana said. "The men told us that some of us will be *vaqueros*. Some will be *marineros*."

I touched Maria's arm. Eliana stopped.

"Sorry," Maria said. "*Vaqueros* and *marineros*. Cowboys and sailors."

Then Eliana continued.

"Some to travel by the desert. Others by the sea. We did not have a choice. They chose for us. I said to them, 'I get seasick. I'm afraid to take such a long trip by boat.' They laughed. 'It's a big boat,' they said. 'You won't even feel like you're on the sea.'

"Then we all got into vans depending on whether we were to travel by land or by sea. My van drove for eight hours or more through the night. Early the next morning, we saw the ocean. Off the coast a large freighter waited. We—"

"Eliana, do you know where on the coast you were?" I asked.

"No," she said. "But we were on the ocean, not the Sea of Cortez. Maybe somewhere south of. . . . Sorry, Señor Noble, but I do not know exactly."

"Were other ships around?" I asked.

"No. This was the only ship. Anchored off shore. Smaller boats awaited us. 'Come quickly. You must hurry,' the men in the smaller boats said. They pushed us into the boats and sped us toward the larger boat. I remember it was big and red, red like the color of the dying sun, red like blood. And I said to myself, 'I will die at sea.'"

"Did you see the ship's name?" I asked.

"Sorry, Señor, I looked to see what was the name of my tomb, but it appeared they had draped cloth over the front of the boat where I expected to see the name."

Eliana began to sob. She shook her head. She said a few words to Maria. Naida gasped. Miguel bit his lip and shook his head as well. Maria hesitated to translate.

"I wish I would have died at sea, Señor Noble. Then I would not have brought this disgrace on my family and on myself."

The subtle, polyrhythmic beat in the background came from Raven tapping his finger against the wall. His eyes remained closed. His lips continued to move.

"No, Eliana," I said. "This is not your fault. Please, can you tell me what you saw on the boat. What kind of cargo did it carry?"

"Precious cargo," she said. "I remember that down below, next to the room where they kept us, I saw many wooden crates marked 'Handle With Care.' They treated their cargo better than they treated us. Twelve men and women, all of us in a room no bigger than this." Eliana pointed around the galley. "There we must sleep and eat and use a small bucket as the toilet. No place to wash. Crammed like cattle into a stall. The smell of human waste and mildew always in the air."

Eliana held her hand to her face, massaging her forehead with her fingertips.

"Do you know how long you were at sea?" I asked.

Eliana shook her head. "No. We had no clocks. No windows to see outside. No light other than a small lightbulb that hung overhead. They fed us occasionally. Rice. A few beans. Two tortillas for everyone to share. A small pitcher of water for everyone to drink from.

"We took turns sleeping on the floor while the others stood. A man wheezed for several days. From asthma, he said. His breathing grew worse, and one day after he slept on the floor we could not awaken him. He had a weak pulse. We called for the ship's men. They came and hauled him away. To get help, they said. A pregnant woman began bleeding from between her legs. They also carried her away. We never saw either of them again.

"Then one day the ship's men knocked on the door and announced that we could take showers. I was to be first, they said. I was so happy to bathe. Then the men said that they must watch as I bathed. When I refused, one man hit me. Two other men grabbed me by the arms. I knew what they wanted. I said, 'Why would you want to have sex with an unclean woman?' They laughed. They stuffed a cloth in my mouth and pulled me into a washroom, where they ripped off my clothes and threw me under a shower. They took turns rubbing me everywhere with soap."

Miguel hit the table with his fist. Naida sobbed. Eliana sniffed back tears.

"'Now,' they said, 'you are a clean woman.' They dragged me to a berth somewhere deep in the belly of the ship, and each man—"

Maria held up her hand for Eliana to stop. She picked up a napkin and wiped tears from her eyes, then she motioned for Eliana to continue.

"Each man took his turn inside me. When they finished, they said, 'It's good practice for your new life in America.' I thought they simply wanted to insult me. When they left, a man turned out the lights and said, 'For your services, tonight you can sleep alone in this bed.'"

Now Eliana also began to sob. In the background, Raven's chanting grew louder.

"The next day they returned me to the room with the others. They came for me and the other women whenever they wanted. When the men tried to stop them, they used clubs and beat the men until they were bloody and bruised. Time stopped. My life stopped. I wanted to die at sea. I tried to kill myself by rushing from the men once when they came for me. I wanted to jump into the sea. Surely, the sea would open her arms for me and let me lie peacefully in them rather than stay in this brutal hell. But the men caught me, and from then on they guarded against my flight.

"Then one day, a man came into our room. He tied our wrists behind our backs with a heavy rope. Blindfolded us. Gagged us. I thought it was just another trick to drag the women away for sex. But the ship shuddered beneath us, the engines slowed, and suddenly I felt little motion other than the sea. They led us all up several flights of stairs. Once on deck, I felt the salt air kiss my face. We were lowered into smaller boats whose engines roared to a start. We bobbed up and down in the sea. I felt myself getting seasick, but I told myself soon we would be on land. But land never came.

"We were taken to another boat, smaller than the freighter, I think. A different kind of boat. My feet walked over carpet as they led us through the boat, then down. Down somewhere in the bottom of this boat. Below the water, I think. The sides of the boat felt cold against my skin. I heard water sloshing against the boat.

"Ten of us were crammed into a long, small room without light. We could not really stand, and we could not really lie down."

Eliana extended her hand back on her wrist. "We leaned against the sides of the boat. Shoulder to shoulder, like sardines in a can."

I closed my eyes as Eliana continued.

"We could not speak. They kept the gags over our mouths. The rope rubbed my wrists raw. No one fed us. But no one bothered us either, at least not at first. I experienced a different motion in this second boat. We moved faster, and I felt the sea more than I had before.

It made me feel nauseous, but I did not vomit. And the smell. I remember the smell of this boat."

Eliana paused, searching for words.

"A strange smell, Señor Noble. Slightly sweet. Slightly pungent. I have been in several new cars since I am here, and their smell reminded me of this boat.

"Thankfully, we did not stay long on this boat. Less than a day. Again we were led from our tiny room and placed into a smaller boat that sped away. And finally, finally, my feet touched the earth. I said a prayer to Santa Maria for carrying me through this ordeal. A man said, 'Welcome to America.' He removed our blindfolds and then said we must be quiet or else risk discovery and return to Mexico by the American immigration authorities."

"Did you see this man? Could you describe him?" I asked.

"No, Señor, it was very dark. Only the twinkling of lights over the water in the distance, like stars floating on darkness. I thought that now I would be taken to see Mama and Papa." Eliana touched her mother's arm. "After so much to go through, I thought finally I would be with my family. Finally, I could leave the horror of this voyage behind me. But this would not be."

She sighed. "We were marched in the darkness for a long time. After little food and little sleep, my body was very weak. I was very tired. Walking up hills and down for maybe two hours. No stars above. Just clouds. No lights. No sounds. Trees all around us. And new smells. A sweet *picante* smell in the air. It reminded me of cherries. I remember thinking, 'This can't be America. Where are the big cities? The lights? The cars? The people?'

"At the end of this march, we came to more water. But now I saw more lights in the distance. An orange glow lit the air. We were placed in small, fast boats that zoomed toward the lights. Then put in cars. I thanked God for leaving the water. I fell asleep in the car, and when I woke up I was in a strange bed.

"The next morning someone knocked on the door. I opened it and saw this short man, Señor Frank. He had a smile and a tray of food. I asked when could I see my parents. 'Soon,' he said. 'But first you must help them out.' When I asked how I can do that, he said, 'Your parents did not have enough money to pay for you to leave Mexico, but I have a job for you that will help them pay what they owe.' When I asked what job that is, he said, 'A nice job. A hostess to see to the needs of my customers. You will be paid very well, and you will soon repay what your parents owe.'"

Miguel stabbed the table with his elbow, then dropped his head into his hands. Eliana reached out to touch him. They spoke. At first, Maria said nothing.

"Please," I asked Maria. "Translate for me."

"Eliana said, 'Papa, it is not your fault, you did not know.'

"Miguel said, 'I sold my baby into slavery. I wish to kill these coyotes and this Señor Frank with my bare hands.'

"Eliana said, 'Papa, it would only result in more sin.'"

Miguel rose from the table. Eliana reached for him. He turned around and spoke to Maria. She translated for me without being asked.

"Miguel said, 'I cannot stay and listen to what happened to my baby.'"

He moved toward the door. Suddenly, Raven stepped forward. He put an arm around Miguel's shoulder, opened the door, and walked him outside onto the rear deck. I didn't hear them speak, but a low, rhythmic tapping sound came from the back of the boat.

Naida spoke to me through Maria.

"We knew something had happened to Eliana when we heard she had made it out of Mexico but we never saw her here. We prayed for the best, but fears of the worst were never far away. Now the truth is worse than our fears. Miguel cannot forgive himself for trying to bring Eliana to be with us. His dream of a better life has become a nightmarish hell." She sighed. "Eliana is our daughter. I will not leave her side."

Eliana squeezed her eyes closed, but she continued her story through Maria.

nineteen

"At first there was no sex. I felt very uneasy in the club. Señor Frank knew this, so he had me work behind the counter and in the kitchen preparing drinks and food for the women who served the customers of his club. Then one night he said that one of the women servers became sick. He asked if I could take her place. So I put on one of those very short dresses and served the patrons.

"A man I served asked if I would accompany him to the backroom. 'What backroom?' I asked. The man laughed and said, 'Go ask Señor Frank.' I did. Señor Frank said it would be all right. So I escorted this man to the back of the club. He took me into a room with a bed and pink satin sheets. When he began to get out of his clothes, I ran from the room back to Señor Frank. But now Señor Frank became a monster. He yelled at me, 'If you don't please my customers you will never see your parents again.'"

Eliana sobbed softly.

"And so my descent into an even worse hell began that night."

Now, she openly wept.

I punched the ceiling in the galley, fighting the urge to act on Miguel's wishes. Then I took in a deep breath. I leaned over the table and touched Eliana's arm. She raised her head, her dark eyes now a fathomless pit of sadness.

"You are a very brave woman," I said, "to endure what you have endured. And, also, to tell the truth about it. Please, I know this is hard but may I ask you some questions?"

I waited for Maria to translate.

Eliana nodded. "*Sí.*"

"On the second boat, you said you moved faster and felt the motion of the sea more than on the first boat. Can you describe the motion of the waves you felt?"

After Maria translated, Eliana shook her head.

"She doesn't understand what you mean," Maria said.

"Did you feel this?" *Clap. Clap. Clap.* I smacked my hands together sharply three times. "Or did you feel this?" I raised my hand and traced the outline of a large wave.

Before my hand dropped, Eliana pointed. "*Sí.*" Then she spoke through Maria.

"Yes, the second." Eliana touched her midsection. "My stomach dropped from under me each time the boat dropped down."

"Thank you," I said. Then I held up a finger. *"Uno momento."*

Eliana smiled.

I stepped down into the stateroom and grabbed a folder with the photographs of the three dead women. I walked back into the galley and laid them on the table.

"Do you know any of these women?"

Eliana closed her eyes and nodded *"Sí."* Then, through Maria, she said, "Señor Frank kept the Chicano girls in the club at all times. We each had our own tiny room. Like a prison—Señor Frank posted a guard in the hall outside. We couldn't leave during the day. We couldn't talk to the other girls. But we found a way. We shared a bathroom. We were not allowed to use it at the same time. So we left messages for each other in lipstick on the toilet paper."

Eliana pointed to the picture of Juanita Gutierrez.

"We called Juanita *Mamasita* because she had been there more than a year. Longer than any of us. Señor Frank told her to use the name Francesca with his clients. A few weeks ago, Juanita left a message that she, Melinda, and Carmela planned to escape. She asked if I wanted to go with them. I wanted to, but I'd heard that if Señor Frank caught a girl trying to escape he beat them badly. So I said no."

Eliana pointed to the pictures. "I did not see any of them for several days. But they returned." Fingers splayed, Eliana moved her hand in the air in front of her face. "Beaten. Bruised. Black eyes. Then one day, all three disappeared again. I did not hear of them until Maria told me they had been pulled from the ocean. I did not see them again until you showed me these photographs."

Eliana dropped her head in her hands. "I would not be surprised if they took their own lives," she said. "Many times I wanted to take mine."

I asked Maria to explain that we found bricks tied to the women, suggesting that they hadn't committed suicide. When she finished, I had another question for Eliana.

"Did Juanita, Melinda, and Carmela share any clients?" I asked.

I'm not sure what Maria said, but Eliana narrowed her eyes and cocked her head. *"No comprende,"* she said.

I tried again. I held up a finger. "One man." I pointed to the pictures. "Three women?"

"Sí. Sí. Some men always wanted the same girl. Some men always wanted a different girl. Some clients liked more than one girl at a time. So it is possible that Juanita, Melinda, and Carmela could have had the same client."

"Off-site?"

Eliana frowned.

"Away from the club," I said.

She nodded. *"Sí. Sí.* Once girls had worked at the club for some time, Señor Frank would send them from the club to visit a client in a hotel room, at his home, or even at his office. You, for example"—Eliana pointed to me—"when I came to your hotel room it was the first time that I had been allowed away from the club."

"Do you know the names of any of the men who paid to be with Juanita, Melinda, or Carmela?"

Eliana shrugged. "Who is to say? I did not use my real name. The men who paid for me I am sure often did not use theirs."

"Would you recognize them?"

She dropped her head and mumbled to the table. "I wish I could forget the face of every man who paid to have sex with me, but I can't. As for those who paid for sex with these women? I probably would not recognize them. Especially if a man paid for all three women at the same time. Very rarely did such men come into the club. These were Señor Frank's more wealthy clients, who paid for the girls to be delivered to them."

I sighed. "Thank you. No more questions from me."

Eliana held up a finger. "*Uno momento.* I . . . have . . . one . . . for . . . you." She struggled through the English, then switched to Spanish, translated by Maria. "Señor Noble, would you promise me that all I have been through and all you have put my mama and papa through has not been for nothing? Would you promise me that no more girls will become sex slaves for bastards like Señor Frank?"

I stared directly at Eliana. "I suppose there are many men in the world like Señor Frank and I cannot stop them all. But I promise you this: I will do my best to see to it that Señor Frank no longer sells young women for sex."

A weak smile spread over Eliana's lips. "*Mucho gracias, Señor Noble. No más. No más.*" And then in English she said, "Thank you, Señor Noble. No more. No more."

Naida wrapped her arm around Eliana and pulled her close. Then she rose and spoke to Maria, who rose as well.

"Naida said they must go and speak with Miguel," Maria said.

Naida opened the cabin door. She and Eliana stepped out. Raven stepped in. I took a seat at the galley table next to Maria. Raven slipped in beside me.

"What happens next for Eliana and her family?" I asked Maria. "They can't go back to their migrant camp."

Maria shook her head. "No, they can't. So, I will make arrangements for them to relocate to a farm in central California. Abadi won't find them there."

"And Eliana will be with them?"

"I hope not," Maria said. "A young woman who's been through what she has needs help. Professional help, and plenty of it. She has to reclaim a feeling that she owns her life and her body, both of which have been owned by Abadi for all these months. She has a long period of healing ahead, but she's a strong, smart young woman. She's a survivor. And she can make it. I mentioned that I knew of a program to help young women like Eliana. It's in Portland. If she agrees to enter it, I'll drop her off there when I drive her parents down to California."

"It's hard to know if what I've done has helped or hindered Eliana and her family," I said.

Maria touched my arm. "In this work, you never really know. All you can do is your best. So you do what you're best at—finding out who killed these women and stopping them; maybe even putting Frank Abadi out of business. And I'll do what I'm best at—helping Eliana and her family take the first steps toward a new life."

Maria slipped out from behind the table and walked to the cabin door. When she opened it, Miguel stuck his head in. He placed his hand over his heart, "*Gracias, Señor Noble.*"

"*Por nada,*" I said.

Miguel smiled, and the *Noble Lady* bowed to starboard as the Morales family, accompanied by Maria, stepped off.

I turned to Raven. "You know what I'm thinking?"

"That a man uses his megayacht to transport undocumented immigrants from an offshore freighter into the United States," Raven said, "and that it's time we found *Longhorn* and put an end to all this."

"You know."

twenty

The following morning I awoke with a gasp, bolting upright in bed. I shook my head and rubbed my eyes, but a dream's gossamer web still ensnared me.

A voice whispering, "Tight packers versus loose packers," whistled through my mind, like the wind through a boat's rigging. I squeezed my eyes closed and shook my head again. An image of the hand-drawn, black-and-white plans of a nineteenth-century slave ship flickered on and off behind my closed eyes. Rows of small, silhouetted figures packed side by side, head to toe filled every available inch of cargo space on a ship specifically designed for carrying human chattel.

"Tight packers" gambled that their loss in profits from slaves dying during the horrors of the Middle Passage would be more than offset by the number of live slaves they delivered. "Loose packers" preferred to arrive in American ports having suffered fewer deaths among their precious cargo.

Sleep slowly drained from me. Through the skylight, a weak shaft of morning light struggled with the darkness in the stateroom. I swung my feet around and sat on the edge of my bed, resting my head in my hands. The *Noble Lady* rocked gently in the wake of a boat leaving its slip.

I felt overwhelmed by darkness. My mind meted out a Promethean torture, serving up images of crab-eaten women one after the other. I pulled the clock from the nightstand and squinted at the glowing red numbers. Seven o'clock. Raven would be here in thirty minutes. I stuffed clothes under my arms and grabbed a small ditty bag.

Halyards clacked against masts as I walked up the dock toward the main gate and the showers. Halfway up the ramp, I turned around and looked out over Bellingham Bay. Urged on by southeasterly winds, dark clouds rapidly advanced against the pale blue sky. I pounded the ramp's aluminum railing. It rang with a dull, hollow sound. That dream about tight packers and loose packers still gnawed at me.

By the time I stepped from the showers and headed back to the boat, I could no longer see the sun. When I reached the *Noble Lady*, I climbed up into the pilothouse and switched on the NOAA weather radio station. Donna and Craig pronounced small craft warnings throughout Puget Sound and the Strait of Juan de Fuca. They also warned of fog, which made me laugh and finally broke the morning's pall.

Both Donna and Craig pronounced the word "fog" with such a hard *f* and short *o* that it came out sounding like . . . well, like what I had said to myself over and over again as I listened to Eliana's story. I punched the channel selector a few times until I reached the Environment Canada weather station. Essentially the same forecast—a low in the north sucking winds up from the south—but at least a human had recorded the broadcast, and the announcer didn't "fuck up" the word "fog."

When I got back down to the galley, I pulled a can of protein powder from the cupboard and a carton of cold orange juice from the refrigerator. Someone stepped aboard the rear deck. The *Noble Lady* dipped to starboard. I opened the cabin door, and Raven walked inside. A dark cloud seemed to follow him in. He walked over to the galley table without speaking. I went back to making my smoothie. I poured the orange juice into a glass, then added a heaping scoop of protein powder. The mixture turned puke green. I raised the glass to Raven.

"You want a protein smoothie?" I asked.

Raven glared at the glass. He didn't say anything.

"It doesn't look very appetizing, I'll admit that," I said.

I took a couple of swallows. Damn. I'd gotten the mixture wrong by adding too much protein powder. It tasted like wet sand. I held my breath, turned the glass nearly upside down, and finished it in a few giant gulps. Then I got some coffee going. I leaned back against the sink, facing Raven. He stared aimlessly out the side window.

"Something on your mind?" I asked.

He turned toward me, eyes narrowed, lips pursed, jaw tight. His expression suggested that either an angry yell or a plaintive wail might follow. His eyes moved back and forth, scanning my face as if to ascertain whether he'd answer my question.

I turned away from Raven and poured two steaming cups of coffee. By the time I'd turned around, he'd gone back to staring out the window. I slid a cup in front of him. He didn't turn back. I slipped into the seat next to him. He finally turned away from the window and picked up his cup. He started to drink it, then set it down.

"I take mine black," I said. "You want sugar, cream, milk?"

Raven stared with a look that penetrated right through me, as though he didn't see me next to him.

"Residential schools," he said.

"Residential schools?"

"My mother and her brother were forcibly taken from their homes when they were children. Split up. She went to a residential school in Alert Bay. He went somewhere in the British Columbia interior."

I squinted. "Who took them from their home?"

"Canadian government. The schools were often brutal. Beatings. Rape. Starvation. No one ever saw him again."

"What happened to your mother's parents?"

Raven spoke into his coffee cup. "My grandparents were forced to move from their coastal village to a town on Vancouver Island. The Canadian government burned the village so no one would ever return."

"That's brutal."

"All Miguel wanted was a better life for his family. But brutality's what he got instead."

I squeezed Raven's shoulder and held it. He dropped his head. After a few minutes, I let go.

"I'll be right back," I said.

I climbed up into the pilothouse again. The *Noble Lady* swayed under me. Wind blew her against the dock. She bounced off her fenders, moving away from the dock until the lines pulled tight and reined her in.

Standing at the wheel, I reached overhead toward my collection of charts, rolled up and fitted into holders. I peeked inside a few charts until I saw the number 3001. I pulled that chart out and partially unrolled it. "Vancouver Island from Juan de Fuca Strait to Queen Charlotte Sound," the title read. I let the chart spring back into a roll, then I climbed down to the galley.

I unfurled the chart on the galley table. Raven's coffee looked untouched. I set his cup on one edge of the unfurled chart. I took a sip of my coffee, then placed my cup on the opposite edge.

"Where do we start looking for *Longhorn*?"

"Big boat," Raven said.

I tapped on the chart. "Bigger ocean."

"Ahab's problem," Raven said. "Finding the white whale." He drummed with his finger on the side of his cup, then he pointed on the chart to the vast area of white off the west coast of Vancouver Island. "You think she's somewhere out here, coming into Puget Sound with another group of immigrants?" He let his finger run in from the Pacific, down the center of the Strait of Juan de Fuca.

"Maybe. Eliana said she landed on one beach, and then she was walked over hilly terrain to another beach, where she boarded a small boat for a trip that eventually put her in a car."

"So *Longhorn* anchors at Smuggler's Cove," Raven said. "A boat picks up the immigrants and ferries them to shore. Then they're marched overland to Eagle Harbor, where they're taken by another boat to the mainland." Raven tapped on Cypress Island. "So we wait at Cypress."

"But what if Kincaid diverts to another location because Cypress no longer seems safe?"

Raven looked at me askance. "You playing devil's advocate?"

"I am."

"In that case, we'd need to find *Longhorn* on her way in from the Pacific, before she gets a chance to unload."

I pointed at Raven. "That's Plan A."

Raven stared at the chart and shook his head slowly. "Port Renfrew. Sooke. Esquimalt. Victoria." He tapped on each Canadian harbor. "Neah Bay. Clallam Bay. Crescent Bay. Port Angeles." He tapped on the American ones. Then he pointed to Cape Flattery, next he pointed to Race Rocks. "More than fifty miles of ocean. Lots of little places for *Longhorn* to slip into." He pulled the blinds back and looked out the window. "On a day like this, big seas and high winds. What if they slip by because we picked the wrong port?"

"That's Plan B," I said. "Where you come in."

Raven picked up his cup from the chart and held down the edge with his hand. He took a sip of coffee, which must have been cold, though he didn't grimace.

"I'll take the *Noble Lady* out looking for *Longhorn*. You'll stay here in case I don't find her and she slips into Cypress with another load of immigrants."

"In case Kincaid does use Cypress Island again?"

"Right. There are other drop-off places he could use. But if I were smuggling undocumented immigrants into this country by boat I'd use Cypress too. Few people live on the island. None at Eagle Harbor or Smuggler's Cove. It's a straight shot up Rosario from the Strait of Juan de Fuca. Close to the mainland. Since boats are frequently in Eagle Harbor, *Longhorn* pulls into Smuggler's Cove, where no one ever anchors. They unload the immigrants in a matter of minutes, weigh anchor, and steam away.

"Then someone else on shore walks the immigrants over the island to Eagle Harbor, where small boats whisk them away to Anacortes. They're placed in cars, and they disappear. With all the trails criss-crossing Cypress, Kincaid could still unload the immigrants at Smuggler's Cove and have them taken overland to someplace other than Eagle Harbor, if he feels it's now unsafe to have them picked up there."

"You want me to stake out Cypress?" Raven asked.

"I do."

"While you hunt for the white whale?"

"Uh huh. We need evidence if we're going to stop Kincaid."

"Catching them with undocumented immigrants on board," Raven said.

"Or catching them in the process of unloading the immigrants."

"Not much catching in this boat." Raven patted the wall beneath the galley window. "*Longhorn* must do at least twenty knots."

"I won't try to catch her. We need to figure out where she'll likely be. If I can intercept her while she's in port, then maybe I can determine if she's carrying undocumented immigrants."

"How?"

I patted Raven's shoulder. "Doing my job . . . investigating."

Raven looked off into space. "A private eye on the water."

I patted his shoulder again. "Not a private eye. A 'fish-eye' maybe. Someone who sees the world a little differently from the rest."

Raven winced, but he finally smiled. I smiled back. I picked up my coffee cup and took a sip.

"It's cold and it's bitter," I said. "You want a hot cup?"

Raven waved me off. I walked over to the stove and lit a burner. The coffee didn't take long to heat. I returned to the table and smoothed the chart out, resting my cup at the edge of the chart, on top of Bellingham Bay. Then I tapped in the middle of the Strait of Juan de Fuca. A gust of wind howled, and the *Noble Lady* shivered on her lines. Raven peeked outside. He shook his head.

"So where's *Longhorn* now, and where's she headed?" I asked.

"Coming in from the Pacific," Raven said.

"When I talked to the captain over the VHF, he said they were taking the boat to Port Alberni to fish." I pointed to Alberni Inlet, a deep gash in the lower third of Vancouver Island, then I ran my finger due west out of the inlet, through Barkley Sound and into the open Pacific. "So, maybe they pick up the immigrants somewhere offshore from Barkley Sound."

"And come back in through the Strait of Juan de Fuca. Means they're in Canadian waters."

"They'd have to clear Canadian customs outbound, and American customs inbound."

"You think clearing customs matters to Kincaid, if he's illegally transporting immigrants into this country?" Raven asked.

"I do," I said. "I think that's the reason this immigrant-smuggling ring uses his boat in the first place. It looks legitimate. Who'd expect a fancy yacht to be a modern-day slave ship?"

"In that case, he's probably got a prearranged clearance number, so he just calls in and doesn't have to stop at an American customs port. That way he can lie about the human cargo he's actually transporting without worrying about a customs inspector boarding his boat, or sniffing around it with a dog."

"But that means fingerprints and a background check," I said. "My guess is that Kincaid might not want all that scrutiny. He might prefer to check in at a customs port, schmooze the agents, and be gone."

Raven ran his finger along the southern edge of the Strait of Juan de Fuca. "Which means Neah Bay or Port Angeles."

"Those'd be my choices. He's coming down from Canada. The question is, does he stay on the Canadian side of the strait and cross over when he nears Port Angeles? Or does he first cross over to the American side at the western entrance of the strait and clear customs in Neah Bay?"

"I've got another question," Raven said. "What if we're wrong about Kincaid and it's someone else who transported Eliana? Why the hell would a wealthy guy like Kincaid get involved in dirty business like this anyway?"

I sipped some coffee. "Yeah. I've been asking myself the same question. I don't know if I have the answer, but I bet I know someone who does."

"Who?"

"Janet."

"Still leaves the question of where *Longhorn* might clear customs unanswered," Raven said.

"I know what I'd do," I said. "Clear customs in Neah Bay. Smaller office. Farther out. Maybe the agents aren't on quite as high an alert as in Port Angeles, where they intercepted Ahmed Ressam entering from Canada with a load of explosives back in 1999."

"Noble, you're crazy. You can't do it," Raven said. "Neah Bay's a hundred miles from here. What does your boat do? Nine . . . ten knots tops?"

"Seven or eight," I said.

"It'd take you twelve to fourteen hours to get there. Besides, you can't leave today. Southeaster's blowing. It's already up to fifteen or twenty knots in the islands. It'll be more in the Strait of Juan de Fuca."

"You sound concerned," I said.

"I am," Raven said.

"I'm touched," I said.

"Too many souls lost to the sea already."

I put a hand on Raven's shoulder. "I hadn't planned on leaving today," I said. "Forecast calls for high pressure building offshore. I'll leave very early in the morning, and catch a ride with the current. It's early summer. Plenty of light. I can make Neah Bay before sunset."

"What if *Longhorn* gets there before you, clears customs, and then leaves?"

"Maybe I can intercept her on the water."

"Big ocean."

"Big boat. *Longhorn*'s over twenty meters in length."

Raven nodded. "So there's a good chance that she'll report into the Vessel Traffic Service."

"Better than a good chance. Coast Guard issued new regs several months ago. Vessels over twenty meters periodically will be required to check in with VTS. If I was the captain of *Longhorn* I'd play by the rules and check into the system the moment I entered U.S. waters."

"Less chance of being boarded."

"Uh huh. The new rules make it easier for the CG to know who's out on the water. They'll also make it easier for me to know if *Longhorn*'s out there. I'll monitor the VTS channels."

"I'll keep an eye on Cypress beginning tonight."

"I'll call you on your cell phone once I get to Neah Bay, or if I cross paths with *Longhorn* before then."

"Don't worry," Raven said.

"About what?"

"Plans. Contingencies. Figuring out everything beforehand. Operational planning," Raven's voice echoed bemusement. He shook his head. "Reminds me of the SEALs. We planned and planned, but no mission ever turned out as we planned."

Raven stared at my chest as though peering deep inside my soul. His unflinching gaze unnerved me. Finally, he nodded.

"Spirit Walker," Raven said. He smiled while nodding. "Yes, Spirit Walker."

I shrugged my shoulders. "Spirit Walker?"

"Someone who goes where the Spirit calls even if he can't hear his name. Noble, take one step in the direction of truth, and truth will take two steps toward you."

"I'll try to remember that," I said.

I removed the coffee cups from the chart and let it roll up. I carried the chart up into the pilothouse and slipped it into its holder. On the way back down, I felt the *Noble Lady* tip to starboard, and when I got to the galley I didn't see Raven. I looked out the window in time to catch him disappearing behind a large sailboat as he turned from my dock and headed down the main walkway toward the gate.

I flipped open my cell phone and called Janet. She agreed to lunch. Then, with a few hours to spare, I pulled my guitar from its case and launched into the *English Suite*. It's a funny thing, not practicing for several days. My fingers took me through the Prelude, and the only time I screwed up was when my mind tried to override what my body already knew. Beginner's mind. Beginner's heart. Beginner's hands. The crisp, buoyant melody brought with it hope that joy still proceeds even amid life's sorrows. I finished the Prelude and laid the guitar across my lap.

What the hell. I picked up my cell phone and called Kate. She answered, but at first I only heard conversation in the background. Then she said to someone nearby, "Pardon me, Sir, I need to use the head."

I chuckled. A minute later, Kate whispered, "I'm in the head. I had my phone on vibrate in case you called. Look, I can't talk long. But I'm really glad to hear your voice. What's up?"

"I miss you," I said. "That's the only reason I called."

A long pause followed.

"Are you all right?" I asked.

"No," Kate said. "I need to be with you soon."

WHEN I WALKED INTO AVENUE BREAD, I waved to Janet, who sat at a round glass table in the far corner of the restaurant. Her tepid wave surprised me. I walked over to the counter and ordered a turkey sandwich on toasted multigrain bread. After I paid, I went to sit down next to Janet.

"What's wrong?"

She seemed near tears. "Ben and I had a fight."

"So what's new? I thought you both liked to fight because you both liked to make up afterward."

Janet shook her head slowly. Her eyes looked red, as though she'd been crying. "No. We had a real fight."

"About what?"

"About who I am, and who Ben is."

"And who are you both?"

"I'm passionate and wild," Janet said.

"I thought that's what Ben liked about you."

"I don't know," Janet said. "He's . . . well, he's even-keeled and steady."

"I thought that's what you liked about Ben."

"I don't know that either."

From behind the counter, someone called Janet's name, then mine. I walked over and grabbed two baskets, one with my sandwich, and the other with her salad. I slipped the plastic basket in front of Janet.

"This really about you being wild and Ben being steady?"

She shook her head. "No. It's about both of us being scared."

"Because the relationship is progressing?"

"Yes. And I don't want to give up a part of me to be with Ben."

"And Ben is afraid of losing a part of himself to be with you."

"You should be a therapist," Janet said.

"I was married to a strong-willed woman, and I now have an equally strong-willed girlfriend."

Janet chuckled as she stabbed some lettuce with her fork. "Damn you," she said. "I'm starting to feel better already. I wanted to stay angry with Ben longer, for what he said."

"What'd he say?"

"That he wanted me to cut down on my activism if we're going to be together."

"To which you took offense."

"Damn right."

"And then he got defensive."

"You know the dance."

"I've done it. And I think you know there's only one solution."

Janet stabbed another piece of lettuce. "Compromise."

"Uh huh."

"That means both of us giving up a little of ourselves to be with the other."

"Uh huh. It's the new math. One plus one equals one *and* one plus one also equals two."

"Confusing."

"Ever been in a relationship that wasn't?"

Janet shook her head, and her hair flew wildly. She sighed. "Damn relationships. . . . I hate 'em and I love 'em."

"Confusing," I said.

"Apart from being my therapist, what did you want to talk about?"

"Confusion," I said. "In particular, I'm confused about Dennis Kincaid, and why a man with money may be involved with undocumented immigrants."

Janet slipped her fork under a piece of blue cheese and delicately balanced it on the tines as she lifted it to her mouth. Then she leaned over the table, and in a contrived, high-pitched, syrupy voice that sounded like that of a gossip columnist, she said, "Darling . . . Dennis Kincaid has no money."

twenty-one

"**K**incaid is nearly broke," Janet said. "We thought we'd negotiated a buyout of his Chuckanut Ridge properties for $14 million. Then, at the last minute, he raised the price to $18 million. It sounded suspicious. We had our lawyer, Nancy, check deeper into his background to see if he'd pulled a stunt like this before in Texas. What she discovered floored us. . . . Sorry, I've got to eat."

Janet paused for some more salad. I took a healthy bite of turkey sandwich. Not enough mustard. I got up and had the woman behind the counter put a good-sized dollop into a tiny paper cup. When I got back to the table, Janet dabbed the corners of her mouth with her napkin.

"He *was* a wealthy Texas developer. But apparently Daddy Kincaid had a huge weakness. He liked to gamble in casinos south of the border. Nancy said she checked with lawyer friends in Texas, who told her that Kincaid had lost most of his wealth to gambling, and what he hadn't lost, he owed to those from whom he'd borrowed plenty."

"That's the reason he wanted to either develop or sell this Bellingham property."

"It was all that remained of his real estate empire." Janet laughed.

"I guess it was hard to place this property on the gambling table. Who down there has heard of Whatcom County?"

"Maybe the coyotes," I said.

"But all they do is howl," Janet said.

"Not these coyotes. They transport human beings across the border from Mexico, and I bet they made Mr. Kincaid an offer he dared not refuse."

I explained to Janet what we'd heard from Eliana. Her face turned red as she listened. Afterward, she pounded the table, which caused our baskets and water glasses to jump. A few people at adjacent tables turned toward us. It didn't faze Janet.

"The bastard won't get anything now," she said. "We'll take that property from him for trafficking in human beings."

"That may be jumping to a conclusion," I said. "We don't know for sure that he's involved."

"I wouldn't put it past him or Bud."

Janet stabbed what remained of her lettuce, while I told her what I planned to do. Afterward, she placed her hand on top of mine.

"I'll go with you," she said.

"I've already got a good lady going."

"Kate?"

"No, I—"

"The *Noble Lady*, of course," Janet said. "Just remember that the strait can be treacherous, especially on summer afternoons when the land heats up, the hot air rises, and colder ocean air rockets down the strait to replace it. Pull in somewhere if you need to."

"Thanks," I said. "I'll remember that."

"When can I expect that you'll return?"

I smiled. "Ma'am. Are you requiring me to file a float plan?"

"Yes, Commander, I am."

"If I'm not back in three or four days, call the CG."

"I will."

I rose to leave. Janet rose as well. Outside of Avenue Bread, she gave me a big hug.

"Are you going back to the gallery?" I asked.

"No, Ben's at the station this afternoon. I'm going over there to needle him about being a jerk."

"To make him more angry than he already is?"

She smiled mischievously. "No. To make him angry enough so he'll want to make up."

I threw up my hands and shook my head.

On the way to my car, my cell phone rang.

"Ray Bob was arrested for assault and battery of a sex-trade worker," Ben said.

"Sex-trade worker?"

"Hey, I'm with Janet. I'm trying to become politically correct."

"No conviction?"

"Case was thrown out because the sex-trade worker refused to press charges after the arrest or to testify against Ray Bob."

"Thanks," I said. "I'm leaving for Neah Bay early tomorrow morning."

"Going after *Longhorn*?"

"Uh huh."

"You got a plan?"

"Investigating. Gathering evidence."

"Call if you need backup."

"I will. I just had lunch with Janet. She insisted that I file a float plan with her."

Ben said nothing.

"By the way, I want to give you a heads-up," I said.

"Shoot."

"Janet's on her way over to see you."

"She is? Is she angry?"

"You asked her to give up a part of herself to be with you. What do you think?"

"I think I'd better call 911."

AT THREE-THIRTY THE FOLLOWING MORNING, I backed the *Noble Lady* from her berth. We glided over liquid darkness past rows of quiet halyards and hulls hunkered down in the shadows of slips. Rounding the breakwater, I saw the pulsing green light of the channel buoy. I set my coffee cup aside and strained out the window to find the two unlit red channel buoys.

A mariner's mantra played in my mind, "Red. Right. Returning." But since I was leaving, that meant I needed to find and keep the red buoys on my left. I'd exited the harbor so many times I didn't really need them to guide me. But I finally spotted both red buoys bobbing gently well off to port. Something I never really understood is why the Coast Guard didn't put a flashing red light on at least one of these buoys so they'd be easier to find in the dark.

Past the buoys, I fiddled with the engine until the rpm's felt just right. We cruised along at seven knots. I set the *Noble Lady* on autopilot, opened the pilothouse door, and looked behind me. A pale blue glow backlit the hills surrounding the city, and overhead a full moon had yet to dissolve in the morning light.

Full moon, ebb tide. I'd meet swift currents today. I'd timed my passage to take advantage of them, particularly the ebb that would flush me down Bellingham Channel into Rosario Strait, and from there out into the Strait of Juan de Fuca.

I gripped my coffee cup tightly. I caught myself checking and rechecking the water temperature, oil pressure, and fuel gauges. I scanned the radar screen several times, even though it showed no other traffic in the bay.

A body of water is like a piece of music. A good mariner learns its tempos and rhythms, its harmonies and discords, practicing the passage until it becomes second nature. I'd never been out on the Strait of Juan de Fuca. So today I'd be sight-reading a body of water for the first time.

I angled slightly left, past the flashing red buoy that marked the shallow area where Bellingham Bay met Hale Passage. Then at the southern tip of Lummi Island, I turned west and cruised past the Devil's Playground.

In the distance off the starboard side, the sky had brightened, marking the horizon over the Strait of Georgia with a rose-colored band. Ahead, the hulking mass of Cypress Island loomed.

The *Noble Lady* lurched under me, as though she'd stepped on a fast-moving conveyor belt. I checked the GPS. The ebb moved us at nearly eleven knots. Small, sharp wavelets blanketed the water around us, reminding me of thousands of tiny shark fins.

Fortunately, no wind fetched the wide expanse of the Strait of Georgia. Wind meeting current here, after a long haul down the strait, kicks up a nasty chop, earning Devil's Playground its fiendish name.

The fragment of a dream replayed in my mind. While at the helm of the *Noble Lady*, I'd spotted someone flailing in the very waters I passed now. I maneuvered the boat closer only to find Eliana struggling to keep her head above the chop. She wore no life jacket. The current in the Devil's Playground pushed the *Noble Lady* away from her. I finally managed to turn around for a second rescue try. But Eliana slipped under the dark waters and I never saw her surface again.

I sighed, then I pounded the wheel with my fist.

Her name was Melinda Corazon, a Mexican immigrant looking for a better life in America. Her parents had come here before her, and when they sent for her the coyotes steered her into a life of prostitution to pay back the money her family owed. That's all the Bayneses asked of me— to find out about the woman they'd brought up on their anchor.

"No más. No más." I heard Eliana's soft voice in my mind. I dropped my head into my hands and rubbed my forehead. I'd made her a promise about stopping Frank Abadi and his human trafficking and prostitution ring. Searching for *Longhorn* in the *Noble Lady* might seem crazy, but it was a step I could take to fulfill that promise. What did Raven say about taking one step toward the truth? The truth will take two steps toward you. I sighed again. I hoped he was right.

The sea, however, wouldn't let me wallow in second-guessing or regret. The current twisted the *Noble Lady* to starboard, pulling me from my thoughts, forcing me to shut down the autopilot, grab the wheel, and steer the boat. A turn to port at Bellingham Channel had me looking at lights flickering along the shore of Guemes Island to my left. To my right, the dark bulge of Cypress Head protruded from Cypress Island.

I veered toward the Guemes side of the channel. The *Noble Lady* shuddered under me as though a giant's hand, thrusting up from the water, had grabbed her bow and shaken it. I'd nipped the outer edge of a whirlpool just beginning to form off the head. It pulled us in toward the center of the channel. I cranked the wheel hard to port and fought the waking giant until we'd traveled beyond its reach. I've never doubted that early mariners imagined monsters living beneath the oceans. Standing on the point at Cypress Head, I've heard this current roar when it's running at full strength.

The ebb flushed me out of Bellingham Channel into "Neptune's Little Trident," my name for the meeting of Rosario Strait and Guemes and Bellingham channels. From Bellingham Channel, the trident's middle prong, I angled starboard toward Rosario Strait, its western prong, which also served as its handle. To port, I passed a ferry, sitting at dock, lit like a tiny city, readying for the day's first run into the San Juan Islands.

The sun rose and the moon dissolved into the day's light. The ebb built.

Passing through a long, narrow body of water is like running a gauntlet. The worst hazards often occur at the beginning and the end. Rosario Strait ends at "Neptune's Big Trident," a place where it meets Haro Strait and Admiralty Inlet, the trident's outer prongs. All three then dump into the huge Strait of Juan de Fuca, the trident's crooked handle.

I gripped the wheel and wrestled with a tide rip at the end of Rosario Strait. After the rip, I nudged the *Noble Lady* west and now faced down the twelve-mile-wide expanse of the Strait of Juan de Fuca. My body tingled from a rush of blood at the sight of the horizon over the strait, leading out to the waters of the open Pacific.

A subtle tremor also rippled through me with the realization that I was now heading into a watery unknown. On my left, the morning sun crowned the majestic, snowcapped peaks of the Olympic Mountains in gold as they stood sentry over the waters of the strait.

With mechanical diction, Donna and Craig reported light winds in the strait of ten to fifteen knots from the west. Canadian weather radio agreed. I checked my course and heading, which had me north of the shoals and kelp patches that extended from Smith Island, then turning gently to port for a straight shot to Neah Bay.

Smith Island, a desolate rock pile, took forever to put behind me. Just as I did, several waves clapped the *Noble Lady*'s bow; not steep waves, but each of them a whitecap. Around me a sea of whitecaps grew, a sign that the wind had already reached fifteen knots. Ten o'clock had not yet arrived, so the land would continue warming and the winds and seas would continue building.

I hit the button marked WX on my VHF radio and tuned to the NOAA weather radio channel. Donna and Craig still predicted light winds in the strait. I punched in the Canadian weather radio station. They still agreed.

I switched back to VHF channel sixteen. I also monitored the vessel traffic channel. Tugs and tankers reported in, but I didn't hear a call to or from *Longhorn*. I could have waited, and watched Cypress Island with Raven. But Kincaid may have decided to divert *Longhorn* to another location. Even if I had only a slim chance of intercepting *Longhorn* at Neah Bay or on the water, I needed to take it. That slim chance might save a young woman's life.

Outside, whitecaps built and wave heights grew. I switched back to VHF channel sixteen. Two-foot waves now came directly at the *Noble Lady*'s bow, which rose slightly, then slapped down on the backside of each wave. My grip on the wheel tightened, but I'd count myself lucky if the sea stayed this way. Suddenly, my VHF radio crackled with static, then came a monotone voice.

"All stations. All stations. All stations. This is Victoria Coast Guard Radio. Victoria Coast Guard Radio. Victoria Coast Guard Radio. For a revised marine weather forecast, listen to VHF continuous marine weather broadcast. Victoria Coast Guard Radio out."

I jabbed the WX button with my thumb and pushed the channel button until I reached the Canadian marine weather station.

"Revised marine weather forecast issued by Environment Canada at Zero Niner Three Five. Strait of Juan de Fuca revised forecast. Small craft advisory. Westerly winds ten to twenty knots, rising to twenty to thirty knots later this morning. With possible gusts higher. Seas to one meter."

I switched to NOAA weather radio, but Donna and Craig hadn't caught up with their human, Canadian counterparts. A gust of wind blew across the sea, knocking the foam off a few whitecaps. I didn't fear a small craft advisory. The *Noble Lady* could easily take thirty-knot winds, though I'd sooner take them from behind than on the nose, to make for a smoother ride. Even four-foot seas posed no problem.

I feared that this first revised forecast might spawn others as meteorologists came to grips with conditions far worse than initially predicted. I thought about turning back, but high winds colliding with a rising ebb tide meant angry waters at the mouths of the channels leading back into the islands. I could ride the winds up Haro Strait and duck into the islands farther north.

The *Noble Lady* rose on the crest of a wave and careened to port as she dropped down into the trough. Below me, plates rattled in their racks. A cabinet door hit the wall with a smart crack. I turned a few degrees to port, away from meeting the wave fronts head-on.

I switched the VHF to NOAA weather radio. Donna and Craig now issued a small craft warning of their own. The *Noble Lady* rolled from side to side as she hobbyhorsed on a wave. The open cabinet door smacked into the wall again.

I hummed a country-and-western tune. Hold 'em, fold 'em, walk away, or run? I'd been through plenty of small craft warnings without a problem, I reminded myself. I couldn't fold. It wasn't time to walk away. And, at eight knots, I couldn't run.

I could, however, lower the stabilizers into the water, although that meant leaving the safety of the wheelhouse and working out on deck. It's a funny thing about passive stabilizers like mine: When you need them most, the conditions are worst for deploying them. The cabinet door crashed into the wall as the boat rolled in another wave.

I clicked on the autopilot. Then I slipped my arms through my life vest. I also slid a portable VHF radio into my pocket. When I opened the pilothouse door, a steady wind beat me back. I grabbed a handrail and pulled myself through the door.

Handhold after handhold, I climbed slowly up to the pilothouse roof, where both long stabilizer poles stood upright, locked into a crossbeam affixed to the *Noble Lady*'s mast. I wrapped my arms around the mast and held on in the wind as though grasping a lover.

From this height, when we rolled I looked down into the troughs of the waves. With one arm locked around the mast, I undid the lines holding the poles in place. Using pulleys, I slowly lowered each pole until they stood out from the boat at nearly a forty-five-degree angle. I cleated the lines. Next I had to get the delta-shaped metal dolphins into the water.

Whitecaps now broke all around the *Noble Lady*. Ahead, a wave larger than any up until now came roaring at us. I dropped to the surface of the pilothouse roof and grabbed the mast with both arms. The bow rose, then crashed into the wave. Salt spray soaked me. The boat rolled first one way, then the other. I needed to get the dolphins in.

I let go of the mast and reached for the railing at the edge of the roof. I inched my way toward the ladder leading down from the pilothouse roof to the roof over the aft deck. Another wave crashed, rolling the boat in its wake. I tightened my grip on the railing. A few more degrees of roll, and I'd be hanging off the side of the boat.

I lay on my stomach on the pilothouse roof with my hands clutching a railing stanchion. I took some deep breaths, closed my eyes, and with my body sensed the height, the roll, and the period between waves. I waited. The next large wave hit. I counted. We rolled to port, then to starboard. I swung my left leg down until my foot found a ladder rung. Then I swung down my right leg. I let go of the stanchion.

For a brief moment, my body, bent in an L-position, poised precariously in the space and time between two waves. My legs locked tight against the ladder. My upper torso leaned over the pilothouse roof. My right foot searched for another rung, but it slipped. I lost my balance and started to fall backward. I lunged for the rails on either side of the ladder and held on as we rose over a wave and crashed down. The forecast may have called for three-foot seas, but the ocean actually called for six.

I dropped to my side on the aft deck roof. I held onto another stanchion while I undid the line locking one dolphin into its holder. I waited until we'd completed the next roll to port, then I grabbed the dolphin's line. We started a roll to port again. I quickly pulled the dolphin out of its holder and let the finned metal wedge fly away from the boat. It tugged on the end of the chain attached to the line from the stabilizer pole, then splashed into the water.

When we next rolled to starboard, the dolphin attempted to dampen the roll, but with only one in the water it ended up pulling us off course. I had to drop the other dolphin or risk losing control of the *Noble Lady*.

I hauled my body along the railing at the edge of the aft deck roof until I reached the other side. Again, I held on with one hand while the other worked the dolphin's locking line, but I'd cinched this line so tightly around the cleat that I needed two hands to work it free.

I waited for that brief moment between two waves and reached up with my other hand. But we rolled quickly again. I slipped across the aft deck roof with the dolphin's line in only one hand. I grabbed the line with my other hand and held on until the roll subsided. Then I pulled myself toward the cleat. But holding on through the force of the roll had only cinched the line tighter.

This time, I turned over onto my back, swung a leg out, and locked it around one of the railing stanchions. This gave me enough stability to work with both hands to free the dolphin from its holder. I lowered it into the water. After the dolphin dived, the *Noble Lady* settled down with the next roll. I scrambled into the pilothouse and yanked the door shut behind me.

I shivered from the cold, the wet, and the fear.

I grabbed the wheel and checked the compass. I steered the *Noble*

Lady back onto course. Then I put her on autopilot again. I climbed down to snatch a change of clothes and warm my cup of coffee in the microwave, which I rarely use unless I'm being bounced around by the sea.

When I got back to the pilothouse, I sat at the helm, savoring the aroma of the coffee and the soothing heat of the cup in my hands. The rush of warm liquid down my throat calmed me.

I switched the VHF to the Canadian weather, where I recognized the announcer's voice. He often interjected a note of humor into his broadcasts. After reporting on nearby areas, he came to the strait.

"Strait of Juan de Fuca." The man's voice dropped low. Absent humor, he continued. "Small craft advisory upgraded to gale warning. Winds twenty to thirty knots, rising to gales thirty-five to forty knots with higher gusts."

twenty-two

The sea built gradually, with only an occasional wave breaking over the *Noble Lady*'s seven-foot bow. Wind blew the foam from the crests of breaking waves in long, wispy streaks. The chains holding the dolphins vibrated with a high-pitched tone and clinked rhythmically, sending eerie sounds traveling through the hull.

The period between the biggest waves shortened. We headed into a stretch of water with fewer whitecaps. With this much wind, neither one a good sign. I flinched as the next breaking wave sent a wall of green water crashing against the pilothouse window. Soon after that, another. Wind-whipped foam blew all around. The windshield wipers barely kept up. My legs quivered.

The *Noble Lady* rolled deeply to starboard. I heard the cabinet door slam, and the crash of dishes on the cabin floor. I grabbed the wheel and pulled myself up to look out at the portside stabilizer. At the end of the taut chain, the dolphin's dorsal fin cut through the water near the surface. With another roll just a little deeper, both dolphins could launch from the water, becoming airborne missiles headed at the *Noble Lady*'s sides. I'd be a fool to go out to lower the dolphins further. But I couldn't continue bucking and rolling in these seas.

If pilots always have in the back of their minds a fix on the closest airstrip, then mariners must have a fix on the closest safe anchorage. I brought up a chart on my navigational computer. Then I smoothed out a paper chart with one hand, while I steered through the angry seas with the other. Port Angeles lay abeam, but nearly six miles away.

Another mountain of green water rushed at me. Even behind the windshield, I ducked reflexively. After the wave, we rolled deeply again. I eyed the starboard stabilizer chain where it entered the water. The dolphin remained submerged. Turning left now would mean exposing the *Noble Lady*'s flank to the wrath of this gale, rolling more with a greater chance of launching the dolphins at the boat.

My body shook from hunger. I hadn't eaten since leaving. I'd anticipated breakfast under way. I needed food. I needed to get out of this gale. Every wave now broke over the bow. My arms tired from clutching the wheel as green water pummeled the pilothouse. I checked my speed. Even with the ebb behind me, I made only six knots into the wind. I decided to fight on for another hour, then turn sharply left and head back to Port Angeles. Though I'd be bucking the dying ebb, I'd be running with the rising wind.

For the next hour, I clutched the wheel. Frothing seas slapped the bow, burying it under tons of water, then picking up the *Noble Lady* and rudely tossing her aside like a mere child's toy before rolling her one way, then the other.

In these wind-whipped, current-churned seas, my arms strained as I cranked the wheel side to side, trying to keep the bow pointed just off a right angle to the wave fronts, trying to keep the dolphins in the water.

An hour out, I'd had enough.

The upwelling of the next wave lifted the *Noble Lady*. My gut also rose in response. I sucked in a breath. At the top of the wave, I jerked the wheel hard to port and gunned the engine. The *Noble Lady* spun left, but not quickly enough. A wave caught her broadside, throwing me from the wheel. My shoulder crashed painfully into the side wall of the pilothouse. Out the window, I looked down into the belly of a beast.

The *Noble Lady* didn't snap back from the roll as I expected. And when I pulled myself up to the helm, it seemed as though we careened broadside along the edge of a wave, in danger of capsizing. That's when I saw the starboard dolphin completely out of the water, swinging close to the hull from the end of its chain. My muscles burned as I threw my entire body into spinning the wheel in the direction of the roll, trying to take the pressure off of the other dolphin. I needed to regain control of my boat.

Another big wave hit, this time from slightly astern. It did what my arms and the rudder couldn't. It pushed the *Noble Lady* around so she faced down the path of the waves. The starboard dolphin dropped back into the sea, and I had control of the boat once again—if control is what you'd call piloting a thirty-six-foot boat in ten- to twelve-foot breaking seas.

I picked a wave and rode it like a surfer, working the throttle to speed up and slow down to match the speed of the water. In the midst of the chaos I chuckled, giving thanks for the *Noble Lady*'s rounded rear, which shed following seas and made her easier to steer.

My heart soared as Ediz Hook came into view. I'd been so focused on the sea that I'd barely noticed the cobalt blue sky overhead, and the snowcapped Olympics in the distance.

In the lee of long, narrow Ediz Hook, the ocean calmed down. Smoke rose at a steep angle from a slender industrial stack ashore. A tug glided across the Port Angeles harbor. Cars moved along roads. A seal popped its head up in front of the boat, then dived as the bow got too close. I said a mariner's prayer, thanking the sea gods and goddesses for releasing me bruised but alive from their dominion.

After rounding the harbor breakwater, I slowed the boat, shifted into idle, and went on deck to pull in the stabilizer poles and the dolphins. Back inside the pilothouse, I called the harbormaster on the VHF radio.

"I can see you now," he said. "Just pulled in your stabi poles, huh?"

"Roger that."

"Stared down the devil out there, did ya?"

"Roger that."

"Look, we don't have much space. Your boat don't look like one of them chichi yachts, so maybe you won't mind rafting to a fishing boat."

"Not a problem."

"Last pier near the shore. You'll see a fifty-eight-foot fishing trawler, the *Juan de Fuca Queen*. You can tie up next to her. She just got in from fishing. She ain't leaving for at least a week. Hey, you need a hand tying up?"

"I'm single-handed."

"Be right down. Port Angeles Harbor out."

I stepped out on deck and threw three round fenders over the side. They bounced against the hull. I eased the *Noble Lady* deeper into the harbor and slid past the *Queen*. Then I spun her around to dock into the wind.

The harbormaster, a short, rotund man with a gray beard and a red face, stood on the rear deck of the *Queen* in front of the large drum-shaped gurdy used to reel in nets.

The wind blew my bow away from the *Queen*. Without me saying a word, the harbormaster knew exactly what to do. I spun the *Noble Lady*'s stern in toward him. He grabbed a line and tied it off. Then I drove the boat forward into the wind and turned sharply to port. The stern line groaned but the bow swung in. By this time, the harbormaster had scurried to the front of the *Queen*. He grabbed my bow line. I shut down the engine. When I stepped off the *Noble Lady* onto the *Queen*, I tied fore and aft spring lines.

I stood on the *Queen*'s deck. The harbormaster walked over to me. With a clap, he wiped one hand against the other, then extended a hand to me. I shook it.

"Name's Al Monroe," he said. "Say, nice boat you got there. No bow thruster, huh?"

"Nope."

He pursed his lips and nodded. "You know how to handle your boat, unlike some of these chichi yachters."

"Thanks," I said.

Al chuckled. "Got one of them chichi yachts coming in off the strait in a little while. Guy's steaming in from Neah Bay, couldn't hack it. Calls me and asks for a reservation." Al's voice rose to falsetto, "'I'm eighty-four feet. I need a portside tie and 100 amp power.'" He chuckled again. "Hell, I damn near asked him if he wanted valet parking. This is a first-come-first-serve marina. I'm gonna raft him up next to that big yacht over there." He pointed to a gleaming white boat taking up a large part of the far end of the visitor's dock. "And if he don't like it, he can go back out onto the strait and ask the devil for a slip."

"Do you remember this chichi boat's name?"

"Hell, I oughta. Guy called me four or five times. Argued about rafting up. Boat's name is *Longhorn*. Guy even spoke with a Texas drawl. Why? You know him?"

"Heard of him," I said.

"What's he, some kinda' high muck-a-muck?" Al asked.

"Boat like that, he probably thinks he is."

"Hell, rules say you gotta raft up. So you gotta raft up. President could come in here on a boat, he'd still have to raft up if we didn't have space. Look, stop by my office when you're squared away and we'll settle up for moorage."

I stepped back onto the *Noble Lady*. Dishes covered the galley floor. I peeked into the stateroom and winced. Books had flown from the shelves, hopping over their wooden retaining strips.

I stepped around the corner into the head. My toiletries lay on the floor. I gingerly lifted the seat. Thank god, nothing had fallen into the bowl.

I had a lot of housework to do to get squared away. I began by scooping up books and placing them back on their shelves. A warm glow of satisfaction flushed through me. I'd made it through some treacherous water. I sat on the edge of the bed, holding a copy of Jimmy Cornell's *World Cruising Routes*. The sea is a great equalizer. Regardless of size or cost, at some point all boats must seek safe harbor, even chichi yachts like *Longhorn*.

I also heard Raven say, "Take one step in the direction of truth, and truth will take two steps toward you."

✦

AFTER A HASTY ROUND of picking up, I climbed over the *Noble Lady*'s gunwale and onto the metal deck of the *Juan de Fuca Queen*. The *Queen*'s pilothouse sat far forward. Her gurdy, a huge empty metal spool, took up most of the rear deck. I walked over large metal hatches that I knew opened to cavernous fish holds below. I swung one leg, then the other, over her gunwale and dropped to the dock below.

I stopped by Al's office, paid for a night's moorage, and then headed to the restaurant at the far end of the marina for some much-needed food. A tall, lanky kid with red hair and freckles sat me at a table overlooking the boats. He handed me a menu. I ordered a salmon burger, a salad, and a bottle of Northwest microbrew.

The beer came first, and I hoisted my glass in the direction of the *Noble Lady*, for getting me through this afternoon on the strait. I worked through the burger and salad in no time. The red-haired kid placed my bill on the table, but as I whipped out my wallet I looked out the window to see *Longhorn* pass through the breakwater. I held up a finger, and when the red-haired kid came over I ordered another microbrew.

Longhorn skulked into the marina. Al, the harbormaster, stood on the dock talking into a handheld VHF radio. He pointed to the large white motoryacht. Exhaust poured from *Longhorn*'s side. The water behind her churned. It looked like she came to a stop.

Al thrust his finger in the direction of the other motoryacht. *Longhorn* didn't move. I sipped the foam off my beer. Al raised the VHF radio to his mouth, then moved it a few inches away. I couldn't hear a word he said, but his face grew redder, he gesticulated with his free arm, and every so often he jabbed the air in the direction of the other large yacht. I took a swallow of microbrew.

Al reminded me of a major league umpire jawboning an unruly coach. He yanked the radio away from his face and stood on the dock with his arms folded. I drank some more beer and watched the stand-off. Al didn't move. Neither did *Longhorn*. But the wind slowly pushed her back toward the breakwater. Al pulled the radio to his face once more, barked into it, and stormed off toward his office. I could almost hear him saying to Kincaid, "Hell, you don't wanna raft up? Then you can go back out onto the strait and ask the devil for a slip."

Longhorn drifted dangerously close to the breakwater rocks. Finally, she belched smoke from her exhaust and slunk forward toward the other motoryacht. A row of beefy fenders dangled from the sides of both yachts. A couple of men on the deck of *Longhorn* tossed heavy lines to a couple of men on the deck of *White Rhino,* the other boat. *White Rhino*'s crew tied the lines, and the exhaust stopped flowing from *Longhorn*.

A man carrying a thick yellow cord climbed over *Longhorn*'s railing, then over *White Rhino*'s until he got to shore. He plugged one end of the cord into a shore power box, then scrambled back over both boats with the other end.

I paid my bill and left the restaurant, taking the roadway above the marina back to the *Noble Lady*. I looked out over the boats as I walked. Windsocks and flags flew straight out. Loose halyards drummed against their masts. Taut rigging, strummed by the wind, vibrated with long, high-pitched notes like plucked guitar strings. Throughout the marina, boats danced against their mooring lines. I stopped and stared at *Longhorn*. How would I get aboard a boat that large, rafted to another boat even larger?

I heard my cell phone ringing as I stepped aboard the *Juan de Fuca Queen*. I hurried past nets and fishing gear, swung my leg over the gunwales of both boats, and hopped onto the *Noble Lady*. I dashed through the cabin door. Too late. The display flashed a message that I'd missed a call. I didn't recognize the number. I pressed Send and called it back. Maria Delarosa answered, but she didn't say hello. I dropped into a seat at the galley table.

"She's gone," Maria said. Her voice sounded weary, strained.

"Who? Eliana?"

"Yes, she's gone. She and her family stayed at my house in Skagit while I made arrangements for their relocation. This morning all four of us left for Seattle, then Portland. We had not been in the car long when her father said, 'No man will want you now. It will be difficult for you to find a husband.' In my rearview mirror, I saw the mask of shame descend over Eliana's face. South of Seattle, we stopped at a market to pick up some food for the long trip. Eliana went in with her family but she never came out. We looked for her everywhere. Even called the police."

"Damn." I pounded the table.

"She's scared, confused, and ashamed," Maria said.

"I'm afraid she'll wander back to Frank Abadi because he's the only security she's known since entering this country."

"I gave her a few hundred dollars. I'm more afraid that when the money runs out she'll use the profession Abadi taught her and try to make it on her own on the streets of a larger city like Seattle or Portland."

"And get eaten alive by sharks."

"Exactly."

"When I get back, I'll come down there and look for her."

"Where are you now?"

I told Maria.

"If you want to help Eliana," she said, "then do what you're doing."

"But we went to all that trouble to extract her from Abadi," I said.

"Eliana must want our help first. We can't force it on her. Seventy percent of the women I bring to the rehabilitation program in Portland don't make it through the first month. Most find their way back to the streets."

"Grim business."

"Even grimmer if we didn't try." Maria hung up.

I let my head fall into my hands. The eagle had once again eaten Prometheus's liver. I held onto Maria's last words as a levee against a rising tide of despair.

I pulled up the blind in the galley to a view across the fairway of moored sailboats bobbing in the wind. I looked toward *Longhorn*, but saw only her radar arm atop a white arch, and next to it the rounded dome of a satellite antenna.

I couldn't walk up to *White Rhino* and ask to board her in order to board *Longhorn*. Maybe I could row my dinghy up to *Longhorn* later tonight and board her from the waterside. If I could fit the dinghy into the tight space between the boats, I might at least be able to peer through a porthole. Though I doubted that much space existed between the two boats. Besides, my dinghy maneuvered like a stuffed pig. I could just imagine scraping the side of *Longhorn* or *White Rhino* with an oar, telegraphing the sound through the fiberglass hulls, and bringing all hands on deck to investigate.

I let the blind drop in place, then I snapped it back quickly. Several of the sailboats had orange inflatable kayaks on their bows, nestled against the hull and tied off to lifelines. I knew those kayaks well. I'd thought about getting Kate and me a pair, but opted for the more expensive Feathercraft kayaks that we had aboard now. I tapped my open palm with the fist of my other hand.

Lightweight, highly maneuverable, and only two feet wide. I walked out to the rear deck and shuffled through gear in the portside lazarette. I grabbed the end of a heavy tote bag and wrestled it free. I unzipped the bag and peeked inside. Aluminum tubing and a heavy outer skin with built-in flotation. Pretty simple kayaks, and a snap to assemble. I zipped the bag up and set it on the floor. I'd be out for a late paddle tonight.

twenty-three

After practicing the *English Suite*, I placed my guitar down and picked up Jimmy Cornell's *World Cruising Routes*. I thumbed through the book and settled on "Voyage D: Three-year circumnavigation from the west coast of North America." He suggested a fall departure from Washington, out the Strait of Juan de Fuca, and south to Mexico or Central America. Then leaving the following March, and crossing the Pacific to the Marquesas and Tahiti. On from there, to winter over in New Zealand.

I read the route through several times, committing the details to memory as though Kate and I would be casting off in a few days as Sharon and I once hoped we would.

That's another thing I loved about Kate. When I mentioned wanting to circumnavigate the globe, she didn't flinch. She said, "Let's not wait until we're too old." I put the book down and reached for my guitar. I worked through the Prelude for the *English Suite* another time. Who knew? Maybe I'd get a chance to play the piece at my second wedding sometime in the future.

I waited until after eight o'clock to leave for dinner. I threw the kayak bag over the gunwale onto the rear deck of the *Queen*, illuminated by bright fluorescent lights. A new pile of netting sat in front of the large roller. A motor idled loudly. Silhouetted human figures moved back and forth across the opening to a cabin door. I hoisted the kayak bag onto my shoulder and walked across the deck.

I swung the kayak bag from my shoulder, poised to toss it onto the dock, when a large hand clapped me on the shoulder.

"Hey buddy, whaddya think you're doing on our boat with our gear?"

I turned to face a beer-bellied seaman who smelled of fish. He thrust a beefy hand into my chest. I staggered back against the gunwale and dropped the kayak bag.

"I'm rafted—"

He thrust his hand at me again. This time I parried with a swift upward flick of my arm. I caught his forearm, pulled down, and with my other hand jammed my palm hard, up and under his shoulder. I held on and turned him until his chest butted up against the gunwale, then I cranked his arm high up his back. The man winced.

"You didn't let me finish," I said. "The harbormaster had me raft up to your boat. And the gear in that bag belongs to me."

"Hey, Calvin," a voice behind me called out. Then, "What the fuck? What's going on here?"

I spun Calvin around to face his shipmate, a taller man with a cigarette dangling from his lips.

"Just a simple little misunderstanding," I said. "Calvin wondered what I was doing with your gear on your boat. I explained to him in detail that the harbormaster had me raft up to you earlier today and the gear belonged to me."

I let go of Calvin's arm and he swung it from me briskly.

"You okay, Calvin?" the other man asked.

"Yeah," Calvin said. Then he turned to me and shook his finger. "We got work to do, mister, just don't get in our fucking way."

I picked up the kayak bag and let it fall onto the dock, then I climbed over the *Queen*'s gunwale and headed off to dinner at the same restaurant where I'd eaten lunch.

I placed the kayak bag underneath a coat rack. The red-haired kid greeted me again. I stopped him from showing me to the same seat and asked for one where I could keep an eye on my bag. He put me in a booth with a view out to the harbor but situated directly across from the entrance to the main dining room.

I ordered a crab-cake dinner and a glass of microbrew. I didn't rush eating. On this early summer evening, it wouldn't get dark until nearly ten. I'm not a big dessert fan, but tonight, to kill time, I had a piece of blueberry pie and a latte.

The red-haired kid wandered over with my bill.

"You work a long shift," I said.

"Gotta," he said. "Working my way through the community college."

"Is there a bar nearby that's open late?" I asked.

"Fish Inn," he said. "Down the road about half a mile. The fishermen hang out there."

I signed the credit-card slip and gave the kid a generous tip. Then I scooped up my kayak bag and slung it over my shoulder. I headed down the road to the Fish Inn.

I PULLED OPEN THE DOOR to the Fish Inn and walked into a vestibule, where a large, red buoy stood on my right with its light flashing. The sign beneath the buoy told the story: "Red, Right, Returning . . . for a Drink." I laughed.

I hauled my kayak bag into the bar. I threw the bag into a wooden booth, then slid in next to it. Fishing nets covered the walls. Pictures of old trawlers and purse seiners, signed by their captains, hung on the nets. Nets also draped from the ceiling with Japanese glass balls suspended in them. An electric brass lamp dimly lit the table.

Pool balls clacked from somewhere in the shadows of the bar. A few men sat on barstools at the counter. In front of them, lights sparkled off the rows of liquor bottles tiered against a long mirror, reminding me of sunlight sparkling from the rippled surface of the sea.

Conversations murmured around me. A waitress headed my way

with a tray of drinks. She stopped at the booth behind me and slapped glasses down on the table. Then she shuffled over to my booth.

"Whaddya drinking?" she said.

The woman had graying blonde hair and I put her in her late forties. I'd gotten a taste for microbrew and I thought about ordering another. But the Fish Inn didn't look like a microbrew kind of place. I also thought about a Guinness. But it didn't look like a Guinness place either.

"Bud," I said, in honor of Ben and his days before Janet.

When the waitress came back with my beer, she set it on the table with a basket of chips smothered in melted cheese.

"A little something on the house," she said.

"Thanks," I said.

She propped an arm on my table. "My name's Maris," she said. "My daddy was a fisherman. He was also a devout Catholic. He named me 'Maris' after 'Stella Maris,' which means 'star of the sea,' another name for the Virgin Mary. Do you mind if I ask you a question?"

I shook my head. "No, I don't mind."

"Are you on a boat?"

"My own, a trawler in the marina."

"I've lived in the Northwest for almost fifty years and I've always wondered why you don't see many African Americans fishing or owning their own boats. Probably count on my fingers all the black captains I've known."

I took a sip of beer.

"Of course, fishing isn't a profession I'd suggest for anyone today."

"Ain't that the truth," Maris said.

"Exposure. Expense. Family history."

"Yeah, I guess so," Maris said. She started to turn away.

"But beyond that," I said.

Maris turned around.

"Beyond that, maybe the sea holds memories for African Americans. If it does, those memories aren't good. Sea's how we got here. Sea's where millions of Africans lost their lives on slave ships. Slave castles in Africa used to have a door called the 'door of no return,' through which dead or dying Africans would be swept out to sea."

Maris looked away for a few moments, then she turned back to me. "Never thought about it that way," she said. She nodded slowly. "Sea holds memories. Sounds like something my daddy used to say. 'Darlin', you can listen to the sea and hear the stories of all those who've traveled her waters.' So can I ask how come you're here in Port Angeles? And on your own boat, no less."

I thought about the trip across the strait. I took another sip of beer and said to Maris, "It got rough on the strait today, and I needed to pull into a port. Sometimes you have to travel over rough waters to reach a safe harbor."

"Ain't that the truth." She chuckled. "Sounds like something else my daddy would say."

Suddenly, a whirlwind blew through the door.

"Maris? Maris, where are you?" the man bellowed.

Al, the harbormaster, yanked a barstool from the counter and dropped onto the seat. "I need a good stiff drink," he said.

Maris raised her hand. "Damn you, Al, I'm over here taking care of a customer."

Al turned toward us. He squinted, then bellowed, "You're the guy what came in and tied up to the *Queen*." He rose from the stool and sauntered over to my table.

Maris whispered, "Don't mind him, he's just an old windbag. Comes in here every night to blow off steam."

Al took a seat across from me. "Had a little run-in with some of the boys, huh? Brady came over and asked me if you were what you said you were. I told him you were."

"I guess that means I am."

Al turned to Maris. "Whiskey. Straight. Two shots. Two glasses." Then he turned to me. "Fucking *Longhorn*."

Al shook his head and stared into space. Before he could say more, Maris came back with two shot glasses, which she set down with short, snappy pops that sounded like a tap dancer toeing a wooden floor. Al grabbed one, leaned back, and flipped the caramel-colored liquid down his throat. He coughed and shook his head. He frowned.

"Damn, I hate the way that liquor tastes." Then he grinned. "But I do like what it does for my nerves."

While Al eyed the other glass, I took a sip of my beer.

"So this fucker comes into *my* harbor, calls on the radio, and says, 'Where's my slip?' I just about had a conniption. I told him the rule is you have to raft up to other boats if there's no space. So what does the fucker say, but, 'Well, then, make me some space.' That's when I lost it and told him—"

I cut Al off. "He could go back out in the strait and ask the devil for a slip."

Al closed his eyes and tossed down glass number two. His eyes twinkled when he opened them. "Nah. I only tell 'em that when I'm being nice. Look, they built most marinas for boats in the thirty- to forty-foot range. Nowadays your average summer captain has a boat forty to fifty feet long. Many are a lot longer. You do the math. Any way you work it, I come up short on dock space. So rafting's the only way."

Al raised his hand. "Maris, I'll have another."

She pretended not to hear him.

"Damn woman," he said. "You'd think things'd be better now that we're divorced."

"Maybe she's worried about you drinking away all of her alimony."

Al yucked. "Or pissing it away. Say, I'm not one to remember names on credit-card slips. Boat names I'm good at. Yours is the *Noble Lady*."

"That's right."

"But what's your name?"

"Charlie Noble," I said.

Maris finally arrived with another shot glass of whiskey. Al pointed to my glass.

"Say, you want another of whatever you're drinking?"

"No." I waved him off.

Al twirled the shot glass between two fingers. "So after *Longhorn*'s docked, this young fellow comes off the boat into my office. Says he's there to apologize for his dad. Told him I appreciated the courtesy. Then I told him another boater had just pulled in and asked about their boat. He asked who, and I said you. Well, I didn't remember your name but I said a tall black guy, and I pointed out your boat. You sure you don't know them folks?"

I sucked in a breath and thought about taking Al up on a second drink. "I've met the son," I said.

"You owe him money or something? He left my office pretty quick. Didn't seem too pleased to know you were here."

"He's never seen my boat before. Maybe it didn't suit his chichi tastes."

Al let out a belly laugh. "Wouldn't be surprised."

I pushed myself up from the booth. Then I leaned back in and grabbed my kayak bag.

Al's eyes got big. "What're ya carrying in there?" he asked. "A dead body or the loot you owe the son?"

I smiled. "A kayak."

"Right, a kayak. One of us has had too much to drink, and I just got started."

I whipped the zipper open and flashed the contents of the bag at Al. He whistled low.

"Well I'll be damned. A kayak in a bag. What'll they think of next? Why, you're not a SEAL or one of them special agent types are you?"

I straightened up and looked down at Al with a hard stare. His lips tightened, and anxiety swept across his face. In my best military voice, I said, "Sir, if I tell you, I will have to kill you."

Finally, I cracked a smile. Al downed his shot of whiskey, then laughed so hard I thought he'd bring it right back up.

I LUGGED THE KAYAK at least half a mile farther down the road from the bar toward Ediz Hook. On the beach, I stepped behind a rock, then kneeled to open the bag. The aluminum frame and outer skin fit together in a matter of minutes. I grabbed the four-piece paddles, slipping a blade onto the end of each shaft, then joining both shafts together. I stuffed the bag behind the seat and dragged the kayak to the water's edge.

Little wind swept across the water. I donned my spray skirt and life vest. Then, I slipped into my kayak and paddled off toward the marina. Moonlight shimmered over the water. Stars and streetlights twinkled in the night. Salt smell filled the air as the kayak sliced silently through the sea.

Rounding the breakwater, I hugged the shore, staying out of *Longhorn*'s line of sight. I slowly worked my way up and down the fairways, slipping between boats and the dock when I could. One fairway from *Longhorn,* I stopped. Poking the kayak's nose out and peeking around the corner, I noticed the radar arm no longer revolved. A few lights lit the inside of *Longhorn*. A lone guard patrolled her decks.

I waited for the sentinel to walk toward the stern, then I paddled hard toward *White Rhino*'s bow. The front portion of both hulls flared up and out, forming an arched tunnel wide enough for me to fit through. Once between the boats, I slipped my paddle under a bungee cord on deck and used my hands to push off on the hulls. I wasn't sure how far back to travel. Eliana's story suggested that immigrants might be held in an area at or below the boat's waterline.

Longhorn's engines and machinery probably sat toward her stern, placing her staterooms, and maybe her below-deck holds, farther forward. Ten feet in from the bow, I put my ear low on her hull. The thin fiberglass transmitted a diesel generator's steady throb. Muffled, laughing voices also traveled through the hull. I guessed at where a forward stowage area might be, then I tapped lightly, but rhythmically, on the hull. Three short taps. Three long taps. Three short taps. Antiquated Morse code for S-O-S.

I didn't expect that immigrants would know Morse code, but the rhythmic pattern might grab their attention. I tapped again. A guard's footsteps echoed through the hull, growing louder. I risked the crew also hearing my taps.

I pulled my ear away and pushed myself farther back along the tunnel between the hulls. Through the narrow gap, I watched the guard lean over the bow railing. He looked my way, then looked out toward the strait. He raised his arm and flicked a finger. A glowing ember fell, and a cigarette butt hissed as it hit the water twenty feet away.

The guard resumed his rounds, walking toward the stern. I used my fingers to work myself back toward the bow, tapping as I went. Three short. Three long. Three short. I put my ear against the hull, but I heard only the generator and the distant voices. I tapped out code once more. This time, a door on the main deck snapped open. A man yelled, "Tommy, Mr. Kincaid says he keeps hearing something tapping against the hull. Is a log banging against us? Maybe near the bow?"

"Don't know," Tommy said. "But I'll walk up there and have a look."

I worked myself deeper into the gap between the boats. Overhead, a flashlight blazed on, and a moving circle of luminous green swept the water only a few feet away from me.

"I don't see nothing," Tommy said. "You want me to lower the skiff and have a look?"

"Nah. Too much trouble to go through for a fucking log," the other man said. "Let's wait."

A door on the deck snapped closed, and Tommy's footsteps faded toward the rear of the boat again.

Maybe Kincaid hadn't picked up any undocumented immigrants on this trip. I inched my way back toward the bow. Or maybe he'd already dropped them off at Neah Bay, Clallam Bay, or some other secluded cove. I'd try tapping one more time.

A current had developed in the marina, funneling between the hulls, pushing me aft, making it hard for me to move forward using just my fingers. I pressed my palm firmly against the smooth surface of the fiberglass, searching for a little more traction. I made a fist of my other hand and I tapped again. In desperation, I must have rapped too hard. Above me, a door crashed open.

"Lower the skiff, Tommy," a man said. "Kincaid wants us to find out what the hell's knocking against the hull."

I pulled my paddle from beneath the bungee cord, but the narrow space between the hulls didn't offer enough room to put the blades in the water. So I rested it lengthwise along the top of the kayak.

Mooring lines groaned in the rising current. I thrust my hand against *Longhorn*'s hull, trying to maintain my position. A winch whined, then stopped.

"A little more to the right," the man said.

The motor turned on again.

"Got it. Got it. Now lower the fucker."

With a splash, the skiff dropped into the water. That's when I heard the feeble knock from the other side of *Longhorn*'s hull. Three short. Three long. Three short. I jammed my ear to the hull. The skiff's engine roared to a start. Pain shot through my knuckles as I rapped out code with all my strength.

"I heard it. I heard it," Tommy said. "Near the bow. Between the boats. Damn log could be caught in there."

Beneath my ear, the hull echoed once more with a weak reply. The outboard motor telegraphed the skiff's location on the opposite side of the hull, traveling forward. Tommy's footsteps moved toward the bow along the side deck above. I ripped my ear from the hull and glanced over my shoulder to see the nose of the skiff turning the corner at *Longhorn*'s bow.

twenty-four

I let go of *Longhorn*'s hull. The current shot me back along the tunnel between the boats, like a bullet from a rifle barrel. When I exited the tunnel, I plunged a paddle blade in the water and held on. I didn't have time for a stroke. Fast water pushed against the blade, forcing the kayak to carve a turn around the stern of *White Rhino*. Finally, I gripped the paddle tightly and dug water, heading into the shadows of a nearby fairway.

Out of sight of *Longhorn*'s skiff, I held onto the edge of a dock. I gave myself time to catch my breath and allow my heart rate to drop. Then I pushed off and wove my way through the maze of boats and docks. The full moon glowed overhead. The ebb tide had returned. It flushed me from the marina, past the breakwater and toward Ediz Hook.

Back on the *Noble Lady*, I lay on my bed in the dark, hands clasped behind my head, looking up. Framed by the skylight overhead, stars moved slowly across the sky, first one way, then the other, in time with the gentle rolling of the boat.

I could go to the local police and ask them to search *Longhorn*. "I tapped on the hull of a boat . . . a few taps came back . . . you need to search it, then arrest the owner for transportation of undocumented immigrants." Somehow I didn't think that would go over too well. If I were local law enforcement, I'd sooner arrest the person who came to me with such a preposterous story.

I could call ahead and have someone intercept the boat. Maybe my buddy, San Juan County Sheriff Ed Sykes. I could hear Ed. "I need a little more to go on than you 'think' a crime's been committed. I need some solid evidence."

Solid evidence meant more than a few taps from the inside of *Longhorn*. It made sense for me to stay in Port Angeles, keep an eye on *Longhorn*, then head out behind her when she left.

A SHAFT OF BRIGHT LIGHT filtering through one of the stateroom portholes awoke me with a start. I pulled myself up and peered out the porthole. A heavy fog had rolled into the harbor. I looked toward *Longhorn*. I blinked my eyes several times and looked her way again. Then I bolted out of bed.

I jumped into my clothes and raced upstairs, shoeless, into the pilothouse. I cranked the *Noble Lady*'s engine over, then I hurried downstairs. While the engine warmed, I slipped on my tennis shoes, tucked my shirttail into my pants, and put on a fleece jacket. *Longhorn*'s radar arm rotated, a sure sign of her impending departure.

I went back up into the pilothouse and turned on the GPS, radar, and VHF. Then I grabbed my binoculars and watched *Longhorn*. No mooring lines attached her to *White Rhino*. Exhaust spewed from her aft. Water gurgled near her bow. She slid slowly sideward, away from the dock. Her big engines groaned. She spun around like a giant pointer on a board game and slipped into the fog, headed toward the breakwater.

I scurried down the pilothouse steps and made my way through the galley onto the rear deck. I stepped off the *Noble Lady* onto the *Queen*. I'd bent down to unravel my stern line from a cleat on the *Queen*'s deck when a heavy, rough hand clamped down on my shoulder. My body shuddered.

"Hey, buddy, where d'ya think you're going?"

I spun around to face Calvin, the beer-bellied fisherman holding onto me. Behind him, his other shipmate stood, glaring. I slapped Calvin's hand away.

"I'm untying my boat."

I reached down for the mooring line. Calvin jammed his fleshy palm into my shoulder. I stumbled away from the cleat.

"Like hell you are," Calvin said. "Some of our gear is missing. Brady and me think maybe we oughta take a look on your boat for it."

"Like hell you are." I mimicked the vague hint of a southern accent in Calvin's voice. "No one comes aboard the *Noble Lady* uninvited."

At the edge of my vision, Brady's tall, slender body disappeared to my right and behind me. These guys hankered for a fight. Why? I spun around. I backed against the gunwale of the *Queen*. Calvin launched a right hand toward me, dumping the heft of his body into the punch. I sidestepped him and threw my elbow into his upper back, sending him sprawling into the *Queen*'s gunwale.

No sooner had Calvin flown by than Brady came at me. Not in a heated rush, but coolly, like a man who'd fought before. He moved from side to side eyeing me, sizing me up. I dropped into a crouch and held my hands up in loose fists, moving away from the gunwale so I could keep both men in view.

Brady threw a few jabs my way. Nothing serious. I got the feeling he'd done so only to measure his reach. His long arms did give him an advantage. Meanwhile, Calvin had pulled himself off the gunwale. His footsteps rang heavily on the aluminum deck. He wandered out of sight, which left me facing Brady.

Brady feigned with his right, then swung a fast left hook. I whipped my right arm up and blocked it, but he came at me quickly with a right jab. I dipped my head, but his fist caught the side of my face. My cheek stung. My ear rang from the blow. He smiled as though proud of himself. Sometimes it takes getting hit to get into a fight, particularly one you'd rather walk away from.

Brady tried a right-hand feign again. When his left arm shot out, I dropped even lower, swung to one side, and kicked hard and fast. My heel caught him at the top of his thigh, close to his groin. He winced. His leg began to buckle. I stood up quickly. He threw a feeble left. I grabbed his wrist and let his body follow through with the motion of his punch. A short upward jab with my palm under his armpit and a downward tug of his arm sent him flying toward the back of the *Queen*. He hit the metal deck with a thud. I turned around, looking for Calvin.

Suddenly, a fishing net descended over me like a spider's web.

"Got him, Brady," Calvin said.

I fought to loosen myself, but each movement only further ensnared me in the net. Calvin came at me with a volley of punches. I dropped to my knees, covering my body as best I could. Calvin sent his boot into my side several times. I winced with each blow. Hot flashes of pain coursed through me.

"He paid us to delay him, not to kill him," Brady said.

"Didn't you see what the fucker did to me?"

Calvin sent another boot my way. It caught me in my lower rib cage. I went face down onto the deck. Calvin pounced on me. The rounded flesh of his belly pressed me further into the deck. He pummeled my back with his fists, and a fiery pain shot through my body. I walked my fingers along the metal deck, searching for the edge of the netting.

"Leave him there," Brady said. "Man's got a fast boat. This guy won't catch up to him now."

"Bastard threw me into the gunwale," Calvin said. He stood up and kicked me again.

My fingers found the doubled-over edge of the net, and I worked my hand free. I rolled over onto my side and curled into a fetal position. Calvin swung his leg to kick me again, but this time I swung my hand with the edge of the net up and caught his ankle just as his boot plowed into my body. I grimaced, but I held on. I yanked with all my strength, pulling his leg out from under him. He plummeted to the deck and fell in a seated position with a clunk. He yelped in pain.

I kneeled on the deck, trying to step out of the net. Brady pushed off the gurdy and dived at me. He drove me down to the deck again, onto my back. I still had a portion of the net in my hand. I wrapped it around his head and his neck. I pulled hard. He raised his hands to get it off, and the moment he did I rolled him over onto his back. I slammed my forearm into his throat. He coughed, wheezing and choking as he struggled for a breath.

I wriggled out of the net. My body ached from top to bottom. I stood bent over, breathing hard. Blood oozed from a gash in my forehead where Calvin had kicked me. I looked down. Brady writhed on the deck, with half of his body caught in the net. Calvin sat, red-faced, tears streaming down his cheeks. Chances are he'd broken his tailbone with a fall like that. I thought about landing a kick in the middle of his fat gut. Instead, I jumped behind him and caught his neck in a choke-hold.

"Who?" I asked.

He remained silent. I tightened my hold a notch. He grabbed for my forearm. I tightened my hold even further.

"Who paid you?"

He pointed out of the harbor. He tried to speak, but little air came from his mouth. I eased up.

"*Longhorn.*" He muttered in a raspy whisper.

I flexed my arms quickly, then let him go. Calvin grabbed his throat. He struggled for a breath.

"Next time, think twice about how you welcome someone who rafts up to your boat," I said.

twenty-five

A spasm of pain shot through me. I squeezed my eyes closed. Then I gritted my teeth and returned to the *Noble Lady*'s mooring lines. It took me much longer than usual to untie her. When I went to push her away from the *Queen*, a stitch of pain knifed into the side of my body. I tumbled over the gunwale onto the *Noble Lady*'s rear deck.

Once inside, I hauled myself up to the pilothouse. I spun the wheel hard over to starboard. Then I gave the engine a shot of forward throttle, followed with a shot of reverse, and finished off with a shot of forward again. Like a horse taking her injured rider home, the *Noble Lady* spun around in her own length and headed toward the marina's entrance.

We rounded the breakwater, and I pulled the throttle back to idle, disengaging the gearshift. The *Noble Lady* pirouetted in the current, then drifted in the pea-soup fog. I stumbled downstairs and into the head to find a bottle of painkillers. I swallowed a couple of pills dry, grabbed a bandage for the gash in my forehead from the first-aid kit, and climbed back up to the pilothouse. I kneaded my temples and forced myself to focus through the pain. A blanket of luminous white enveloped me. I couldn't see past the *Noble Lady*'s bow. Forget following *Longhorn*. I'd be happy just to find her on radar in this fog.

I checked my GPS and brought up my location on my navigational computer. I'd already swung around nearly 180 degrees. I engaged the forward gear and brought the engine rpm's up. Then I spun the wheel, the boat twirled, and we headed off through the fog.

A nearby ship's horn blasted two long, mournful pleas. The deep, throaty sound vibrated through my body. Off in the distance, another ship answered. I punched in the Vessel Traffic System channel on my VHF radio. Tankers, container ships, and tugs pulling barges radioed that they'd slowed down several knots entering the bank of fog, which apparently had socked in most of the Strait of Juan de Fuca.

I switched on my radar and zoomed-out the view to a distance of sixteen miles. The gash on my forehead throbbed. But the painkillers must have kicked in. Only a dull ache persisted in my back and the sides of my body. I counted eight glowing spots of green light ahead of me, any one of them possibly *Longhorn.*

Another ship's horn sounded. I braced for the second blast. It came loud and close by. I scanned the radar screen. A large target closed in on me from behind, now about half a mile away. The ferry from Port Angeles to Victoria, I guessed. I verified my position on radar, then swung the *Noble Lady* sharply in toward land. I knew I'd appear on the ferry's radar screen. I hoped this abrupt turn would telegraph to the captain that he should pass on my port side.

The ship's horn blared twice again. My body responded, vibrating like a struck tuning fork. I strained to see out the forward and side windows, but fog dispersed the sound, making it impossible to determine the vessel's location.

I hit a button on the radar to zoom-in the view. A large green blob now appeared almost on top of me. I revved the engine higher and headed farther in toward shore. When the depth sounder read twenty feet, I stopped.

The low grumble of large diesel engines pulsed through me. The diesels pounded louder, as though the fog itself breathed. I heard the ship's bow wave before I felt it, like the sound of a thousand fallen leaves crushed under foot and rushing at me. I braced against the wheel, unsure from which direction to expect the wave. It hit the *Noble Lady* abeam, rolling her heavily. I held onto the wheel. Two more waves slapped her side in short succession.

Down below, cabinet doors crashed open. Books jumped their retaining strips again and hit the floor with a cascade of plops. Outside, the chains attached to the dolphins rattled violently, even though the dolphins sat securely in their holders. Then the *Noble Lady* regained her composure. Fog swallowed the sound of the diesels. I never did see the vessel that passed. Far away, ship horns brayed, warnings of giants still hidden in the mist.

With my eyes fixed on my instruments, I turned the wheel slowly, gently bringing the *Noble Lady* back on course. On the radar screen, the number of targets within sixteen miles had now grown from eight to twelve. I headed toward the eastern entrance of the Strait of Juan de Fuca, back toward the San Juan Islands.

I thought about trying to find my cell phone amid the mess I knew awaited me in the *Noble Lady*'s cabin. I could call Kate and ask if she'd have her CO divert *Sea Eagle* to intercept *Longhorn*. But I couldn't leave the helm, not in conditions like this. Navigating by radar in blinding fog is like playing a video game with real lives at stake. Then again, calling Kate might not be such a good idea. I'd risk putting her position as a junior officer in jeopardy by asking her to request something highly irregular from her CO.

I gazed at the glowing green dots on the radar screen. Maybe I could tease them apart. Vessel traffic follows predictable sea-lanes, which are laid out plainly on nautical charts. Only pleasure craft and vessels like water taxis or ferries traveled outside of those lanes. I turned up the VHF radio, tuning it to the vessel traffic channel.

"Victoria Traffic. This is Ocean Challenger."

"Ocean Challenger. Traffic."

"Traffic. We're at Race Rocks. Slowing to eight knots in heavy fog. Estimating Victoria Harbor at One Two Three Zero."

"Ocean Challenger, Roger. Ahead of you is the one-hundred-foot fishing vessel *Pacific Warrior,* leaving Victoria Harbor and heading for

Sydney via Baynes Channel. Behind you, and possibly overtaking, is the tug *John McCormack*, towing two empty barges. Estimated speed is fourteen knots. Well behind the *John McCormack* is the *Pacific Nomad*, a tug with two full container barges, and behind her the *Ocean Titan*, a tug making twelve knots. Opposing is the oil tanker *Alaskan Rose*, estimating Race Rocks at One One Four Five, and the *Victoria Clipper* on her regularly scheduled run from Seattle, estimating Victoria Harbor at One Two One Five."

"Roger, Traffic, thank you. Ocean Challenger standing by Eleven and Sixteen."

I found Race Rocks on the radar and the blip representing the *Ocean Challenger*. I tapped on the *John McCormack*, the *Pacific Warrior*, the *Alaskan Rose*, and the *Victoria Clipper*. I also tapped on a dot that sped northeast across the top of my radar screen. Probably the ferry from Port Angeles to Anacortes.

"Roger, Traffic, thank you," I said silently to myself. I'd already accounted for six out of twelve targets.

With the *Noble Lady* headed east, three of the remaining six targets actually traveled toward me from behind and about two miles north. I estimated their speed at about twelve knots. A double blip flickered on and off for the middle target of this trio, the telltale signature of a tug towing a barge. This looked like *Pacific Nomad*, and the other blip like the *Ocean Titan*.

Suddenly, one of the three remaining unidentified targets changed course, turning south and racing across the screen ten miles ahead of me toward Admiralty Inlet. It's dangerous to estimate the size of a vessel simply based on the size of its blip. But this tiny blip traveling at such high speed suggested an inflatable or a small boat, perhaps a coast guard patrol boat. I counted how long it took for the target to cross the concentric rings on my radar screen, estimating its speed at twenty-five knots. I didn't believe that *Longhorn* could move that fast.

Of the remaining blips, one moved slowly east from Smith Island, and the other headed north up Haro Strait, by my calculations making somewhere between ten and fifteen knots. I nodded and tapped atop the second blip, which I believed was *Longhorn*. Then I pushed the throttle forward. The engine whined, and the *Noble Lady*'s speed rose to just over eight knots. While I couldn't catch up to that blip, at least I could stay within range to keep it on radar and determine its probable destination.

A flood current built, at times pushing me to over ten knots. The VHF radio crackled with the static-filled conversation of ship captains and Vessel Traffic Control. Little wind blew, and the morning sun had yet to burn off the fog. The faster target, which I presumed to be *Longhorn,* continued its northerly course up Haro Strait, while the slower target appeared not to have moved much from its previous position off Smith Island.

Fog stopped me in my early days of cruising. I'd tuck into a little nook, throw out the anchor, and wait for it to lift. Perhaps the captain of that boat off Smith Island felt a similar reluctance to venture out today.

I neared Smith Island and looked right into a dense white cloud. I couldn't see a slow-moving boat. I couldn't see anything. I located the faster target on my radar and adjusted my screen so it would continue to stay in view.

A small, scintillating point of green light appeared near the target off Smith Island. It vanished, then it reappeared, then it vanished again. I adjusted the radar to filter out clutter. Afterward, I didn't see the dot. Then a moment later it reappeared, its radar image merging with the outer edges of Smith Island. I adjusted my radar again, this time to keep the faster-moving target I thought was *Longhorn* on the screen. The tiny spot of light flickered on again. A ship's horn broke the silence. My body tensed. I scanned radar again. *Ocean Titan* moved past my port side, and *Pacific Nomad* steamed along not far behind.

Suddenly, two sharp cracks sounded off my starboard side. Instinctively, I ducked. The first bullet chuffed into the outside wall of the pilothouse. The second bullet splintered the window of the pilothouse door and dived, whining, into an upper sidewall above my head. I reached up and pressed the autopilot button with my fingertips. Then

I crawled to the window and raised my body slowly to peek out. That's when I saw the small white boat with a large black outboard motor, barely visible in the fog. It looked like *Longhorn*'s high-speed skiff.

I scooted down the pilothouse stairs and into the stateroom, looking for my pistol. Damn. The nightstand drawer lay on its side, its contents strewn over the floor, mixed with the pile of books. My pistol lay somewhere beneath that clutter. Two muffled cracks sounded. Two slugs bit low, into the hull. I didn't have time to search for my gun.

Empty-handed, I scrambled back into the pilothouse. Fired at just the right location, a bullet could puncture the hull or, worse, hit the fuel tank and set off an explosion. I switched off the autopilot, then snatched the wheel. I spun the boat around and headed into the fog. I zoomed-in my radar view as far as I could, but the small boat lurked too close to distinguish it on the screen.

And I'd thought about a boater afraid of the fog? That slow-moving target had been *Longhorn,* and she stood off Smith Island—not to wait out the fog, but to wait for me. Perhaps Brady or Calvin had called Kincaid on his cell phone.

Another dull thud struck the *Noble Lady*'s hull on the other side. I peered out the port window just in time to see *Longhorn*'s skiff disappear into the fog.

With small patches of varying visibility, a fogbank is much more like a maze than a solid wall, particularly as it begins to lift. I opened the throttle wide, headed out toward the shipping lanes, and steered into and out of the thickest fog based on how much of the ocean I could see in front of the boat.

From the size of its outboard motor, I bet *Longhorn*'s skiff could easily attain a speed of thirty knots. I felt like a sitting duck. I opened the pilothouse door and looked behind me. The *Noble Lady*'s stern tucked into thicker fog just as the skiff's bow pierced through into a clearing. I ducked back into the pilothouse and grabbed the wheel. I spun the *Noble Lady* around sharply. If the men in that small boat tracked me on radar, this close they'd have trouble distinguishing me turning 180 degrees and heading back at them.

I slammed the throttle forward, aiming for the spot where I thought the skiff would reappear. A moment later, the small boat broke through the fog directly in front of my bow. I leaned into the *Noble Lady*'s foghorn.

Terror stormed across the faces of the two men. They dived into the water. I held onto the wheel. Fiberglass met fiberglass with a jarring crash. The *Noble Lady* rammed the skiff just beyond its bow. The skiff tipped precipitously, then veered off sharply to starboard. I swung the wheel to port so we'd miss the rest of the small boat. When I looked back, I saw the skiff upside down in the water. One man clung to the hull. The other swam furiously toward him.

The *Noble Lady* had more than an inch of fiberglass in the forward sections of her hull, so I wasn't worried about serious damage. I noted my position from the GPS, then I radioed the Coast Guard to let them know where they'd find two cold, unhappy mariners in the water.

I checked my radar. I no longer saw *Longhorn*'s blip sitting off Smith Island. But a target making about twenty knots now headed for Cattle Point. Hunters know that tracking prey that moves faster than they do is exhausting and often futile. So the smart ones split duties, some herding prey, others lying in wait where the prey is likely headed. I set the *Noble Lady* on a course for the Lawson Reef buoy at the southern end of Lopez Island. I'd managed to herd *Longhorn* from the Strait of Juan de Fuca into the San Juan Islands.

I knew the exact spot to lie in wait.

twenty-six

I rounded the southeast tip of Lopez Island and entered Rosario Strait. The fog lifted, revealing a multicolored world beyond the pilothouse. I stuck my head out from the pilothouse door and looked behind me. A dense white veil rose from the water beyond Lopez, blocking the view of the monochrome world that I'd left.

Ahead of me, dark green waters capped with a layer of sparkling sunlight surrounded chunks of sun-drenched, dark green land. A deep blue sky reigned overhead. The flood swept me along.

I called Raven on his cell phone. He didn't answer. The call transferred to his business voice mail. I left a message telling him what I intended to do.

At Neptune's Small Trident, I continued up Rosario. Tiny Doe Island lies in Rosario Strait, just off the southeast coast of huge Orcas Island, like a misplaced period on a page. The island's all of six acres, but it's a state park equipped with a thirty-two-foot-long dock. I threaded my way through the rocky entrance. Boats tied to private buoys bobbed in front of the few homes lining the Orcas Island shore across from Doe Island.

The current ran hard around the tiny island. I spun the wheel into it and gunned the engine forward and back a few times. It took several passes to maneuver into a position where the current pushed me into the dock. I tied the *Noble Lady* with her stern facing the island and her prominent bow sticking out past the end of the dock.

I hadn't eaten since breakfast, and the thick mass of Kate's protein smoothie slid slowly down my throat, comforting my stomach. Afterward, I grabbed a pair of binoculars and jumped down to the dock. My adrenaline level dropped a notch with each step along the short path through the woods to the other side of the island. The sharp, sweet aroma of cedar scented the air. A crow's cackle floated above the screams of seagulls. Though the gash on my forehead throbbed once again, the path ended at a view that took my breath away.

I sat with my back propped against a rock and gazed out to the water. To my left lay a clutch of rocks known as the Peapods. Across the wide expanse of Rosario Strait stood Eagle Bluff, the high promontory at the north end of Cypress Island. I raised the binoculars to my eyes. A colony of seals lazed in the sun on the Peapods. Then, turning the glasses to Cypress Island, I stared directly into Smuggler's Cove.

I lowered the binoculars and closed my eyes, sucking in a deep breath of salt air laced with the piquant sweetness of cedar. I nuzzled my back into the rock. A breeze blew across my face. The last thing I remember is imagining Kate resting her head in my lap.

When I opened my eyes and checked my watch, I'd given up forty-five minutes to the water, the wind, the trees, and the earth.

I strolled back to the *Noble Lady*. I picked up books and put back the spilled contents of cabinets and drawers. Then I flipped my cell phone open to call Raven again. The bars on the tiny screen indicated that I had minimal service. I pressed Send, and the call went through. Raven answered. We exchanged "Hello" and "Can you hear me?" several times. Frustrated, I yelled into the phone, "I'm at Doe Island keeping an eye on Smuggler's Cove." The connection dropped. I tried to call again, but now a message on the screen indicated I had no service at all.

After dinner I dropped the dinghy into the water and tied it to the dock. Then I slipped into a windbreaker and grabbed my night-vision binoculars and a flashlight before heading back over to the other side of the island. Once there, I propped myself up against the rock. The setting sun tinged the sky above Obstruction and Blakely islands a deep orange. Out of sight, two kingfishers bantered with high-pitched staccato calls that sounded like the rattling of miniature machine guns. The breeze died. A cormorant on a log floated by. North of the Peapods, a big tanker turned the corner at Point Lawrence, plowing through the waters of Rosario Strait.

I watched and waited.

Shimmering stars arrived overhead first, followed by an orange moon just past full. A satellite sped across the face of the night sky. On the other side of Rosario Strait, a red light moved against the dark landmass of Cypress Island. I picked up my night-vision binoculars, which transformed the darkness into a world of garish yellow-green light. The running light belonged to a boat maybe forty feet long, shaped like a Grand Banks, heading east along Rosario. Smuggler's Cove still lay empty. I pulled the binoculars away, enjoying the darkness again after my eyes adjusted.

The Lydia Shoal buoy flashed green. In the distance, other buoys flickered red and yellow. No lights moved along the water. Put me at the helm of *Longhorn* tonight, and I'd run with my lights off. I stood up to stretch and decided to head across the island to the *Noble Lady* for some coffee.

As I walked back to the rock with the thermos, my flashlight beam danced among the trees, sending eerie shadows bouncing through the woods. I sat against the rock and took a few sips of coffee. Through the binoculars I saw Smuggler's Cove still empty. I'm sure that many a hunter has sat in a blind waiting for prey, wondering if he'd staked out the right spot. Maybe I'd been wrong about *Longhorn* returning to Smuggler's Cove. One step toward the truth, I reminded myself. I exhaled deeply.

In short succession, two shooting stars etched trails of fire across the sky. The moon, once orange, now cast an undulating silvery path over the water. Kincaid could have run back into Canada with *Longhorn*.

A twig broke behind me. My body stiffened and I pushed back into the rock. Tiny feet scurried over fallen leaves. I chuckled to myself. What is it about darkness that feels so ominous and threatening? Earlier today I'd been in near-zero visibility in the midst of vessel traffic along the Strait of Juan de Fuca. Now I sat on an island, gazing at the stars, with houselights visible twenty miles away. Yet, I felt more vulnerable than I had earlier, encased in thick fog.

Every few minutes, I peered through the binoculars, scanning Rosario Strait and the eastern entrances to Peavine and Obstruction passes. Nothing moved over the dark, still waters.

I pulled out my cell phone again. When I opened it, a shaft of neon blue light arose from the screen. But the bars showed I didn't have any better service than before. I pressed the key for Raven's number, then I hit Send. The cell phone tried to make the connection, but after a few minutes it gave up. If *Longhorn* came into Smuggler's Cove tonight, it looked like I'd be going after her alone.

Suddenly, a loud pop preceded a sharp splash, like the precision entry of a high diver into the water. The seal's tail hit again. I trained the binoculars in the direction of the sound, past the green flashing buoy at Lydia Shoal toward Peavine Pass. A small yellow-green fountain of water erupted with the seal's next tail slap. I held the glasses steady on the site. The seal never surfaced again, but the gossamer image of a boat slowly moved into view. I focused the binoculars on the entrance to Peavine Pass.

Once the full profile of the boat emerged from the shadows, I stripped the glasses from my eyes and tucked them in their case. I scooped up the thermos and twisted the flashlight on. I moved quickly through the woods, back to the dock.

I leapt aboard the *Noble Lady*. I snatched my gun and tucked it into the small of my back. Then I shoved my arms through my life vest, fastening it as I hurried out the cabin door. I jumped into the dinghy, untied it, and pushed myself away from the dock. The outboard motor started with the first pull of the cord.

I headed out toward Rosario Strait, and once clear of Doe Island I brought the motor to idle. I raised my binoculars to my eyes. The

ghostly green silhouette still moved slowly across the water. I brought
the motor's speed back up and continued toward Smuggler's Cove to
intercept *Longhorn*.

A mile off the Cypress Island coast, I stopped the motor and drifted
in the moonlit strait. *Longhorn* turned the corner and ducked into
Smuggler's Cove. The dim blue glow of instrument lights emanated
from her helm windows. I raised the outboard motor from the water.
Then I unhooked the oars from their holders. I set the oars in the oar-
locks and sat facing the stern. I started rowing, using a fisherman's
row, pulling one oar through the water, followed by the other. I angled the dinghy east, away from the mouth of Smuggler's Cove, fer-
rying across the ebb that pushed me west.

Half a mile away from the cove, I listened to chain rattling as *Longhorn* dropped her anchor. Her engines whined as she backed down on
it, allowing it to bite into the seafloor. Suddenly, the engines cut off
and a foreboding stillness gathered. I rowed hard through the ebb.

At times it seemed I made no headway, but I finally reached the
coast of Cypress just as a loud splash announced that *Longhorn* had
dropped a tender into the water. Voices floated in the darkness. On-
shore, a flashlight pulsed on and off three times. Then three times
again.

Washing away from the land, the ebb kept *Longhorn's* bow pointed
at the shore of Smuggler's Cove. I spotted the tender against the starboard side of the boat. I pulled with my right oar, turning my dinghy
toward *Longhorn*, rowing to her. Moments later, my inflatable bounced
gently off the aft port side of her hull. I reached out for the edge of a
porthole, holding on with a few fingers against the ebb.

"Bud, let's do this, boy." Anxiety infused the Texan's drawl. "Coast
Guard plucked Jim and Tommy Lee from the water. Let's get these
goddamned people off this boat, so if the Coast Guard stops us, there'll
be nothing for them to find."

"I can only fit two at a time in the small inflatable. I'll have to make
several trips." I recognized Bud Kincaid's voice. He breathed hard.
"Hey, this way. You, step down on that platform, then into the boat.

You understand? *Comprende? Habla* English? Shit. I don't speak Spanish, Jim does."

"Just shove 'em into the damn boat," the elder Kincaid said.

Bud grunted. "This way."

Footsteps shuffled over the swim step. Whispered Spanish wafted through the night air. A woman whimpered.

"In, dammit. Kneel down once you get in the boat."

"Bud, you take 'em in and come right back. He's waiting for you on shore. Don't fuck with any of them young things. You got me, boy?"

"Going in, then coming back," Bud said.

"Good, I'll be waiting for you on the rear deck."

"Untie me," Bud said.

A moment later, an outboard motor whined. The light on shore flashed again. The Spanish whispers faded as the sound of the outboard disrupted the quiet of the night.

Since I wouldn't be stepping aboard *Longhorn* from the swim step, I pulled myself forward against the current. Once the portholes ended, my fingers strained against the smooth hull.

From shore, an eighty-four-foot boat looks big. From the water, it looks even bigger. *Longhorn*'s bow towered over me. I stretched out for the anchor chain, but it plunged into the water beyond my fingertips. So, I pushed off from the bow and grabbed an oar. Instead of rowing, I rose onto my knees and paddled the inflatable like a canoe toward the anchor chain.

I grabbed the chain and twirled the dinghy's painter around it in a quick hitch. Then I stood and reached high on the chain. One thing about a big yacht is that it usually carries a big anchor chain, which makes for good handholds. My hands wrapped around the cold metal links as I hoisted myself up the anchor chain, catching it between my feet as I went.

At the top of the anchor chain, I swung a leg onto *Longhorn*'s deck and locked my arm around a stanchion to haul my body aboard. The other thing about a big yacht that weighs a hundred tons or more is that it doesn't sway much under the addition of a mere two hundred pounds. I doubted that Kincaid would realize that anyone had just boarded his boat.

I slid my pistol from the small of my back and tiptoed along the side deck. At *Longhorn*'s stern, I peeked around the corner. Kincaid's tall frame leaned against the stainless steel railing. Light from inside the cabin reflected off his silver white hair. A few quick steps, and I stood behind him. I jammed the muzzle of my pistol into his back and put a hand on his shoulder. He flinched, then stiffened. I whispered in my best Texas drawl.

"Don't y'all turn around or say anything. You got me, boy?"

Kincaid's body trembled. "I'm a rich man. If it's money you're after, I'll get you whatever you want. Just don't shoot me."

"The way I understand it, you're broke. And if you don't pay back your friends in Vegas, Reno, Juarez, or wherever they are, they'll see to it that you're dead broke."

"Who the hell are you?"

"Maybe we should step inside for a chat."

I peeled Kincaid from the railing and pushed him toward the cabin door. I reached around him for the door handle and slid the large glass door open. Kincaid looked down at my hand and went rigid. Then he hissed, "You're that goddamn nig—"

I slammed the butt of my pistol into the soft flesh between his neck and his shoulder. Kincaid groaned. His knees buckled. His head slumped forward. I shoved him into the cabin, then spun him around. I stiff-armed him down onto a couch. He sunk into the soft leather. I stood back with my gun pointed at his chest. A cold look set into his blue eyes.

"Maybe you need a history lesson," I said. "You lost the Civil War. Slavery's over. And you don't use the N-word when you refer to African Americans like me."

Kincaid squeezed his eyes closed tightly, accentuating his crow's feet and the furrows traversing his brow. His hand went to his shoulder and he rubbed it. I dropped into a couch across from him. The soft leather swallowed me.

With his eyes still closed, Kincaid asked, "Look, what do you want?"

"To shut you down. Like I said, slavery's over. *Longhorn*'s nothing more than a fiberglass slave ship."

His eyes popped open. "Hell, son, this ain't no slave ship." He nodded toward the front of the boat. "These fucking wet—"

"Watch it." I held up a finger and thrust my gun at Kincaid. He reared back into the couch.

"These damn Mexicans," he said. "They wanna come to this country. There's nothing for them in that hellhole south of the border."

"So you're doing them a favor, right?"

"Something like that."

"Taking their money. Transporting them like animals. Forcing them to work off debt. Turning young women into prostitutes. Welcome to America. Land of the free, home of the brave. Whatever happened to 'Give me your tired, your poor, your huddled masses yearning to breathe free?'"

"Fuck you."

"Don't think that's going to happen."

Bud yelled from outside the boat. "Hey, I need some help tying up."

I looked at Kincaid and whispered. "Tell him to keep his voice down and tie up on his own. Tell him you're in here doing something important."

Then I leaned over and slid the cabin door open.

Kincaid yelled, "Bud, get the hell out of here, now. We got troub—"

I slammed a forearm into Kincaid's throat. Then I cracked my pistol against the side of his skull. He crumpled to the carpeted cabin sole. I raced outside and leaned over the railing. Bud roared away in his dinghy. I blinked several times and squinted. I aimed my gun into the night. But by the time my eyes adjusted to the darkness, Bud had made it halfway to shore.

Kincaid groaned. I stepped back into the salon. Blood oozed from the side of his head, streaking his silver hair pink. From his fetal position, he looked up.

"My boy'll be back."

Kincaid winced, closing his eyes. But he opened them quickly and forced a grin. My leg twitched. I wanted to kick the grin off of his face. Instead, I stepped back outside and rummaged through a lazarette, looking for heavy line. I didn't find any. But I did find something even better—a roll of duct tape. I yanked Kincaid's arms behind him and spun the tape around his wrists and ankles. Finally, I tore off a piece and mashed it over his lips.

I raced from the salon down the side deck of *Longhorn* and forward to the bow pulpit. I swung my legs over the railing and dropped down the anchor chain into my dinghy. I unhitched the dinghy, then jerked the starter cord. The outboard motor sputtered. I took a deep breath and pulled the cord with a steady, easy motion. The motor coughed several times, but it finally engaged. I opened the throttle wide and sped to shore.

Close to the beach, I stopped the motor and rocked it up on its hinges. I let the inflatable glide onto the gravel of Smuggler's Cove. I jumped out and grabbed the painter, tying it to the first piece of drift-wood I found.

I stood in the darkness turning my head, listening, looking. Above me and to my right, a light flickered through the dense trees. Subdued voices floated my way. I twisted my flashlight on and found the rem-nants of Zoe Hardy's cabin. I quickly twisted the flashlight off, letting my eyes adjust to the darkness while I tried to recall the location of the trail in relationship to the cabin.

I walked a few feet in the direction I remembered, but I tripped over a downed limb. I switched my flashlight on again. This time, two shots rang out and two bullets dived into the bark of nearby trees. I ducked low and dowsed the light. I'd only glimpsed the trailhead. I crouched, walking forward, swinging my arm down and out in front like a blind man without a cane, feeling for branches and large rocks.

I looked up at the night sky, barely able to make out the dark forms of treetops against the stars. I stumbled in the direction where, overhead, a wide swath of stars met with the edges of treetops on either side. Finally, I felt hard earth and small rocks under my feet instead of the spongy cushion of the forest floor.

I moved quickly up the trail, sharpening my senses, projecting them away from me out into my surroundings. The sound of my footsteps came at me differently when I walked straight down the middle of the trail, or veered off to the forest on either side. When I felt the rough edge of the trail under my feet, I moved back toward the center.

I must have looked like a drunk in a hurry, but I staggered along, doing my best to keep an open view of the sky over my head. Perhaps my imagination played tricks on me. I thought I could even smell a difference between the damp earth of the forest and the drier dirt of the trail. The hairpin switchbacks proved hardest to navigate, and several times my shoulder crashed into a rock wall as I careened off the trail. Occasionally, a flashlight flickered far ahead.

When I stumbled into a signpost, I walked my fingers over the pointed wooden signs. I didn't dare switch on my flashlight. From the distance I'd already walked and the signs pointing in three directions, I realized I'd made it to the juncture of the Smuggler's Cove, Pelican Beach, and Eagle Harbor trails. I continued straight ahead to Eagle Harbor.

That's when I heard voices ahead of me, louder than before. It sounded like they were arguing. I moved faster. I wanted to get to Kincaid before he got the immigrants onto another boat.

Suddenly, the voices stopped and an eerie silence prevailed. An inner voice warned me to slow down, and I did. Off to my left, an occasional light from a distant island shone through wavering branches. Then, to my right, footsteps crashed in the forest. I froze in place. The footsteps neared. I sucked in a breath and held it. I reached for my pistol. A dark form leapt from the trees. The deer stopped and huffed once toward me before trotting across the trail and tromping through the woods on the other side.

I moved cautiously. My mind created monsters out of the dark boulders and rock faces on the right side of the trail. My leg muscles tightened. Under my feet, the ground angled down as the trail descended toward Eagle Harbor.

Small rocks clattered to my right. Suddenly, the air grew heavy. I turned to my right, but too late. Someone leapt on top of me, flattening me on my back on the ground. My pistol skittered away.

twenty-seven

My assailant held me down with one arm. Instinct told me to reach for his other arm. I grabbed his wrist and found his fingers wrapped around the hilt of a large knife. He leaned on my outstretched arm, locked at the elbow. I tried to move my other arm out from under his knee, but I couldn't.

I held the knife away, but my arm quivered under the weight of his body. Then my elbow bent, and my arm quivered even more. I could only move one leg, so I bent my knee and brought it up hard under the man, catching him in the crotch. He groaned, and I used my knee and my arm to push him off my body.

I sprang to my feet in the darkness. I heard him jump to his feet as well. I whipped my flashlight from my pocket and shined it momentarily into his eyes, closing my eyes as I did. I got a glimpse of Ray Bob, dressed in blue jeans and a white hooded jacket, crouching with his knife drawn.

I jumped to the side of the trail. RB saw me, but I hoped that my eyes would adjust to the darkness before his did. RB moved toward me. His knife swished as he sliced wildly through the night air. I backed away from the sound of his blade, crouching low, a few yards down the embankment that plunged to the water.

RB must have heard me moving. He turned in my direction and headed blindly toward me. His dark outline hovered above me. He continued to strike out with his knife. He must not have realized that he'd come to the edge of the trail. He took another step. His foot slipped. I rolled out of the way. Branches snapped as he tumbled down the side of the trail.

Then, a blood-curdling scream rose from below me, echoing through the night. I shined my flashlight down the embankment. RB lay amidst a tangle of branches and downed limbs. He writhed in pain. A crimson stain soaked his white jacket. He moaned low. I couldn't tell if he'd fatally wounded himself, and I didn't have time to find out. I scrambled back up to the trail. RB would have to wait. I needed to get to Bud Kincaid.

A brief flash from my flashlight revealed my pistol lying farther down the trail. On my hands and knees, I crawled toward it, sweeping my hand over the dewy earth until I found it. I slipped the gun into my pocket and moved as fast as I could in the darkness down the trail to Eagle Harbor.

Once I got to the clearing at the head of the harbor, the soft glow of lights from Guemes Island helped guide me along the remainder of the trail. I went to the pocket beach where I guessed RB might have pulled his boat in to pick up *Longhorn*'s human cargo.

When I got there, I didn't see Kincaid. I didn't see the immigrants either. I shined my flashlight out into the harbor. It illuminated the numbers 3-4-7-4-2-8 on the side of a native fishing boat.

Farther out, anchor lights from pleasure craft swayed in the night. Closer in, my flashlight beam reflected off the small aluminum boat belonging to CJ, the park ranger, tied between the old wooden pilings. Then I scanned the beach. An inflatable had RB's boat number stenciled on its side. CJ's wooden dinghy rested higher up above the sand. I thought she said she'd be gone for several days.

Absent a boat, there aren't many choices for getting off Cypress Island. In the middle of the night, I couldn't see playboy Bud bushwhacking through the forest with frightened immigrants in tow.

I switched on my flashlight and headed up the road to Reed Lake, the road that also led to the compound where CJ worked and lived. My legs burned, climbing the steep grade after making the journey over from Smuggler's Cove. The thought of Bud holding CJ hostage played in my mind. After all, those buildings provided the closest shelter. A place to hide out and regroup.

Near the park compound, the road flattened out. I stopped walking and leaned over. I propped my hands on my thighs and rested to catch my breath. Close by, a generator hummed. A bright green light shone through the trees. I rounded a corner and entered the compound. The green light hung from atop the garage in the center of the buildings. A dimmer, yellow light leaked from a crack where the garage's large bay door had been rolled back slightly.

I pulled my gun from my pocket and crept up to the garage door. I peeked around the corner, and what I saw made me nearly burst out laughing.

Bud sat with his hands tied behind his back and his feet bound, propped against the wheels of a large yellow dump truck. CJ stood watch over him with a rifle, her back to me. I still didn't see the immigrants. Bud saw me first. He yelled.

"She's a crazy bitch. You'd better be careful."

"I'd be careful what I said if I were you. Seems like CJ's the one calling the shots."

CJ turned around to face me. I slipped my gun into the small of my back. I pointed to the rifle in CJ's hands.

"You know how to use one of those?" I asked.

"I do," she said.

She wore a gray sweatshirt with the red letters A-W-O-L emblazoned on the front. I didn't doubt that she knew how to use the rifle, but she aimed it at my chest. My heart clenched.

"Throw your pistol down," she said. "And kick it over to me."

"What's going on, CJ?"

She yelled. "Just take your damn pistol out from behind your back really slow, with two fingers. Drop it on the floor and kick it my way."

Bud hollered. "Told you she was one crazy bitch."

My hands went up in front of me. "Put the rifle down, CJ."

I took a step in her direction. Her finger tightened around the trigger. My heart rate climbed, and I backed off.

"Throw out your gun, now." Her voice sounded calmer this time, but it didn't lack resolve.

"Okay, two fingers." I reached behind my back with my thumb and index finger, grasping the handle of my pistol, sliding it from the small of my back, all the while watching CJ. She never blinked. A cold, hard stare set into her eyes. I dropped the pistol to the ground and kicked it toward her. She kept the rifle pointed at me while she reached down and scooped up my gun. She stuck it into the pouch of her sweatshirt. Then she waved me away from the door.

"Move over there next to Bud. I don't have anything to lose now," CJ said, "so I'd just as easily kill you too."

I moved slowly to the hood of the dump truck. CJ stood with her back to the door.

"What do you mean? Of course, you have everything to lose," I said.

CJ sneered. "What the hell do you know about me? What do any of you know about me?"

Tears welled in CJ's eyes. My heart raced, but I forced some slow, deep breaths.

"What's going on, CJ?" I asked.

"Fucking lunatic. That's what," Bud said.

I waved my hand toward Bud. "Shut up, Bud," I said.

"Bud, you fucking prick. I intend to kill you first," CJ said.

"Whoa." I held up my hands. "Look, CJ, we caught them. Bud transferred some immigrants onto the island. I don't think they've gotten off yet."

I looked at CJ, but spoke to Bud. "Where are they, Bud?"

"Fucking wetbacks escaped."

I held out my hands to CJ. "We can find them. They can't get far on this island. There're still immigrants aboard *Longhorn*. Bud and his father will stand trial for illegally transporting them here, and for killing those young women in Eagle Harbor."

"I may've screwed 'em but I didn't fucking kill no women."

"Shut up, Bud," I said.

CJ whimpered. "He didn't kill them."

"What do you mean?"

"See," Bud said. "You heard it for yourself. I didn't kill them. She probably did."

"Shut up, you bastard," CJ said. "Before I blow your balls off."

She twisted in Bud's direction, aiming the rifle at his crotch. He reared back. I started to move toward CJ, but she whipped around and held the rifle on me. I put up both hands again.

I spoke calmly. "Put the rifle down, CJ," I said. "And then tell me what happened."

CJ's eyes had glazed over. She stared right through me, though she kept the rifle leveled at my chest.

"He said, 'If you like adventure, I'll take you anywhere on the face of the earth. Exploring the Amazon. Hiking the Himalayas. An African safari.' We flew to the Galapagos. I thought I'd finally found a man I could be with. But he only said those things, did those things, because he needed me to look the other way while he transported undocumented immigrants across the island. Isn't that right, you bastard?"

"Who'd want you anyway?" Bud said. "You're more like a mountain man than a woman. What turns you on is tracking grizzly bears, or being dropped in the middle of some fucking jungle and hacking your way out."

"Shut up, you fool," I said.

"Hell, crazy bitch's probably gonna kill us both."

I took a step toward Bud. He rolled back and stuck his feet up, as though ready to kick me. CJ sighed. I turned back to her.

"I heard through friends in Bellingham that Bud slept around. I didn't want to believe them. I asked him about it. He said he loved me. He assured me I was his only lover. I wanted to believe him, needed to believe him. I spend most of my time on this island or in some remote corner of the globe. There aren't many men who understand my lifestyle, not many willing to join me on adventures without limits. He said he loved what I did. He wanted to join me on my adventures. Lying son of a bitch. All he loved was seducing me into turning a blind eye. He said he helped poor Mexicans gain a foothold on a better life here."

"That's all we do," Bud said.

"Bullshit," CJ said. "Rumor was that Bud liked kinky sex, twosomes and threesomes, preferably with younger women. Then, about two weeks ago, *Longhorn* pulled into Eagle Harbor. I heard the noise and thought his daddy was throwing a party. Through the binoculars, I saw some of Bud's friends on deck. I rowed my dinghy over and climbed aboard. I didn't see Bud. Then I went below and opened his stateroom door. I found him in bed with three young Mexican women."

"You killed them. You killed them," Bud said.

CJ sneered. "Just like I'm gonna kill you." She sniffed back tears. "He sent the women from the room and tried to talk his way out of the situation. He said they didn't mean anything to him, they were mere toys, playthings. He loved me. Look at me." CJ ran a hand down the front of her body. "I'm almost forty. I've never been an attractive woman. I traveled early to escape the dating scene. I've never been married. Never had a man who understood my need for adventure.

"On my way from the stateroom that night, I passed the women and in Spanish I told them I'd meet them later. Help them escape. That's all I really wanted to do. Help them escape from Bud and their lives of prostitution. Late that night, after the partying ended, I took my dinghy back to *Longhorn* and brought the women ashore." CJ began to cry. "I only wanted to help them escape. You've gotta believe that. I only wanted to help them."

The rifle trembled in her hands. I took another step toward her.

"I believe you, CJ. Now, give me the rifle," I said.

She snapped. "Stay back. I'm the one in control here."

I stepped back. "You killed the women to get back at Bud. Is that what happened?"

CJ looked at Bud. Her gaze hardened. "Pathetic bastard. He sank his cock into every woman he could." Then she looked at me, and her tears returned. Desperation crept into her eyes. "They were so young. They had such beautiful bodies. I wanted to be them. To have a body like theirs. To feel what it was like to have a man desire me so much that he'd pay for my body. Can you understand that?"

"Bud's betrayal must have been hard," I said.

CJ's eyes narrowed. She shook her head. "You don't understand. You're a man just like Bud. Out after the same things. You're all like that. All of you men. Thinking with your dicks." Her voice had a dull, flat, monotone ring.

Suddenly, CJ's eyes snapped open. Her voice rose to almost a scream. "They slept. Bud's pretty little playthings slept in my bed." Then her voice grew soft. "I didn't mean to kill them. I swear, I only wanted to touch their skin, to feel their perfect bodies. So smooth. The skin around their necks felt so smooth. Not weather-beaten like mine. And their bodies were so fragile. So easily broken. Not tough and hard like mine. They slept. Bud's pretty little playthings slept in my bed."

CJ kept her eye and her gun on me, but she pointed to Bud. "He didn't understand that all beauty eventually decays. He had to see that. I had to make him see that."

"So you strangled them in their sleep?" I asked.

CJ spoke in a high-pitched monotone as if to some invisible witnesses in the room. "They were tired. They didn't put up a fight. One tried to run, but I caught her. Such fragile bodies. So easily broken."

She glanced at Bud, wildness now inflaming her eyes. "I planned it to look like Bud killed them. That'd teach him to fuck with me. I loaded their bodies into the truck. Drove them to the water, and dumped them where *Longhorn* had anchored."

CJ spun the rifle barrel toward me. "It would have worked until you came along. It would have worked." Then CJ's voice dropped. "Now I have to kill you both." She put her hand into the pouch of her sweatshirt. "Maybe I'll use your gun. Make it look like you killed Bud and then killed yourself."

Sweat beaded over my forehead. "You don't want to do anything more that you'll regret. You have to hand me the rifle," I said.

CJ couldn't hear me. She seemed completely self-absorbed, as if many people were simultaneously conversing in her mind, and occasionally she narrated one of their conversations.

"You're just like them . . . just like them," she said to me.

Then she turned the rifle on Bud. He cried like a child, cringing up against the dump truck's huge black tire. "Don't shoot me. Please don't shoot me."

"Don't, CJ," I said.

Her trembling finger wrapped around the trigger. She muttered now, more than she spoke. "You can't treat me like that. Adventure without limits. That's me. You can't treat me like that."

"Don't compound the tragedy and the sorrow," I said.

She turned the rifle back on me, that wild look still in her eyes. "You pathetic bastard."

I couldn't tell which of us she meant. She whipped the rifle around to Bud.

Suddenly, a shadowed figure stole through the door, then flew through the air at CJ's legs. I lunged for the rifle barrel and pushed it up and away. All three of us tumbled to the ground. The rifle went off. Bud screamed. The shot rang in my ears. An acrid smell of gunpowder stung my nostrils. I ripped the rifle from CJ's hand. Bud lay crying on the ground, but the shot had only shattered a window of the dump truck above his head.

Raven buried his knee between CJ's shoulder blades, trapping her arms beneath her body. With his palm on the back of her head, he pressed her face into the ground. She sobbed. "You can't treat me like that. . . . You can't treat me like that."

I yelled. "She's lying on my gun."

Raven rolled off of CJ's back and reached beneath her. I lunged toward her. But we were both too late. A muffled shot rang out. I flinched. CJ's body heaved.

Bud sang out. "She shot herself. That crazy bitch shot herself."

A pool of blood seeped from beneath CJ. A dark red gurgle ran from her mouth. I grasped both of her arms and spun her over. Blood soaking through the front of her sweatshirt obliterated the red letters. I pulled my gun from her limp hand. I checked her neck. She had no pulse. I shook my head. CJ's lifeless eyes now looked toward an otherworldly adventure.

Raven stood. He closed his eyes and sighed. "Too much sadness on this island. Too many lost souls trying to find their way home." Then he kneeled and whispered into CJ's deaf ear.

"Told you she was a crazy bitch. Told you I—"

I put my hand out to Bud. "Shut up," I said.

I grabbed Bud's bound legs and dragged him outside, propping him up against the garage wall. Raven joined us.

"I have to get back to *Longhorn*," I said to Raven. "There are other immigrants on the boat."

"I need to stay with her," Raven said. "To help her soul find its way home."

"I understand."

Bud blurted out. "But what about me? What are you—"

"Shut up, Bud," I said.

Raven reached into his pocket, whipped out a cloth, then stuffed it into Bud's mouth. Finally, Bud shut up.

Raven stepped back into the garage. I set out for Eagle Harbor. Behind me, tremulous chanting echoed through the night.

ONCE BACK AT EAGLE HARBOR, I pulled RB's inflatable into the water. I started the motor and headed around the north end of Cypress to Smuggler's Cove.

When I got aboard *Longhorn*, I moved quickly through the salon past Dennis Kincaid, who craned his neck up and mumbled a string of incoherent imprecations.

I walked up a few steps into the wide, sweeping galley, then through it to a narrow passageway toward the helm. Just before the helm, I took the companionway down and found myself in a carpeted corridor with doors on either side. I followed the soft strains of music emanating from behind one door.

I pulled my gun out. I twisted the handle and burst in. I swept my pistol in a wide arc. Wrinkled light-blue satin sheets fell from a king-sized bed. Julio Iglesias and Willie Nelson serenaded an empty stateroom with "To All the Girls I've Loved Before."

I moved forward from the stateroom, shouldering open each door I passed and scanning each room with my pistol. The carpeted passageway ended at the crew's quarters. Inside the small, V-shaped cabin, a built-in chest of drawers protruded from one teak sidewall, upper and lower bunks from the other.

Alternating stripes of teak and holly covered the floor. I eyed a small door ahead of me, then yanked it open. The musty smell of mud and saltwater met me. I stuck my head inside, but I only saw anchor chain piled into a mound. I slammed the small door shut and turned away.

The other immigrants had to be somewhere nearby. I twirled around and tapped the anchor locker door with the barrel of my pistol. Three short taps. Three long taps. Three short taps. I waited. Nothing. I tapped again. This time, I heard a faint reply. Three short. Three long. Three short. It sounded like it came from beneath the cabin sole.

I dropped to all fours and stuck my ear to the teak and holly. I tapped again. The wood resonated with the reply. I looked around but I didn't see a latch, a hinge, or anything to suggest an entrance to a space below this deck. Maybe a doorway from the engine room? That couldn't be. The engine room sat too far aft. I ripped out the bottom dresser drawers and peeked into the opening. I felt around, but I didn't find anything there.

Then I remembered the fifty-four-foot Krogen trawler that Sharon and I had liked so much. The berth in the forward stateroom folded up and a shelf dropped down to make a desk, turning the space into a convenient floating office.

I reached up and under the bottom bunk. My fingers walked back and forth until finding their way over a small latch. I tripped it with my trigger finger. The bunk popped up. I pushed it higher until it mated with a latch on the sidewall that secured it in place. Then I lifted and twisted the stainless steel O-ring embedded in the floor. A large section of the cabin sole swung up on hinges. Muffled voices called from the darkened space below.

I stuck my hand down into the hold, where I felt a bony arm. With one foot propped against the sidewall, I braced while I pulled a man up. He sat on the edge of the hold. I stripped the gag from his mouth, then whipped out my pocketknife to cut the rope from around his wrists.

The drawn brown skin of his face suggested he hadn't eaten in some time. Still, his dark eyes sparkled, and the corners of his lips curled into a tight smile. He balled his hand into a fist and rapped his knuckles on the floor. Three short. Three long. Three short. He bowed his head toward me more than once.

"Muchas gracias, Señor. Muchas gracias."

Then he brought his legs up and he kneeled down. He reached back into the hold. I reached my hand down again, and together we lifted a young woman out. She couldn't have been more than sixteen, with dirty, matted, jet-black hair and a tiny mole in the middle of her right cheek. Her body trembled as we set her on the edge of the hold. After we untied her, she pushed herself up, and with shaky legs she moved to the other side of the small cabin. She leaned against the dresser and stared at us with dazed eyes.

The man and I reached down into the darkness again and again, until we'd brought up four men and two women.

"Una más," he said. He pointed down. *"Una más."*

We reached down one more time and raised another tired, frightened teenage girl from *Longhorn*'s hold.

twenty-eight

A summer high had finally taken hold. Treetops swayed in the stiff northwest wind. In the distance, puffy columns of white smoke rose angularly from long industrial stacks. I'd anchored deep in Mark Bay, so deep that the *Noble Lady* rested in calm, glassy water, the current swaying her more than the wind. The flood pointed her bow away from the land while only a hundred yards farther out the bows of other anchored boats pointed toward us like weathercocks turned by the wind. One against many. The *Noble Lady* stood proud.

I checked my watch. Almost eleven in the morning. I imagined the captain of Kate's big British Columbia ferry radioing Vessel Traffic Control about now, reporting they'd just passed Entrance Island, heading for Duke Point. I hopped in my dinghy and rowed the short distance over to Newcastle Island.

The small red water taxi bobbed at the dock. Inside, passengers filled the benches. The taxi's captain untied the boat and pushed off. We darted in and out of the boats anchored in the bay. Then, closer to Nanaimo, we waited while two bright yellow planes landed, throwing trails of water from their floats.

After arriving at Nanaimo Harbor, I headed up the ramp to the harbormaster's office. Perfect timing. A yellow taxi rolled down the hill and pulled into the circular driveway. The door opened. Kate stepped out. My heart soared. She had on jeans and a T-shirt. The brim of her wide, floppy straw hat partially hid her face. The driver hurried around to the back of the cab. He popped up the trunk and swung two duffels onto the sidewalk.

Kate smiled as she walked toward me. We fell into each other's arms, and she had to pull up the brim of her hat so we could kiss. I arched back and lifted her off her feet. I let her down, and we each grabbed a bag. Then we walked back to the water taxi.

"Great idea," Kate said, "your taking the boat up here to Canada, and my joining you by ferry. It buys us at least one extra day."

"Wind's blowing out of the north. Perfect conditions for anchoring in Tribune Bay. We'll make Hornby Island well before dark," I said.

"I'm good to go the minute we get back to the *Lady*," she said.

On our way down the metal gangway, I took a deep breath of salt air laced with the smell of fish. Way in the distance, the snowcapped peaks of the British Columbia Coastal Range danced in a jagged line across a crystal blue sky. Closer in, the *Noble Lady* still held her own against the fleet of anchored boats in Mark Bay. Closer yet, in the inner harbor, sun glinted off the windows of a large police catamaran and a row of megayachts. Still closer, Kate walked ahead of me. Now that view excited me most. She swiveled around.

"Did you hear that?"

"Hear what?"

"I thought I heard someone call your name."

"Pretty common name."

She pointed. "There, isn't someone waving at us from the flybridge of that boat?"

I looked down and over the gangway and out past the gleaming white tops of a few rows of boats. A woman waved from her flybridge while calling out, "Charlie."

She patted down her wide-brimmed floppy straw hat to keep the wind from whisking it away. A man arose beside her wearing the same hat. He stared without waving, then took the hat off, revealing a shock of white hair that sparkled as bright as the finish on their boat's hull.

"It's the Bayneses," I said.

"The people who—"

"Uh huh. I thought they'd be further north by now."

"You don't sound that excited to see them."

"I had other exciting things on my mind."

Kate raised her eyebrows. "Like?"

I let my eyes run the length of her body.

"Oh, I see." Her voiced dropped to a whisper. "I can assure you, those exciting things will be waiting for you once we get back to the boat. I'm also sure the Bayneses would appreciate hearing from you." She smiled.

We strolled along the docks to *Sarabande*. Strains of a Bach cantata grew louder as we approached the boat. When I realized that I had a guitar transcription of the same piece, a hot flash of guilt shivered through me. I hadn't practiced much in the last few weeks.

Marvin stood on deck. He reached over the handrail for our bags. He tossed them inside the cabin, then reached down to help Kate aboard.

"Up here," Angela said. She peaked over the railing of the flybridge above us. Her voice quivered joyfully.

I let Kate climb the ladder to the flybridge first.

"Thought you'd be further north by now."

"I had an epiphany," Marvin said. "Tell you about it in a moment."

We sat around a teak table underneath the green flybridge awning. In the short time it had taken us to walk to their boat, Angela had prepared a feast of smoked salmon, cheese, olives, carrots, and snap peas. She'd arranged all this in strips pointing out from the center of a clear glass plate like the spokes of a bicycle wheel.

Marvin pulled a wine bottle from the shade beside him. He'd just begun to let the deep red liquid flow into Kate's glass when her hand shot out as if to stop him.

"I'm sorry," he said. "I should have asked if you drank wine. It's quite good, you know. One of our favorites. A bottle of—"

"Red Mountain Reserve," Kate said.

Marvin flinched. "Yes, Hedges. You know it?"

"We do."

Kate glanced my way and smiled. I chuckled. Angela and Marvin raised their eyebrows.

"And?" Marvin asked.

He seemed steeled for the worst.

"I bet you know Wagner's *Tristan and Isolde*," I said.

"Know it? Why we've both performed it from the pit many times," Angela said. "But I—"

I held up a hand. "Then you remember when they are mistakenly given the love potion."

"The potion was meant for the king," Marvin said, "so he would fall in love with Isolde, but instead Tristan did."

"But Tristan and Isolde already loved each other and that potion simply allowed them to realize it," Angela said. She looked between Kate and me. "Oh, that's so dear. This wine was your love potion."

Kate put her hand on my thigh. "I left a bottle of Red Mountain Reserve for him," she said.

"With a note not to drink it alone," I said.

"I didn't tell him with whom."

"And I didn't drink it alone."

Kate slapped my thigh playfully, then wrinkled her nose slightly. "But at least he made the right choice."

We all laughed.

"Then let's toast to magical potions," Marvin said.

"And to falling in love," Angela said.

Marvin finished pouring the wine. Our glasses clinked together. Sharon would have liked the Bayneses.

"Perhaps you have some news of that poor girl we brought up from Eagle Harbor," Angela said.

"I do. But first I want to know why you're not further north and what that has to do with Marvin's epiphany."

Angela chuckled. She shook her head. "What epiphany? It has to do with his mistress."

"Mistress?" Kate and I both said.

"Through all the years we've been in love, Marvin's always had his mistresses."

"And you have enjoyed them too, dear."

"That I have."

Kate and I now took our turns at raised eyebrows.

"And *Sarabande* was to be our last," Angela said.

"This was to be our last summer aboard her," Marvin said. "But anchored off that lovely white sand beach outside of Montague Harbor the other night, with dark seas shimmering under an almost full moon, I said to Angie, We're not selling *Sarabande*. Even if we are a pair of old sailors. I'd rather go down with a boat than without one." He reached for Angela's hand.

Kate smiled through moist eyes.

"A toast, to old boaters," Marvin said.

We raised our glasses.

"And to boaters who will someday be old," I said.

Our glasses clinked again.

I told Angela and Marvin about the human-trafficking ring Raven and I ended; about the women drowned at Eagle Harbor; about the Kincaids, Frank Abadi, Eliana and her family, and Maria Delarosa; and about CJ.

"You saved lives, Charlie, and prevented more suffering."

Images of Eliana Morales flashed through my mind. "I only wish I could have done more."

"You did do more," Angela said. "Knowing this lifts a forty-year-old burden from my heart. I think I can finally say good-bye to our darling, Amy, knowing we helped other parents find out the truth about their daughters' fate when we were never able to find out the truth about our own."

"What do we owe you?" Marvin asked.

I took a deep breath and looked at Kate. "How about another bottle of wine?"

"B . . . But," Angela said.

Marvin put an arm gently on her shoulder. "I've got another bottle down below, and we'd be glad for you two to have it."

After Kate and I stepped off *Sarabande*, Marvin swung Kate's bags over the railing. "Be careful, wine's in the large duffel."

twenty-nine

Kate rested her head on my shoulder as we rode the water taxi back to Newcastle Island.

"I like what you did back there." She squeezed my arm. "Asking for a bottle of wine rather than for money."

"Janet would tell me that I'm a poor businessman."

"And I would tell you that money isn't everything."

Once back at the *Lady,* Kate took the helm. I popped the engine hatch and checked the oil and water. She fired up the *Lady*'s engine while I went out on deck and washed down the anchor chain as it rose. We steamed out of Mark Bay and headed down Newcastle Channel. After dodging a ferry lumbering into Departure Bay, we threaded our way among the rocks lining Horswell Channel and finally entered the Strait of Georgia. The *Noble Lady*'s bow rose up, then slapped down in the three-foot seas. I sat on the bench behind the helm. Kate turned to me.

"Sea's nothing," she said. "Last week we were out in near gale-force winds on the *Sea Eagle* in the Strait of Juan de Fuca in ten- to twelve-foot seas."

I nodded. "I know. I was out there too."

Kate smiled. She kept one hand on the wheel and reached her other

266

hand back for me. We held hands. She turned around. "And I'm glad that you and the *Noble Lady* made it back safely."

The dark, smoky-blue silhouettes of Texada Island and the British Columbia mainland loomed across the strait. Ahead of us, the Ballenas Islands appeared as two bumps on the horizon.

Kate let go of my hand. She brought up the course to Tribune Bay on the navigational computer. She flipped a switch and set the boat on autopilot. Then she stepped up and sat next to me on the bench. She rested a hand on my thigh.

"You're quiet," she said.

"I'm happy to be out on the water with you, heading off on an adventure."

"Raven drove me to catch the ferry," Kate said. "He doesn't talk much, but I like the feeling I get when I'm around him. He hummed softly as we drove."

"Chanting," I said. "He's constantly chanting. Prayers to the spirit world to aid those of us living and those who are dead, he says."

"Had you told him that my mother was part Inuit and part Kwakiutl?"

"No."

"That's strange because out of nowhere he encouraged me to reconnect with my Northwest Indian roots as though he knew. He offered me his help. What's even stranger is that just a few days earlier I'd been thinking about making a trip north to learn more about my mother's family. Raven seemed to have the words I needed to hear at just the right time."

"In Raven's world everything happens at the right time, even if it seems wrong to others at the moment."

"Like the way he appeared on Cypress at the right time? I noticed you didn't tell the Byneses all of the details, like what really happened that night."

"I didn't think they needed to know the full extent of the tragedy and the gore." I took a deep breath. "Yes. Raven'd been on Cypress all along, hidden in the brush near Eagle Harbor. I couldn't reach him on his cell phone. He followed RB from Eagle Harbor to Smuggler's Cove. While RB waited for Bud to ferry another group of immigrants in from *Longhorn,* Raven slipped away with the first two that Bud had brought in. He took them to his boat, which he'd tied to a mooring buoy off Pelican Beach.

"Then he hurried back to Smuggler's Cove. He saw my dinghy there and figured I'd gone to Eagle Harbor after Bud and RB. Along the way, he even stopped to help RB, who'd fallen on his own knife. When Raven didn't see me at Eagle Harbor, he walked up to the compound where CJ stayed. He's still pondering why he didn't realize that she had my gun in her sweatshirt."

"It wasn't his fault," Kate said.

"I don't think he feels it was his fault as much as he's trying to fathom why he was called to be part of CJ's tragic death."

"Called?"

"Spirit Walkers," I said. "In Raven's world, there are people called to help others even if they do not hear their names. He calls these people Spirit Walkers. I believe he feels that he was called to Cypress to help the souls of CJ and the other women find their way home."

"Called to help others even if they do not hear their names? . . . Does that also make you a Spirit Walker?"

"In Raven's world it does."

Kate shook her head. "What happened to those young women, and then to CJ, really was tragic. A misdirected crime of passion," she said. "Bud deserved CJ's rage, not those young women, but she took it out on them anyway, and then she took it out on herself." Kate sighed. "And in CJ's troubled world it probably made sense. Beauty. Desirability. Those young women represented what she wanted but thought she didn't have. It seems like she did have low self-esteem. She didn't realize that her real beauty lay within."

"It was Raven's observation that she traveled far in the outside world to escape traveling deep within herself."

"Adventure as a way of running from inner demons?"

"Perhaps."

Kate patted my leg. "When I'm old, and my beauty has faded, will you still love me?"

I placed my hand on top of hers. "You will then be my Sea Maiden."

"Your what?"

"The *Sea Maiden* is an old wooden trawler that I fell in love with. She's berthed near Raven's boat."

"You're comparing me to a boat again."

"I am."

Kate smiled. "I like old wooden boats."

"So do I."

She squeezed my leg. "I'm glad because someday we will both be living with one."

I laughed. "Ben's chief prevailed on the Skagit County sheriff's department to shut down Abadi's club. Abadi must have known that something was coming. He had no young Mexican women in the club when the police arrived. Kincaid, his son, and Ray Bob are in jail for illegally transporting immigrants into the country. My hope is that the DA will get the Kincaids to testify against Abadi, shutting him down permanently and sending him to jail. *Longhorn* was confiscated."

Kate chuckled. "Yeah, it's sitting at Station Bellingham's dock. Everyone's joking about the 'gin palace' boat, and when can they take it out on patrol." She sighed. "What'll happen to the Mexicans that Kincaid had on his boat?"

"I brought the immigrants I found on *Longhorn* around to Raven's boat, where I gathered the others. Then I carried them all back to Bellingham while Raven stayed with CJ's body, and with Bud. I called Maria Delarosa the moment I got into port. Now there's a bulldog. She swept the immigrants away and hid them. Then, through a lawyer, she made the Skagit County DA an offer he couldn't refuse: If he wanted their testimony in convicting the Kincaids, he'd have to come up with a plan for them to stay in this country legally. I haven't heard the outcome, but Maria's nothing if she's not persuasive. She'll find a way to make it happen. I only wish she'd been able to persuade Eliana to seek treatment."

"And you didn't want to take a few days to see if you could find her?"

I stared straight ahead. Hornby Island now appeared, like a tiny swelling of the horizon. I sighed. "I wanted to go after her, but Maria said it wouldn't work. Even if I found her, it would be a struggle to pry her away from the streets. Maria said the chances were that, given the choice between treatment and the streets, she'd choose the streets again."

Kate squeezed my leg again. "You did what you could. You heard Angela. You accomplished even more than you know."

"Still, it wasn't enough for Eliana."

"But maybe it'll prove to be enough for the people you rescued from Kincaid and his smuggling ring. Maybe it'll also help the Bayneses finally move on from the loss of their daughter."

"It feels like a tiny drop in an ocean of need."

"You know how to start filling an ocean of need?"

I put my arm around Kate and pulled her closer. "One drop at a time," I said.

Kate leaned her head on my shoulder. "You also made a new friend," she said.

"Raven?"

"Yes. Something tells me that this friendship will be significant for you both."

"I look forward to knowing Raven, and his world, better."

Kate raised her head and turned to kiss me, but she yawned in the middle of the kiss.

"Is that a message that my kissing's boring you?"

"It's a message from my body to me that I've gotten little sleep since being on the *Sea Eagle*. During the training mission, the CO made me his exec."

"Good experience," I said.

"But not good sleep."

I stood up and gently guided Kate down to the bench. She folded her legs up. I grabbed a blanket and a pillow from a shelf above and tucked her in.

"I wish you could join me," she said.

"Someone has to stand watch."

"But the boat's on autopilot."

"Lieutenant. You know the rules."

"A vessel under way must have a watch-stander at all times." She yawned.

"I'll join you when we get to Tribune Bay," I said.

"I'll dream about it until we get there," she said.

I stepped up to the helm and took the boat off autopilot. I swung the *Noble Lady* around so her bow cut the wave fronts at an angle, which made for a smoother ride.

Four hours later, the wind had died as we approached Tribune Bay. The sunset backlit the mountains to the west in shades of deep orange and blue.

With the *Lady* on autopilot, I climbed downstairs to pull the anchor bridle from a rear port lazarette so I'd have it ready once we anchored. Kate's bags sat atop the starboard lazarette. I almost flung them inside the cabin when I remembered the wine. So I carefully placed the larger duffel on the galley table and pulled out the bottle of wine.

Marvin had duct-taped a check onto the neck of the bottle—a check for more money than I made in a month's service in the Coast Guard. A note on the check read, "A peaceful heart is priceless."

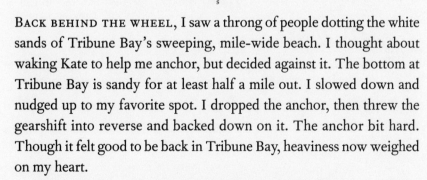

BACK BEHIND THE WHEEL, I saw a throng of people dotting the white sands of Tribune Bay's sweeping, mile-wide beach. I thought about waking Kate to help me anchor, but decided against it. The bottom at Tribune Bay is sandy for at least half a mile out. I slowed down and nudged up to my favorite spot. I dropped the anchor, then threw the gearshift into reverse and backed down on it. The anchor bit hard. Though it felt good to be back in Tribune Bay, heaviness now weighed on my heart.

We'd arrived at the place where Sharon and I had once watched a Tibetan monk pour sand from an elaborate painting into the water to bless all beings under the sea; the place where, a year later, Sharon, sick from cancer, died in my arms on an evening just like this; the place where I returned the following year to let her ashes join the monk's blessed sand.

After bridling the anchor, I walked back into the pilothouse and shook Kate gently. She woke with a smile. "There's someone I want you to meet," I said.

We slipped into the dinghy, and I rowed to the spot where I'd spread Sharon's ashes. We drifted in the water. Blue smoke curled upward from a fire on the beach. Kate said nothing. I spoke to the water.

"Sharon," I said. "I want you to meet Kate Sullivan."

I thought I'd have more to say, but I didn't. I just sat, allowing memories of the monk, Sharon's death, and her ashes wash over me. Finally, Kate spoke.

"Hi, Sharon," she said. "I want you to know that I love Charlie and he loves me. I also know that he still loves you. I hope he always will. Real love sustains life and survives death. You were a remarkable woman. One whom I could never replace. Nor would I want to. What I want is for Charlie and me to spend the time we have together creating a new life and nurturing our new love."

Kate reached for me. We squeezed hands tightly, drifting in silence as darkness gave birth to the evening's first star. Later that night, with the *Noble Lady* swaying gently beneath us, Kate and I made love. And for the first time since we'd been together, I thought only of her.

acknowledgments

Natasha Kern, my agent, for staying the course until we'd found a great home for this book. Roger Cooper, Peter Costanzo, Georgina Levitt, Amanda Ferber, Francine LaSala, Sandra Beris, Kathy Streckfus, and the rest of the "dream team" at Vanguard Press. Virginia Martin, my publicist. Morgan Freeman, Ruby Dee, Roscoe Orman, and Swil Kanim for the generous donation of their time and talents in creating a special-features DVD to accompany the book. The East Coast film crew: Bill Toles, Ruth Goldberg, Bobby Shepard, Naje Lataillade, Cherrie Shepherd, Corky Moore, and Gloria Allen. The West Coast film crew: Max Kaiser and Hand Crank Films. William Kimley of Seahorse Marine for his generous support. Myrna Colley-Lee and the SonEdna Foundation. Christopher Moensch and Jennifer Hahn for their friendship and compassion. And lastly, the love of my life, Chara Stuart, whose many sacrifices made this book possible.

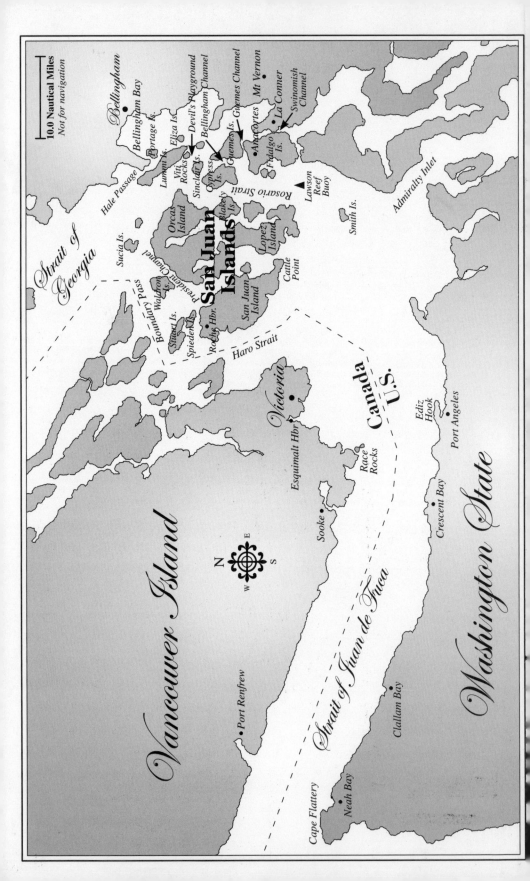